Stories
for
Summer

and days
by the
pool

BRITISH LIBRARY

This anthology first published in 2024 by
The British Library
96 Euston Road
London NW1 2DB

Cataloguing in Publication Data
A catalogue record for this publication is available
from the British Library

ISBN 978 0 7123 5515 5
e-ISBN 978 0 7123 6862 9

Series editor Alison Moss
Series consultant Simon Thomas

Text design and typesetting by JCS Publishing Services Ltd
Printed and bound by CPI Group (UK), Croydon, CR0 4YY

Contents

Introduction

Vengeful words in the blazing sunshine, sandcastles built on the beach, honeymoons gone awry and holiday romances misunderstood. Lust, joy, regret, revelation: whatever comes to mind when you think about the sunshine and heat of a summer short story can be found in this collection. From glimpses into contented lives, to those which are about to drastically change forever, the women and girls in these entertaining stories are experiencing summer days to remember one way or another.

Some of their authors are household names, while others are likely to be new discoveries – so you'll find Virginia Woolf, Daphne du Maurier and Muriel Spark alongside lesser-known writers such as G. B. Stern, Sylvia Lynd and Angela Huth. In this collection, the stories are ordered by date of initial publication. As with all the books in the British Library Women Writers series, *Stories for Summers* aims to throw new light on a wide range of women's experiences throughout the twentieth century, highlight their attitudes and agency, and celebrate the women writers who created these innovative, enjoyable and often moving stories.

We start in a classroom with a group of schoolgirls who would probably rather be out, enjoying a summer's day of playing or exploring. Instead, in 'Carnation' by New Zealand writer Katherine Mansfield (1888–1923), they are enduring a French lesson. 'Curious Eve' is known for bringing a flower to class – sometimes a rose, which she might even eat – and, today, it's a

＊　＊　＊

deep-red carnation. The story is particularly short, and open to interpretation: what might the flowers be metaphors for and what are the girls beginning to explore and discover? 'Carnation' was published in 1918 and included by Mansfield's husband, John Middleton Murray, in *Something Childish and Other Stories* the year after Mansfield died of tuberculosis at the age of 34. In her short life, she published several collections of short stories that have long been regarded as among the finest examples of the genre.

Mansfield moved in the same literary circle as the novelist Virginia Woolf (1882–1941). Indeed, Woolf wrote in her diary shortly after Mansfield's death, 'I was jealous of her writing – the only writing I have ever been jealous of'. Woolf's story, 'Kew Gardens' (1919), takes up the mantle of flowers from 'Carnation'. It starts with a detailed examination of the plants, explored with an intensity that makes the reader feel immersed in a new, vivid, miniature landscape:

> The petals were voluminous enough to be stirred by the summer breeze, and when they moved, the red, blue and yellow lights passed one over the other, staining an inch of the brown earth beneath with a spot of the most intricate colour.

Then the scene pulls back, and our attention is drawn to the different groups spending their summer afternoon in the gardens, their relationships revealed in brief snapshots of their memories, pleasantries and anxieties. 'Kew Gardens' was among the first stories that Woolf and her husband Leonard privately printed in their own printing press, Hogarth Press, and was later collected in *Monday or Tuesday* (1921). Woolf is one of the most admired writers of the modernist movement, and novels including *Mrs*

Dalloway, *To The Lighthouse*, and *The Waves* remain regarded as among the most important of the twentieth century.

The Irish writer Elizabeth Bowen (1899–1973) provides the collection's first trip to continental Europe in 'Requiescat' (1923). Mrs Majendie is staying in her villa near Lake Como, Italy, and is reunited with her late husband's friend. Bowen weaves together the awkwardness of stilted conversation, the inability to properly express long-held emotions, and the incompatibility of two people's recollections of an earlier period. Among the lemon trees, climbing roses and summer heat, Bowen's subtlety creates a quietly devastating story that is all the more effective for taking place in a quintessentially idyllic summer landscape. Appropriately, 'requiescat' is a prayer for the deceased – the word is found most often in the Latin '*requiescat in pace*', meaning 'rest in peace'. 'Requiescat' appeared in Bowen's first collection of short stories, *Encounters*, and she went on to write several other volumes of stories and well-regarded novels, including *The Last September*, *The Heat of the Day* and *The Death of the Heart*.

Staying in Italy, 'Exile' (1925) by Sylvia Lynd takes place in Florence during the dying days of summer in September. A young man meets a woman he has known in England – and is surprised by how pleased she is to see him.

He had known her to be gracious and pretty as she spoke a few words with him when they met at parties in London; but she had never asked him to her house, never shown any personal interest in him whatever. So little had she been interested, indeed, that he had been unable to feel anything but the remotest admiration for her—a tribute as formal as the passing of a vote of thanks at a committee.

❋ ❋ ❋

The title 'Exile' is our first warning that Mrs Alladale isn't entirely content with her new choice of home, and she remains fascinated with the gossip and intrigue of society figures in London – and with one man in particular. While the setting is beautiful, the inhabitants are living in a form of purgatory. Sylvia Lynd (1888–1952) was born in London to Irish parents, and she was involved with the Inghinidhe na hÉireann, an Irish nationalist women's organisation. She wrote stories, novels and poetry and was an influential book reviewer for periodicals such as *Time and Tide*, as well as co-founding The Book Society, the first book-of-the-month club in the UK.

But summer isn't solely a time for Italian vistas, of course. G. B. Stern's 'Black Cat for Luck' (1933) finds the characters at a fashionable garden party in London. As Stern writes in the story's opening paragraphs: 'London in early June hints that this is going to be the loveliest summer, the only summer, the summer of gay adventures and desires come true.' This particular adventure involves a quick-thinking young woman called Barbara, who gets suddenly embroiled in a young man's white lie when he turns up outside her house and does her best to save the day. G. B. Stern (1890–1973) was a prolific novelist, short-story writer, and memoirist, as well as writing widely about Jane Austen and R. L. Stevenson.

Perhaps few people have this sort of serendipitous adventure on a summer afternoon; rather more likely to strike a chord is Mary Lavin's story of a family going to the beach. 'The Sand Castle' (1945) focuses on a trio of competitive siblings, Emily, John and Alexandre who, at 4½, is the youngest of the three and made to remember it.

✻ ✻ ✻

"You can play what you like," said Emily. "You won't play with us!"

"Why?" said Alexandre. "Why won't I play with you?"

"You're too small," said Emily.

Alexandre accepted this familiar insult. He stared at his plate. The tears began to splash on to the surface of the shining porcelain.

'The Sand Castle' is perhaps the gentlest story in *Stories for Summer*. The plot is simple – the children build a sandcastle – but it is an opportunity for Lavin to delve into the everyday rivalry, cohesion and unspoken love between brothers and sisters that is the pattern of so much family life. Mary Lavin (1912–1996) was an Irish short-story writer and novelist: her first collection of stories won the James Tait Black Memorial Prize for fiction, and she would later be awarded the Katherine Mansfield Prize and two Guggenheim Fellowships.

Phyllis Bottome also takes us to the seaside for 'The Shark's Fin' (1948), but this time the location is the Caribbean, and the tone is much less contented. Dorothy is displeased with her new husband when he leaves her alone on their honeymoon to visit a nearby island. The island is at a just-about swimmable distance across the channel and Dorothy decides to make that swim to teach her husband a lesson: 'after a sparkling month of unsullied felicity, with no fin of a shark showing like a sinister shadow in the translucent sea of her bliss, came this sudden appalling shock'. Metaphorical and real sharks are both, it turns out, threats in this story. Phyllis Bottome (1884–1963) wrote many short stories and novels, including the spy thriller *The Lifeline* (1946) which, it has been suggested, directly influenced Ian Fleming in his creation of James Bond.

＊　＊　＊

Mary Norton's 'The Lovely Evening' is one of a number of stories later collected and published together in *The Bread and Butter Stories* (1998) – so-called, her daughter remembers, because the publication of short stories 'earned our bread and butter'. It takes us back to Italy, where Sarah is on holiday with her daughter, Miranda, and Miranda's friend Brigitta. The girls are on the cusp of adulthood, talking about night clubs and flirting with the cautious maturity of teenagers experimenting at being grown-up. One local young man becomes involved with the party – with unexpected results. Norton (1903–1992) was most famous for writing about a very different family, the Borrowers – tiny people living secretly in humans' homes, 'borrowing' what they need to survive. She also wrote the children's book *The Magic Bedknob*, later adapted into the Disney film *Bedknobs and Broomsticks*.

The scene for Daphne du Maurier's 'The Pool' (1959) is a blazing heatwave at a country house, with Deborah and her brother Roger visiting their grandparents. It is a much-anticipated summer respite from life at their boarding schools: 'the fact that the garden waited for them was a miracle known only to herself'. Deborah is about 13, still grieving the loss of her mother years earlier, and deeply attached to the natural world in a way that is initially touching and, in du Maurier's sure hands, becomes increasingly disconcerting and mysterious. Deborah is particularly drawn to the pool – that 'demanded sacrifice'. Daphne du Maurier (1907–1989) came from a noted theatrical and artistic family and is well remembered for novels including *Rebecca* and horror stories such as 'The Birds' and 'Don't Look Now'. This story borrows elements of creepiness from that genre, distorting the idea of childhood summers as halcyon days.

In Elizabeth Taylor's 'A Different Light' (1961) Barbara has travelled to a Greek island to visit her sister Jane, and scenic boats, tavernas and brilliant sunshine are the backdrop for the story – but it is not a typical summer holiday. Jane's husband 'had died that spring and Barbara had come from England to be with her sister for a time and eventually take her home'. While there, she also gets to know a visiting architect and an unlikely friendship starts up: they spend afternoons swimming together or going by mule to visit the island's convent.

> It was an odd, holiday companionship they shared, founded on nothing but what had happened in the last few days—the mistakes they had made from not understanding the language, their delight in their new experience and, now, the hazards of riding their mules down a rocky, dried-up river bed.

For both of them, life at home – he with his wife, she with her husband and children, in the everyday streets and landscape of England – begins to feel curiously distant and distorted. In Taylor's subtle story, nothing takes place that would count as a scandal. But Barbara's summer has left her altered, unable to think about her home life in the same way, yet also unable to sustain the new friendship that so unexpectedly changed her. The bittersweet final line leaves the reader unsure; Taylor is too clever a writer to give any absolute conclusions. Alongside Taylor's (1912–1975) short stories, her novels, including *Angel* and *Mrs Palfrey at the Claremont*, have established her reputation as one of the most adept writers of her generation.

'In and Out of Never-Never Land' (1963) by Maeve Brennan takes place on a landmark day of summer, at least in the USA

– the fourth of July, with its attendant fireworks leading to the story's climax. Mary Ann lives by the ocean in East Hampton, with her dog and cats for company – and, at slightly further remove, the large family living in a nearby mansion of 'hundreds of rooms'. Their lives cross over, though Mary Ann remains at something of a distance, doubting her place in the little community, and even doubting the house she lives in: 'the house seemed to enjoy the summer sun cautiously, as though it knew it wasn't a summer house, and not a seaside house, and, in fact, not a real house'. Maeve Brennan (1917–1993) was Irish, though moved with her family to the US as a teenager. She went on to work as a fashion writer at *Harper's Bazaar* and later a social diarist for *The New Yorker*, where her short stories were mostly published.

'Afternoon in Summer' (1972) by Sylvia Townsend Warner can perhaps lay claim to the most striking opening lines in *Stories for Summer*:

> He became aware that Sally had emerged from her book and was about to say something.
> "Murder is an occupational risk for prostitutes."

Sally is spending her summer afternoon reading about 'all the murders committed in the last thirty years'. She and Willie set off for tea in a pub but instead find themselves seeking cool sanctuary in a village church. It is the sort of story that is distinctively from the pen of Sylvia Townsend Warner (1893–1978), whose short fiction often takes unexpected turns while still being piercingly observant about everyday human behaviour. Though a British author who lived in Dorset for much of her life, 'Afternoon in Summer' was published in *The New Yorker*, like much of her short

*** *** ***

fiction. Warner is now best remembered for her first novel, *Lolly Willowes* (1926) about a spinster who makes an unconventional choice to avoid being dependent on her male relatives.

While Sally and Willie's marriage is content, the marriages depicted in 'The Fortune Teller' (1983) by Muriel Spark are not. Lucy is on holiday in France with two friends and:

> The marriage between Raymond and Sylvia was already going bad [...] I had already decided after the third day of our travels that I would never again go on holiday alone with a married couple, and I never have since.

As a pastime Lucy tells fortunes – oblivious to the future predictions being made about her by others. Muriel Spark (1918–2006) was a Scottish writer who lived for much of her life in Italy, and is known for sharp, odd novels like *The Prime of Miss Jean Brodie*, *The Driver's Seat*, and *Memento Mori*.

The final story in *Stories for Summer*, 'Men Friends' by Angela Huth (b.1938), appropriately ends the collection with a funeral. The deceased is Louisa, and the mourner we first encounter is Conrad, who had an adulterous affair with her, first meeting on 'one of those smudged summer afternoons when the tremor of heat makes everything illusory'. As the story continues, we see Louisa brought to life through the recollections of the other mourners of the story's title. Angela Huth is a writer and journalist known for the 1995 novel *Land Girls* and was one of the BBC's first female TV presenters, hosting the 1960s documentary series *Man Alive*.

The floral motif that opened the collection and appeared throughout the stories continues here. What started as Katherine

✳ ✳ ✳

Mansfield's carnation among schoolgirls is now 'expensive wreaths of flowers at the foot of yews' and a single gardenia laid on the coffin by Louisa's husband. Through the course of the characters and worlds of *Stories for Summer*, the sunny days of June and July, August and September have borne witness to a wide range of joys and tragedies in the lives of the women and girls featured – some major, some unnoticed by anybody else. Whether on a Greek island, in a French chateau, or at Kew Gardens, each summer story shows a significant day, hour or moment in the life of women from many walks of life. And whether you're able to take this book to a beautiful beach or are reading for some summery escape, I hope you'll enjoy meeting new authors and perhaps re-encountering much-loved ones.

Simon Thomas

Series consultant **Simon Thomas** created the middlebrow blog Stuck in a Book in 2007. He is also the co-host of the popular podcast Tea or Books? Simon has a PhD from Oxford University in Interwar Literature.

※ ※ ※

Publisher's Note

These stories, like the original novels reprinted in the British Library Women Writers series, were written and published, for the most part, from the 1910s to the 1950s. There are many elements of these stories which continue to entertain modern readers, however, in some cases there are also uses of language, instances of stereotyping and some attitudes expressed by narrators or characters which may not be endorsed by the publishing standards of today, and we acknowledge may continue to make uncomfortable reading for some of our audience. With this series, British Library Publishing aims to offer a new readership a chance to read some of the rare books of the British Library's collections in an affordable paperback format, to enjoy their merits and to look back into the world of the twentieth century as portrayed by their writers. It is not possible to separate these stories from the history of their writing and as such the stories are presented as originally published with minor edits made for consistency of style and sense. We welcome feedback from our readers, which can be sent to the following address: British Library Publishing, The British Library, 96 Euston Road, London, NW1 2DB.

Carnation

KATHERINE MANSFIELD

On those hot days Eve—curious Eve—always carried a flower. She snuffed it and snuffed it, twirled it in her fingers, laid it against her cheek, held it to her lips, tickled Katie's neck with it, and ended, finally, by pulling it to pieces and eating it, petal by petal.

"Roses are delicious, my dear Katie," she would say, standing in the dim cloak room, with a strange decoration of flowery hats on the hat pegs behind her—"but carnations are simply divine! They taste like—like—ah well!" And away her little thin laugh flew, fluttering among those huge, strange flower heads on the wall behind her. (But how cruel her little thin laugh was! It had a long sharp beak and claws and two bead eyes, thought fanciful Katie.)

To-day it was a carnation. She brought a carnation to the French class, a deep, deep red one, that looked as though it had been dipped in wine and left in the dark to dry. She held it on the desk before her, half shut her eyes and smiled.

"Isn't it a darling?" said she. But—

"*Un peu de silence, s'il vous plait,*" came from M. Hugo. Oh, bother! It was too hot! Frightfully hot! Grilling simply!

The two square windows of the French Room were open at the bottom and the dark blinds drawn half way down. Although no air came in, the blind cord swung out and back and the blind lifted. But really there was not a breath from the dazzle outside.

Even the girls, in the dusky room, in their pale blouses, with stiff butterfly-bow hair ribbons perched on their hair, seemed to give off a warm, weak light, and M. Hugo's white waistcoat gleamed like the belly of a shark.

Some of the girls were very red in the face and some were white. Vera Holland had pinned up her black curls *à la japonaise* with a penholder and a pink pencil; she looked charming. Francie Owen pushed her sleeves nearly up to the shoulders, and then she inked the little blue vein in her elbow, shut her arm together, and then looked to see the mark it made; she had a passion for inking herself; she always had a face drawn on her thumb nail, with black, forked hair. Sylvia Mann took off her collar and tie, took them off simply, and laid them on the desk beside her, as calm as if she were going to wash her hair in her bedroom at home. She *had* a nerve! Jennie Edwards tore a leaf out of her notebook and wrote "Shall we ask old Hugo-Wugo to give us a thrippenny vanilla on the way home!!!" and passed it across to Connie Baker, who turned absolutely purple and nearly burst out crying. All of them lolled and gaped, staring at the round clock, which seemed to have grown paler, too; the hands scarcely crawled.

"*Un peu de silence, s'il vous plaît,*" came from M. Hugo. He held up a puffy hand. "Ladies, as it is so 'ot we will take no more notes to-day, but I will read you," and he paused and smiled a broad, gentle smile, "a little French poetry."

"Go—od God!" moaned Francie Owen.

M. Hugo's smile deepened. "Well, Mees Owen, you need not attend. You can paint yourself. You can 'ave my red ink as well as your black one."

How well they knew the little blue book with red edges that he tugged out of his coat tail pocket! It had a green silk marker embroidered in forget-me-nots. They often giggled at it when he handed the book round. Poor old Hugo-Wugo! He adored reading poetry. He would begin, softly and calmly, and then gradually his voice would swell and vibrate and gather itself together, then it would be pleading and imploring and entreating, and then rising, rising triumphant, until it burst into light, as it were, and then—gradually again, it ebbed, it grew soft and warm and calm and died down into nothingness.

The great difficulty was, of course, if you felt at all feeble, not to get the most awful fit of the giggles. Not because it was funny, really, but because it made you feel uncomfortable, queer, silly, and somehow ashamed for old Hugo-Wugo. But—oh dear—if he was going to inflict it on them in this heat …!

"Courage, my pet," said Eve, kissing the languid carnation.

He began, and most of the girls fell forward, over the desks, their heads on their arms, dead at the first shot. Only Eve and Katie sat upright and still. Katie did not know enough French to understand, but Eve sat listening, her eyebrows raised, her eyes half veiled, and a smile that was like the shadow of her cruel little laugh, like the wing shadows of that cruel little laugh fluttering over her lips. She made a warm, white cup of her fingers—the carnation inside. Oh, the scent! It floated across to Katie. It was too much. Katie turned away to the dazzling light outside the window.

Down below, she knew, there was a cobbled courtyard with stable buildings round it. That was why the French Room always smelled faintly of ammonia. It wasn't unpleasant; it was even part of the French language for Katie—something sharp and vivid and—and— biting!

Now she could hear a man clatter over the cobbles and the jing-jang of the pails he carried. And now *Hoo-hor-her! Hoo-hor-her!* as he worked the pump, and a great gush of water followed. Now he was flinging the water over something, over the wheels of a carriage, perhaps. And she saw the wheel, propped up, clear of the ground, spinning round, flashing scarlet and black, with great drops glancing off it. And all the while he worked the man kept up a high bold whistling, that skimmed over the noise of the water as a bird skims over the sea. He went away—he came back again leading a cluttering horse.

Hoo-hor-her! Hoo-hor-her! came from the pump. Now he dashed the water over the horse's legs and then swooped down and began brushing.

She *saw* him simply—in a faded shirt, his sleeves rolled up, his chest bare, all splashed with water—and as he whistled, loud and free, and as he moved, swooping and bending, Hugo-Wugo's voice began to warm, to deepen, to gather together, to swing, to rise—somehow or other to keep time with the man outside (Oh, the scent of Eve's carnation!) until they became one great rushing, rising, triumphant thing, bursting into light, and then—

The whole room broke into pieces.

"Thank you, ladies," cried M. Hugo, bobbing at his high desk, over the wreckage.

And "Keep it, dearest," said Eve. "*Souvenir tendre,*" and she popped the carnation down the front of Katie's blouse.

Kew Gardens

Virginia Woolf

From the oval-shaped flower-beds there rose perhaps a hundred stalks spreading into heart-shaped or tongue-shaped leaves half-way up and unfurling at the tip red or blue or yellow petals marked with spots of colour raised up the surface; and from the red, blue or yellow gloom of the throat emerged a straight bar, rough with gold dust and slightly clubbed at the end. The petals were voluminous enough to be stirred by the summer breeze, and when they moved, the red, blue and yellow lights passed one over the other, staining an inch of the brown earth beneath with a spot of the most intricate colour. The light fell either upon the smooth, grey back of a pebble, or, the shell of a snail with its brown, circular veins, or falling into a raindrop, it expanded with such intensity of red, blue and yellow the thin walls of water that one expected them to burst and disappear. Instead, the drop was left in a second silver grey once more, and the light now settled upon the flesh of a leaf, revealing the branching thread of fibre beneath the surface, and again it moved and spread its illumination in the vast green spaces beneath the dome of the heart-shaped and tongue-shaped leaves. Then the breeze stirred rather more briskly overhead and the colour was flashed into the air above, into the eyes of the men and women who walk in Kew Gardens in July.

The figures of these men and women straggled past the

flower-bed with a curiously irregular movement not unlike that of the white and blue butterflies who crossed the turf in zig-zag flights from bed to bed. The man was about six inches in front of the woman, strolling carelessly, while she bore on with greater purpose, only turning her head now and then to see that the children were not too far behind. The man kept his distance in front of the woman purposely, though perhaps unconsciously, for he wished to go on with his thoughts.

"Fifteen years ago I came with Lily," he thought. "We sat somewhere over there by a lake and I begged her to marry me all through the hot afternoon. How the dragonfly kept circling round us: how clearly I see the dragonfly and her shoe with the square silver buckle at the toe. All the time I spoke I saw her shoe and when it moved impatiently I knew without looking up what she was going to say: the whole of her seemed to be in her shoe. And my love, my desire, were in the dragonfly; for some reason I thought that if it settled there, on that leaf, the broad one with the red flower in the middle of it, if the dragonfly settled on the leaf she would say 'Yes' at once. But the dragonfly went round and round: it never settled anywhere—of course not, happily not, or I shouldn't be walking here with Eleanor and the children. Tell me, Eleanor. D'you ever think of the past?"

"Why do you ask, Simon?"

"Because I've been thinking of the past. I've been thinking of Lily, the woman I might have married ... Well, why are you silent? Do you mind my thinking of the past?"

"Why should I mind, Simon? Doesn't one always think of the past, in a garden with men and women lying under the trees? Aren't they one's past, all the remains of it, those men and women, those ghosts lying under the trees, ... one's happiness, one's reality?"

"For me, a square silver shoe buckle and a dragonfly—"

"For me, a kiss. Imagine six little girls sitting before their easels twenty years ago, down by the side of a lake, painting and water-lilies, the first red water-lilies I'd ever seen. And suddenly a kiss, there on the back of my neck. And my hand shook all the afternoon so that I couldn't paint. I took out my watch and marked the hour when would allow myself to think of the kiss for five minutes only—it was so precious—the kiss of an old grey-haired woman with a wart on her nose, the mother of all my kisses all my life. Come, Caroline, come, Hubert."

They walked on past the flower-bed, now walking four abreast, and soon diminished in size among the trees and looked half transparent as the sunlight and shade swam over their backs in large trembling irregular patches.

In the oval flower bed the snail, whose shell had been stained red, blue and yellow for the space of two minutes or so, now appeared to be moving very slightly in its shell, and next began to labour over the crumbs of loose earth which broke away and rolled down as it passed over them. It appeared to have a definite goal in front of it, differing in this respect from the singular high stepping angular green insect who attempted to cross in front of it, and waited for a second with its antennae trembling as if in deliberation, and then stepped off as rapidly and strangely in the opposite direction. Brown cliffs with deep green lakes in the hollows, flat, blade-like trees that waved from root to tip, round boulders of grey stone, vast crumpled surfaces of a thin crackling texture—all these objects lay across the snail's progress between one stalk and another to his goal. Before he had decided whether to circumvent the arched tent of a dead leaf or to breast it there came past the bed the feet of other human beings.

This time they were both men. The younger of the two wore an expression of perhaps unnatural calm; he raised his eyes and fixed them very steadily in front of him while his companion spoke, and directly his companion had done speaking he looked on the ground again and sometimes did not open them at all. The elder man had a curiously uneven and shaky method of walking, jerking his hand forward and throwing up his head abruptly, rather in the manner of an impatient carriage horse tired of waiting outside a house; but in the man these gestures were irresolute and pointless. He talked almost incessantly; he smiled to himself and again began to talk, as if the smile had been an answer. He was talking about spirits—the spirits of the dead, who, according to him, were even now telling him all sorts of odd things about their experiences in Heaven.

"Heaven was known to the ancients as Thessaly, William, and now, with this war, the spirit matter is rolling between the hills like thunder." He paused, seemed to listen, smiled, jerked his head and continued:

"You have a small electric battery and a piece of rubber to insulate the wire—isolate?—insulate?—well, we'll skip the details, no good going into details that wouldn't be understood—and in short the little machine stands in any convenient position by the head of the bed, we will say, on a neat mahogany stand. All arrangements being properly fixed by workmen under my direction, the widow applies her ear and summons the spirit by sign as agreed. Women! Widows! Women in black—"

Here he seemed to have caught sight of a woman's dress in the distance, which in the shade looked a purple black. He took off his hat, placed his hand upon his heart, and hurried towards her muttering and gesticulating feverishly. But William caught him by the sleeve and touched a flower with the tip of his walking-stick in order to divert the old man's attention. After looking at it for a moment in some confusion the old man bent his ear to it and seemed to answer a voice speaking from it, for he began talking about the forests of Uruguay which he had visited hundreds of years ago in company with the most beautiful young woman in Europe. He could be heard murmuring about forests of Uruguay blanketed with the wax petals of tropical trees, nightingales, sea beaches, mermaids, and women drowned at sea, as he suffered himself to be moved on by William, upon whose face the look of stoical patience grew slowly deeper and deeper.

Following his steps so closely as to be slightly puzzled by his gestures came two elderly women of the lower middle class, one stout and ponderous, the other rosy cheeked and nimble. Like most people of their station they were frankly fascinated by any signs of eccentricity betokening a disordered brain, especially in the well-to-do; but there were too far off to be certain whether the gestures were merely eccentric or genuinely mad. After they had scrutinized the old man's back in silence for a moment and given each other a queer, sly look, they went on energetically piecing together their very complicated dialogue:

"Nell, Bert, Lot, Cess, Phil, Pa, he says, I says, she says, I says, I says—"

"My Bert, Sis, Bill, Grandad, the old man, sugar,

Sugar, flour, kippers, greens,

Sugar, sugar, sugar."

The ponderous woman looked through the pattern of falling words at the flowers standing cool, firm, and upright in the earth, with a curious expression. She saw them as a sleeper waking from a heavy sleep sees a brass candlestick reflecting the light in an unfamiliar way, and closes his eyes and opens them, and seeing the brass candlestick again, finally starts broad awake and stares at the candlestick with all his powers. So the heavy woman came to a standstill opposite the oval-shaped flower bed, and ceased even to pretend to listen to what the other woman was saying. She stood there letting the words fall over her, swaying the top part of her body slowly backwards and forwards, looking at the flowers. Then she suggested that they should find a seat and have their tea.

The snail had now considered every possible method of reaching his goal without going round the dead leaf or climbing over it. Let alone the effort needed for climbing a leaf, he was doubtful whether the thin texture which vibrated with such an alarming crackle when touched even by the tip of his horns would bear his weight; and this determined him finally to creep beneath it, for there was a point where the leaf curved high enough from the ground to admit him. He had just inserted his head in the opening and was taking stock of the high brown roof and was getting used to the cool brown light when two other people came past outside on the turf. This time they were both young, a young man and a young woman. They were both in the prime of youth, or even in that season which precedes the prime of youth, the season before the smooth pink folds of the flower have burst their gummy case, when the wings of the butterfly, though fully grown, are motionless in the sun.

"Lucky it isn't Friday," he observed.

"Why? D'you believe in luck?"

"They make you pay sixpence on Friday."

"What's sixpence anyway? Isn't it worth sixpence?"

"What's 'it'—what do you mean by 'it'?"

"O, anything—I Mean—you know what I mean."

Long pauses came between each of these remarks; they were uttered in toneless and monotonous voices. The couple stood still on the edge of the flower bed, and together pressed the end of her parasol deep down into the soft earth. The action and the fact that his hand rested on the top of hers expressed their feelings in a strange way, as these short insignificant words also expressed something, words with short wings for their heavy body of meaning, inadequate to carry them far and thus alighting awkwardly upon the very common objects that surrounded them, and were to their inexperienced touch so massive; but who knows (so they thought as they pressed the parasol into the earth) what precipices aren't concealed in them, or what slopes of ice don't shine in the sun on the other side? Who knows? Who had ever seen this before? Even when she wondered what sort of tea they gave you at Kew, he felt that something loomed up behind her words, and stood vast and solid behind them; and the mist very slowly rose and uncovered—O Heavens, what were those shapes?—little white tables, and waitresses who looked first at her and then at him; and there was the bill that he would pay with a real two shilling piece, and it was real, all real, he assured himself, fingering the coin in his pocket, real to everyone except to him and to her; even to him it began to seem real; and then—but it was too exciting to stand and think any longer, and he pulled the parasol out of the earth with a jerk and was impatient to find the place where one had tea with other people, like other people.

Requiescat

Elizabeth Bowen

Majendie had bought the villa on his honeymoon, and in April, three months after his death, his widow went out there alone to spend the spring and early summer. Stuart, who had been in India at the time of Howard Majendie's death, wrote to Mrs Majendie before starting for home and her reply awaited him at his club; he re-read it several times, looking curiously at her writing, which he had never seen before. The name of the villa was familiar to him, Majendie had been speaking of it the last time they dined together; he said it had a garden full of lemon trees and big cypresses, and more fountains than you could imagine—it was these that Ellaline had loved. Stuart pictured Mrs Majendie walking about among the lemon trees in her widow's black.

In her letter she expressed a wish to see him—in a little while. "I shall be returning to England at the end of June; there is a good deal of business to go through, and there are several things that Howard wished me to discuss with you. He said you would be willing to advise and help me. I do not feel that I can face England before then; I have seen nobody yet, and it is difficult to make a beginning. You understand that I feel differently about meeting you; Howard wished it, and I think that is enough for both of us. If you were to be in Italy I should ask you to come and see me here, but as I know that you will be going straight to Ireland I will keep the papers until

June, all except the very important ones, which I must sign without quite understanding, I suppose." In concluding, she touched on his friendship with Howard as for her alone it was permissible to touch. Stuart wired his apologies to Ireland and planned a visit to the Italian lakes.

Three weeks afterwards found him in the prow of a motor-boat, furrowing Lake Como as he sped towards the villa. The sky was cloudless, the hills to the right rose sheer above him, casting the lengthening shadows of the afternoon across the luminous and oily water; to the left were brilliant and rugged above the clustered villages. The boat shot closely under Cadenabbia and set the orange-hooded craft bobbing; the reflected houses rocked and quivered in her wake, colours flecked the broken water.

"Subito, subito!" said the boatman reassuringly and Stuart started; he did not know that his impatience was so evident. The man shut off his engines, let the boat slide further into the shore, and displacing Stuart from the prow, crouched forward with a ready boat-hook. They were approaching the water-stairway of the villa.

For a few moments after he had landed, while the motor-boat went chuffing out again into the sunshine, Stuart stood at the top of the stairway looking irresolutely through the iron gates. He was wondering why he had come to Italy, and whether he even cared at all for Mrs Majendie. He felt incapable of making his way towards her under the clustered branches of those trees. If there had been a little side-gate it would have been easier to go in; it would not have been so difficult, either, if he had ever been here with Howard Majendie. But this was *Her* place; she had loved it because of the fountains.

He pushed open the big gate, already cold in the shadow, and followed the upward curve of the avenue among the lemon trees. Beyond the villa disclosed itself, unlike all that he had expected; he was surprised at his own suprise and did not realize till then how clearly he must have visualized it. There was a wide loggia, a flight of steps, a terrace on a level with the loggia running along the side of the hill. Cypress trees rose everywhere, breaking up the view. He passed under the windows, climbed the steps and crossed the loggia, not looking to left or right for fear that he might see her suddenly, or even one of her books. The loggia had an air of occupation; it was probable that on any of those tables, or among the cushions, he might see her book, half open, or the long-handled lorgnettes that Majendie had given her in France.

The servant said that Mrs Majendie was in the garden. She showed Stuart into a tall, cool parlour and disappeared to find her mistress. Stuart, distracted by a scent of heliotrope, made an unseeing circle of the room; he was standing before a Florentine chest when the girl came back with a message. Mrs Majendie would see him in the garden. It would have been easier to meet her here; he had pictured them sitting opposite to one another in these high-backed chairs. He followed the girl obediently out of the house, along the terrace, and down a long alley between hedges of yew. The white plume of a fountain quivered at the end, other fountains were audible in the garden below. He could hear footsteps, too; someone was approaching by another alley that converged with his beyond the fountain. Here they met.

She was less beautiful than he had remembered her, and very tall and thin in her black dress. Her composure did not astonish him; her smile, undimmed, and the sound of her voice recalled to him the poignancy of his feelings when he had first known her, his resentment and sense of defeat—she had possessed herself of Howard so entirely. She was shortsighted, there was always a look of uncertainty in her eyes until she came quite near one, her big pupils seemed to see too much at once and nothing very plainly.

"I never knew you were in Italy," she said.

He realized that it would have been more considerate to have written to prepare her for his visit.

"I came out," he said, "quite suddenly. I had always wanted to see the Lakes. And I wanted to see you, but perhaps I should have written. I—I never thought … It would have been better."

"It doesn't matter. It was very good of you to come. I am glad that you should see the villa. Are you staying near?"

"Over at Varenna. How beautiful this is!"

"The lake?"

"I meant your garden." They turned and walked slowly back towards the house. "I hope I didn't take you too much by surprise?"

"Oh no," she said. It almost seemed as though she had expected him. "Yes, it is beautiful, isn't it? I have done nothing to it, it is exactly as we found it."

They sat down on a stone bench on the terrace, looking a little away from one another; their minds were full of the essential things impossible to be said. Sitting there with her face turned away from him, every inch of her had that similitude of repose which covers tension. His lowered eyes took in her hands and long, thin fingers lying against the blackness of her dress. He remembered Howard telling him (among those confidences which had later ceased) how though he had fallen in love with the whole of her it was her hands that he first noticed when details began to detach themselves. Now they looked bewildered, helpless hands.

"I took you at your word," he said; "I wanted to help; I hoped there might be something I could do, and in your letter—"

"I took you at your word in asking for help. There is a great deal I must do, and you could make things easier for me, if you will. I shall be very grateful for your help about some business; there are papers I must sign and I don't understand them quite. There were things that Howard had never explained." She looked full at him for a moment and he knew that this was the first time she had uttered her husband's name. It would be easier now.

"He had told me everything," he said quickly, as though to

intercept the shutting of a door. "I was always to be there if you should need me—I had promised him." She must realize that she owed him nothing for the fulfilment of a duty. He thought she did, for she was silent, uttering no word of thanks.

"Why did you so seldom come and see us?" she asked suddenly. "Howard had begun to notice lately, and he wondered."

"I was in India."

"Before you went to India." A little inflection in her voice made him despise his evasion.

"There is a time for all things, and that was a time for keeping away."

"Because he was married?"

Stuart did not answer.

"We wanted you," she said, "but you didn't understand, did you?"

She did not understand, how could she? She must have discussed it all, those evenings, with the Majendie that belonged to her; he had not understood either.

"I was mistaken, I suppose," he said. "I—I should have learnt later."

There was a slight contraction of her fingers, and Stuart knew that he had hurt her. If he hurt her like this a little more, it would probably be possible to kill her; she was very defenceless here in the garden that Majendie had bought her, looking out at the unmeaning lake. He had crowded out all tenderness for her, and her loneliness was nothing but a fact to him.

"There were messages for you," she said, turning her head again.

"Were there?"

"He said—," her lips moved, she glanced at him a little apprehensively and was silent. "I have written down everything that he said for you. And I believe he left you a letter."

"Can you remember the messages?" he asked curiously.

"I wrote them down; I have them in the house." She looked at him again with that short-sighted intensity; she knew every word of the messages, and with an effort he could almost have read them from her eyes.

"Did he expect to see me?"

"Yes, once he knew that he was ill. He knew that you could not possibly leave India before April, but he kept on—expecting. I wanted to cable to you and he wouldn't let me. But I know he still believed, above all reason, that you'd come."

"If I'd known, if—"

"You think I should have cabled without telling him?" She thought he blamed her and she evidently feared his anger. Curious … He had been so conscious of her indifference, before; he had been a person who did not matter, the nice friend, the family dog—relegated. It was that that had stung and stung. After all he need never have gone to India, it had been a resource of panic. It had saved him nothing, and there had been no question of saving *her*. He wondered why she had not cabled; it was nothing to her whether he went or came, and Howard's happiness was everything.

"Yes, I wonder you didn't cable."

"I am sorry; I was incapable of anything. My resource was—sapped."

He looked at her keenly; it was a doctor's look.

"What have you been doing since?" he asked (as the medical man, to whom no ground was sacred). "What are you going to do?"

"I was writing letters, shutting up the house. And here I'm trying to realize that there's nothing more to do, that matters. And afterwards—"

"Well?"

"I don't know," she said wearily; "I'd rather not, please … Afterwards will come of itself."

He smiled as now he took upon himself the brother-in-law, the nice, kind, doggy person. "You should have somebody with you,

Ellaline. You should, you owe it to yourself, you owe it to"—he realized there was no one else to whom she owed it—"to yourself," he repeated. "You must think, you must be wise for yourself now."

She looked, half-smiling, at him while he counselled. He had never achieved the fraternal so completely.

"It's not that I don't think," she said. "I think a great deal. And as for wisdom—there is not much more to learn once one has grown up. I am as wise as I need be—'for myself.'"

"When are you going back to England?"

"If you would do one or two things for me I needn't go back until the autumn."

"You can't stay here all the summer."

"No," she said, looking round at the cypresses—how pitiful she was, in Howard's garden. "They say I couldn't, it would be too hot; I must go somewhere else. But if you could help me a little this autumn I could finish up the business then."

"I may have to be in Ireland then." He tore himself away from something brutally, and the brutality sounded in his voice.

She retreated.

"Of course," she said, "I know you ought to be there now—I was forgetting."

Because he was a person who barely existed for her (probably) she had always been gentle with him, almost propitiatory. One must be gentle with the nice old dog. It was not in her nature to be always gentle, perhaps she had said bitter things to Howard who mattered to her; there was a hint of bitterness about her mouth. At himself she was always looking in that vague, half-startled way, as though she had forgotten who he was. Sometimes when he made a third he had found her very silent, still with boredom; once or twice he had felt with gratification that she almost disliked him. He wondered what she thought he thought of her.

Now it was the time of the Angelus, and bells answered one

another from the campaniles of the clustered villages across the lake. A steamer, still gold in the sun, cleft a long bright furrow in the shadowy water. The scene had all the passionless clarity of a Victorian water-colour.

"It is very peaceful," Stuart said appropriately.

"Peaceful?" she echoed with a start. "Yes, it's very peaceful … David" (she had called him this), "will you forgive me?"

"Forgive you?"

"I think you could understand me if you wished to. Forgive me the harm I've done you. Don't, don't hate me."

How weak she was now, how she had come down! "What harm have you done to me?" he asked, unmoved.

"You should know better than I do. I suppose I must have hurt you, and through you, Howard. An—an intrusion isn't a happy thing. You didn't give me a chance to make it happy. You came at first, but there was always a cloud. I didn't want to interfere, I tried to play the game. Now that we've both lost him, couldn't you forgive?"

"I'm sorry I should have given you the impression that I resented anything—that there was anything to resent. I didn't know that you were thinking that. Perhaps you rather ran away with a preconceived idea that because you married Howard I was bound to be unfriendly to you. If you did, you never showed it. I never imagined that I had disappointed you by anything I did or didn't do."

"It was not what you didn't do, it was what you *weren't* that made me feel I was a failure." (So *that* was the matter, he had hurt her vanity!)

"A failure," he said, laughing a little; "I thought you were making a success. If I didn't come oftener it was not because I did not think you wanted me."

"But you said just now—"

"A third is never really wanted. I had set my heart on seeing Howard happy, and when I had, I went away to think about it."

"Oh," she said hopelessly. She had guessed that he was putting her off. "Shall we walk a little down the terrace? There is a pergola above, too, that I should like you to see." She was taking for granted that he would not come to the villa again.

They rose; she stood for a moment looking irresolutely up and down the terrace, then took a steeper path that mounted through the trees towards the pergola. Stuart followed her in silence, wondering. The world in her brain was a mystery to him, but evidently he had passed across it and cast some shadows. For a moment he almost dared to speak, and trouble the peace of the garden with what had been pent up in him so long; then he knew that he must leave her to live out her days in the immunity of finished grief. The silence of imperfect sympathy would still lie between them, as it had always lain; his harshness could no longer cast a shadow in her world, that was now as sunless as an evening garden. His lips were sealed still, and for ever, by fear of her and shame for his dead loyalty to Howard. The generosity of love had turned to bitterness within him, and he was silent from no fear to cause her pain.

"Beautiful," he said, when they reached the pergola and could look down on lake and garden through the clustered roses.

"Will you be long at Varenna?"

"I don't expect so, no. Some friends want me to join them on Lake Maggiore, and I think of going on tomorrow afternoon."

"That will be better," she said slowly. "It *is* lonely seeing places alone—they hardly seem worth while."

"I'm used to it—I'm going back to India in six months," he said abruptly.

"Oh, I didn't know." Her voice faltered. He had not known himself till then. Her face was whiter than ever in the dusk of the pergola, and her hands were plucking, plucking at the creepers, shaking down from the roses above white petals which he kept brushing from his coat.

"I'm sorry you're going back," she said. "Everybody will be sorry."

"I won't go until I have finished everything that I can do for you."

An expression came into her eyes that he had never seen before. "You have been a friend," she said. "Men make better things for themselves out of life than we do."

"They don't last," he said involuntarily.

"I should have said that so far as anything is immortal—" He watched a little tightening of her lips.

"It takes less than you think to kill these things; friendship, loyalty—"

"Yours was unassailable, yours and his;" she spoke more to herself than to him. "In those early days when we three went about together; that time in France, I realized that."

"In France?" he said stupidly.

"Yes. Don't you remember?"

He remembered France; the days they had spent together, and the long evenings in starlight, and the evening he had strolled beside her on a terrace while Majendie tinkered with the car. It was a chilly evening, and she kept drawing her furs together and said very little. The night after, he had lain awake listening to her voice and Majendie's in the next room, and making up his mind to go to India.

"Yes," he said. "Now, will you let me have the papers and we could go through them now? I could take any that are urgent back to town with me; I shall be there in a week."

She twisted her hands irresolutely. "Could you come tomorrow, before you go? I would have them ready for you then, if you can spare the time. I'm tired this evening; I don't believe I would be able to understand them. Do you mind?"

"No, of course not. But may I come in the morning? I am going away early in the afternoon."

She nodded slowly, looked away from him and did not speak. She was evidently very much tired.

"I think I ought to go," he said after a pause.

"If you hurried you could catch that steamer down at Cadenabbia."

"Then I'll hurry. Don't come down."

"I won't come down," she said, holding out her hand. "Good-bye, and thank you."

He hurried to the end of the pergola, hesitated, half turned his head, and stopped irresolutely. Surely she had called him? He listened, but there was no sound. She stood where he had left her, with her back towards him, leaning against a pillar and looking out across the lake.

Turning, he pushed his way between the branches, down the overgrown path. The leaves rustled, he listened again; somebody was trying to detain him. As the slope grew steeper he quickened his steps to a run, and, skirting the terrace, took a short cut on to the avenue. Soon the lake glittered through the iron gates.

She leant back against the pillar, gripping in handfuls the branches of the climbing rose. She heard his descending footsteps hesitate for a long second, gather speed, grow fainter, die away. The thorns ran deep into her hands and she was dimly conscious of the pain. Far below the gate clanged, down among the trees. The branches of the roses shook a little, and more white petals came fluttering down.

Exile

Sylvia Lynd

Across the crowded teashop he was aware of two eyes watching him, large dark eyes that were brilliant with excitement. At the same moment he recognized Mrs. Alladale and his pleasure was mingled with a little unexamined puzzle of surprise that her recognition of himself was so unfeignedly joyous. He had known her to be gracious and pretty as she spoke a few words with him when they met at parties in London; but she had never asked him to her house, never shown any personal interest in him whatever. So little had she been interested, indeed, that he had been unable to feel anything but the remotest admiration for her—a tribute as formal as the passing of a vote of thanks at a committee. His vanity saw to that. He understood perfectly the attitude of the poet who said: "If she be not fair for me, what care I how fair she be?" As soon think of falling in love with Mrs. Alladale as with—as with—oh, well, say Mary Pickford. Grown men did not do these things. If a photograph that moved, and rolled its eyes, and laughed, could become suddenly a creature of flesh and blood, descend from the screen, advance upon him through the auditorium, cry out his name with a delighted voice and seem about to fling her arms round his neck—that would be another matter. He realized as he rose from his chair that that was what was happening. Only Mrs. Alladale was not advancing towards him. He was advancing towards her.

"How delightful," she cried, really too soon, while he was still twisting his way among the little tables, "how delightful to see you in Florence."

It made him glow with pleasure to be welcomed so ostentatiously. Yet he was conscious of being puzzled. He could find in himself no reason for her pleasure. Without excessive modesty he knew that little George Bingham of the Education Office was not the sort of person to cause delight to the beautiful Mrs. Alladale. The embarrassing possibility occurred to him that she had mistaken him for someone else. But no, she was saying to her companions, "Let me introduce Mr. Bingham," and he found himself shaking hands with a little old Englishman with an eyeglass, Captain Wallace, a young Italian whose name he did not catch, and a crop-haired girl in a bright red jumper whom he perceived at a glance to be an American and an art student. Her name was Miss Bolst. "Have you been here long?" Mrs. Alladale was asking him, and, while he answered that he had only arrived that morning, was threading her voice through his with little ecstatic exclamations of pleasure. "This is too delightful. We must find you a chair. What a crowded place this is," and in Italian to the proprietor who was standing near in a tightly-buttoned, tight-waisted frock coat, "A chair for this gentleman, please."

George Bingham shook his wits awake. However surprised, he was at least man enough to make the most of his good fortune.

"How splendidly lucky for me to meet you here," he said.

"Oh, everyone meets at Doney's sooner or later," cried Mrs. Alladale, and added: "Ah, here's a chair for you. Now we can all have tea together."

"How do you like Florence?" asked little old Captain Wallace. "Been here before?"

George admitted that it was his first visit and that he had been to the Uffizzi that morning.

"Seeing those pictures for the first time," said the American girl; "why, it's like falling on old friends' necks."

"Yes, yes, like meeting them alive and well," said Captain Wallace, "after a long separation."

They asked George Bingham if he were making a special study of anything. And George replied that he was a simple tourist, a borrowed Baedeker for the year 1909 in one pocket and "Italian Self-taught" in the other. "Tourists—well, there's nothing better than just watching the life in the streets of a new country. Better than a theatre."

Though he sat silent for the most part, putting into his mouth at intervals one of the little mouth-sized cakes that Miss Bolst had gone to the counter to choose for them, George Bingham felt himself to be the success of the party. Mrs. Alladale's dark eyes constantly enveloped him in happy glances, however her lips and ears might be engaged with the other three. It was as if he and the beautiful mature woman shared a secret unknown to the others. George Bingham wished he could guess what the secret was.

When tea was finished and they rose to go, Mrs. Alladale told him that she was living in a villa out at Fiesole. In the street she bade good-bye to the others and, "Mr. Bingham will put me into my tram," she said.

With a feeling of being an impostor George accompanied her. If it hadn't been for that feeling his pleasure would have been intense. But there was no reason, none, why this tall, beautiful, graceful woman in her dark, distinguished clothes should make him the object of her conspicuous favour. He felt altogether inadequate. His pale grey eyes could not provide any reflex for the intense glances her dark ones gave him. The brilliance of her presence increased his sense of dullness and futility.

She was talking to him about Florence, telling him what he must not miss and wherein his Baedeker was now out of date and unhelpful. She told him how the noontide siesta would cut into his time for sightseeing, pointed out the Strozzi lamp and the Palazzo d'Avanzati, and so brought him to where the Fiesole tram starts beside the great marble cliff of the cathedral.

"You'll come and see me ?" she said, taking leave of him. "There are such heaps of things I want to talk about, I've been away more than six months, you know. You'll have to come to Fiesole. Come and dine with me. We'll dine at the hotel and then come back and make coffee at my little villa—Villano Margherita—just at the back of the Villa Medici. I live all alone there. You can't miss it. I haven't much to offer you but a superb view. And the jasmine is still in flower. I was in the mountains all the summer, and I'm going down to Rome and on to Sicily soon. When will you come?"

George with great presence of mind said, "To-morrow." Mrs. Alladale was obviously pleased. "How lovely—how very nice of you—I shall look forward to seeing you so much."

The little tram tattered away, hugging the cliff of the Duomo, and George Bingham walked to his hotel in the twilight. How beautiful it was, how romantic! If only he could by some efflorescence of the imagination become part of its romance and beauty! Mrs. Alladale was part of it. The secrets of night, of jewelled light, of whispering, laughing voices, or rose-red carnations were her secrets. But he was only an onlooker, an outsider. If he were not shut out he should not be so aware of the beautiful appearance of things and the contrasting cold emptiness that took the place of a bounding warmth in his breast. The fine pure beauty of Florence and the rich cosmopolitan beauty of Mrs. Alladale made him feel like a pressed flower among growing ones.

Hitherto he had not been unhappy. He had lived safely and uneventfully. He had played reserve in the house eleven and taken a scholarship at Merton. He had passed with requisite efficiency into the Education Office. His only anxiety had been the health of his invalid mother, a charming old lady to whom he was devoted. During the war he had learned to drill and shoot with the utmost sincerity, but he had never been called on to do more than sit beside a searchlight for the last twelve months of the conflict. He lived in rather elegant rooms in Queen Anne Street. His housekeeping was done for him by an excellent widow who had been cook to his mother and had married a policeman. He spent the week-ends with his mother at Weybridge. He was thirty-two and looked about twenty-six. His health never troubled him except for heavy colds in the winter, and even those never went on to his chest. Reviewing his life he could not call himself unhappy, and he had hitherto called himself happy; now seeing the lights in the dark Arno and listening to the plucking of the inevitable guitars, he realized that his had been a purely negative existence—neither happy nor unhappy—just nothing at all. Deeply discontented with himself, he went to bed.

Next morning, returning from the San Marco, and going for lunch into a restaurant on the Piazza Vittorio Emmanuele, he found Captain Wallace seated in a corner reading an Italian newspaper.

"Ah, ha, my dear chap," the brown-skinned, crumpled little man hailed him, "looking for something to eat ? Come to my table and let me expound the mysteries of the menu—*la carta.*"

George Bingham obediently sat down opposite him, and Captain Wallace discoursed about food for the next twenty minutes, chose his lunch for him, and ordered for them both a flask of chianti. George marvelled at his friendliness, at his unfeigned desire to talk to his young compatriot. The Captain was a dapper old man. George Bingham wondered how long ago he had left the army, and why he had left it. Perhaps in Crimean days, George thought. He was very ancient. George was sure that he had done no work for fifty years. He had the garrulousness and the inquisitiveness of the idler. Probably a small fixed income and a life spent in following the English colony from Bordighera to Florence, and from Florence to Naples, thought George. Captain Wallace talked of the exchange, and with considerable excitement of the shocking increase in prices.

"Those who remember Italy in pre-war days, my dear boy—you could live in a Palazzo like a prince for three hundred a year—and how much do you think one paid a servant ?"

Rome, he told his young friend, was too dear and too noisy for life to be pleasant in it. "Now here in Florence there isn't a stranger comes to the place without your seeing him. Tea-time in Doney's, sooner or later there he'll be. We are one big house-party. Rome's too big, too big and noisy altogether."

And now, George Bingham felt sure of it, the old man was approaching the nucleus of the conversation. He leant confidently across the table and settled his eyeglass in its socket with a little flourish that indicated indubitably the direction of Fiesole.

"*La bella Signora*, she's goin' on to Rome next month, she tells me. Know her well in England, I suppose? When do you dine with her ?"

George Bingham said briefly that he was dining there that night. He had a desire to be reserved with this old man, though he knew there was no danger of his giving away a confidence, since nothing can be got from nothing.

"A charming creature," said Captain Wallace decisively, "a charming creature," and then returning to the attack: "Known her well in England, I suppose?"

George, increasing his air of caution, replied that he had known her very little.

"A woman of considerable social standing," said Captain Wallace. "Bound to have been. Not a doubt of it."

George said he always had the impression that Mrs. Alladale was a great success socially.

"Not a doubt of it," said Captain Wallace. "Mrs. Leslie Alladale, I've seen her picture in the papers—a very pretty picture. What's she doing out here?"

The question was sudden.

George, impenetrable as ever, said he did not know.

The Captain screwed his face into sceptical wrinkles.

"*Une mystère*," he said with great satisfaction; "a very easily solved mystery. Now what is the only possible reason for a charming woman like that to be trapesing about the Continent all alone?"

He posed the question. George Bingham, feeling at once inquisitive, a blockhead, and resentful that Mrs. Alladale should be made the subject of prying chatter, replied with an almost snubbing indifference again that he did not know.

"Ah, my dear boy," said Captain Wallace, "when you've seen as many days in the world as I have, you'll find there is only one answer to every question where a beautiful woman is concerned. The answer to the Question Woman, my dear boy, is Man. There's a Mister Alladale, I may suppose?"

George replied that he believed there was and found himself adding that Mr. Alladale, he believed, was rich—something in the City—and that Mrs. Alladale had always gone about alone.

"Alone?" Up went the Captain's eyebrows.

"Without Alladale," George said with irritation.

"Ah, ha," said the Captain, refixing his glass. George had the sensation that he was being pumped. Until that moment he had not recollected the existence of a Mr. Alladale.

"Now, what is the reason," said Captain Wallace, his eyes bright with the disinterested joy of the scandalmonger, "what is the reason for the absence of Alladale from the side of his lovely and alluring spouse?"

George remained sulkily and ignorantly silent.

"Obviously because they don't get on together. And why do they not get on together? Clearly you or I would get on admirably with Mrs. Alladale. The reason must be—well, we can guess the reason."

George could not guess. He felt base, but he was curious. "We haven't seen Mr. Alladale, you know," he said.

"True," said Captain Wallace, "we have not seen Mr. Alladale. But we will assume for purposes of argument that his wife is not particularly interested in him. But, then, who is she interested in? Not a breath of scandal, not one breath of scandal has attached to her out here, I assure you," he dropped his voice. "If it had, I should have heard it. All the same," he added, "there is bound to be someone. Beautiful creature in the prime of life—I'll tell you something else about her."

George loathed himself for what he felt to be eavesdropping, and yet, in reality, his yesterday's acquaintance with Captain Wallace was already a more intimate one than his five years' acquaintance with Mrs. Alladale.

"She lives up there," the Captain was saying, "in a little *villano* all by herself. Pretty little place. Has a maid in to mend and dust and that sort of thing; but sleeps by herself at night. It isn't safe. There isn't a country in Europe where that sort of thing is safe since the war. Doubt if it ever was safe. Gambling with destiny, I call it. Simply gambling with destiny. A beautiful woman all alone up there. Reported rich—all foreigners reported rich. It isn't safe. I've said to her half a dozen times, 'Dear lady, it isn't safe. I lie awake at night on account of it.' She laughs at me. But she knows that I'm perfectly right." He leant across the table. "She doesn't care," he said emphatically, "she simply doesn't care. Now, what," he asked, "could make a woman like that not care whether someone broke in, stole her pearls, and battered her brains out?"

George was unable to guess.

"Why—because she's unhappy," the Captain expounded, still triumphantly. "There's only one reason for such senseless recklessness. It's damnable. The husband ought to have more decent feeling. Still, it's not on his account she has come out here—since you tell me they've been more or less separated for years."

George made a sound of protest, but the Captain did not heed him. "There's the heart of my story," he said in triumph, "there's the one and only inevitable explanation—an unhappy love affair—a love affair—there's never any other explanation where a beautiful woman is concerned. Of course," he gave a little laugh, "it isn't always necessarily the same love affair."

George was relieved at the arrival of the waiter with the bill. He would have been chagrined had the interruption come sooner; but, as it was, he felt he still retained a wrapping of spiritual dignity. He had not, at any rate, attempted to prolong the Captain's conversation. "Well, we shall meet again," said the old man lifting a hand in benediction, "in Doney's or somewhere else. One is always running into people in Florence." He resumed the reading of his paper and George Bingham walked away. The Captain's gossip, though it was only the expression of a theory, filled the young man's heart with tenderness for Mrs. Alladale. Why had she been so friendly to him? It was not, as the old man perhaps hinted, that she perceived in him the outline of a new lover. No, George was too honest a fellow for such self-flattery as that.

Why, then? Why, then? It struck him that Captain Wallace was jealous of the singular honour of Mrs. Alladale's notice. Oh, well— let it remain a mystery. All he wanted was to protect and adore her.

He was impatient for dinner-time. He could not attend to churches and pictures until he had seen her. He felt that she had some message for him, some communication to make to him, some use to put him to—but he could not guess what. The Captain's speculations aroused all his recollections of Mrs. Alladale in London. Had any name been coupled with hers there? He could not recollect it. Crowded rooms came before his eyes—the Moffats,

Lady Moreton's, a concert in Wigmore Street, a private view of the London Group—but if she had been accompanied anywhere George had never noticed her companion. He had gazed at her as if she were a star—a thing impersonal and splendid. And now, however close to him she might stoop out of the evening sky, he could not change his vision.

When at last the little tram had trailed up the hill to Fiesole, he found Mrs. Alladale waiting for him on the hotel terrace in the yellow evening sunshine. She was wearing a white dress and a white shawl and a sprig of white jasmine in her dark hair. It was with the enthusiasm of the day before that she welcomed him.

"It's so warm and beautiful still, I said we'd dine out of doors. I was sure you would like it."

Spring is the "season" in Fiesole, so the hotel in September was empty. They had the terrace to themselves. George Bingham looked down across the valley at Florence, across the smoke of grey olive-trees and the black geometrical shapes of the cypresses, black triangular cypresses, smoke-vague olives—and the white-walled houses with their flat roofs, golden in the evening light. The vine-wreathed canopy of the terrace made a dark frame for the landscape. Just below, steeply and deeply below, was a little garden, paved with grey flagstones. There were stone bowls containing little pools of water, dark-leaved tropical plants in grey stone vases, and thin pale grey cats prowling about softly as smoke among them. Mist covered the distant Arno. The copper-red dome of the cathedral glowed above it. George Bingham gazed at the landscape and Mrs. Alladale gazed at George Bingham with rapture in her eyes.

They dined upon sardines, soup, spaghetti, roast chicken, salad and cheese. They drank Orvieto wine. And Mrs. Alladale talked eagerly the whole time—of food—the exchange—the sights and customs of the country—as she had talked the day before—as Captain Wallace had talked at lunch-time—as all travellers talk at all times. But while she talked her face had the disproportionate eagerness and excitement that the young man had noticed from the beginning.

"Come," she said at length, "it will soon be getting chilly. Come and have coffee at my *villano*."

She moved across the garden with steps that seemed to restrain her eagerness. A dusty lane leading from the dusty road brought them to a little white-walled, flat-roofed house, folded in between two taller houses. Mrs. Alladale opened the door with her key and led the young man into a slip of shadowed hall.

"I hire this place furnished," said Mrs. Alladale; "it belongs to a friend of Miss Bolst's. It's pretty, I think. There's the terrace view again, you see. This is my living-room. Do sit down. Do smoke. The coffee will be ready—well, it won't be ready for at least twelve minutes."

She moved about the room lighting four candles and the blue wisp of flame beneath the glass funnel of a coffee machine. George smoked and watched her. Beside him the large open window showed a translucent sky and yellow lights became every moment more numerous in the plain. Suddenly out of the intense shadow and small stabbings of light she addressed him.

"Well, I've talked enough. It's for you to begin now. Tell me who you've seen in London. I've been away a lifetime."

Without Captain Wallace's interpretation George Bingham might have been careless in his answering. As it was he felt like an actor who has heard his cue.

"All the people in London that I've met," he began, "seem very dull, colourless creatures compared with … Florence …" He was too shy to say "you" with frank gallantry.

"But distance lends enchantment, you know."

George saw an obvious opening for something about enchantment not necessarily needing distance; but he was not clever at that sort of thing. He said: "Who is it I'm to tell you about?" and his brain cried silently, "Who? Who?"

"Oh, about everyone," said Mrs. Alladale lightly, tapping the glass funnel of the coffee machine with her fingers. She was smiling; but those tapping fingers said "Hurry up."

"I was at Alice Moffat's a week ago."

"A week ago," murmured Mrs. Alladale.

"She was in very good form. She told several amusing stories."

"New stories?"

He laughed. "Well … most of them were new."

"What was she wearing?" said Mrs. Alladale.

George Bingham felt that he was not being a success.

"Some sort of bluish thing, I think," he said lamely, "and she'd a gold thing tied round her head."

Mrs. Alladale's laugh made the spirit flame flicker.

"Splendid," she cried. "Who else was there?"

"Oh, the Crouches, the O'Rourkes, Tom Dyce, all the usual people. Jack Moreton brought his bride. Elmer Seton was there, fatter than ever. O'Rourke is in business now and says he prefers City men to gentlemen any day of the week."

"He can afford to say so with his father in the House of Lords," said Mrs. Alladale. "Tell me about them. Go on."

"Mrs. O'Rourke's dress," said George Bingham, "was a sort of tube the colour of those flowers they grow in cottage window-boxes. You know the kind—shaped like convolvuluses—but they aren't convolvuluses—striped a sort of red-purple colour."

"Petunia," said Mrs. Alladale. "Go on."

George Bingham knew he had not told the essential thing yet. He wished Mrs. Alladale would say warm, warmer, or cold, cold, free-eezing as the children do when they play "Hunt the thimble." When he talked about Mrs. O'Rourke he knew that he was freezing.

"Crouch has published a new novel," he said hopefully.

"Yes, I saw it reviewed somewhere," said Mrs. Alladale, blowing out the little spirit flame and drawing the coffee cups nearer to her.

"It seems to be better than his last one," said George ("Freezing, simply freezing," he shouted at himself).

Mrs. Alladale poured out the coffee with a meditative smile. "So Elmer Seton's fatter than ever," she said. "He must be *very* fat."

"He is," said George (could this be the explanation?). He sought about for a phrase and said: "He has the Continental shirt front—shaped like a robin's, you know."

Mrs. Alladale laughed merrily. The thing was incredible—yet George was old enough to know that the fancies of love nearly always are.

"The Continental shirt front," she repeated enjoyingly.

"Alice Moffat said that of him," said George, honest as ever.

"Yes. It's the sort of thing Alice Moffat does say." She handed the little cup to George Bingham. "Who else did you say was there?"

"That's everyone, I think," said George, wrinkling his forehead vaguely, "except Jack Moreton and his brand new bride."

"Oh yes," said Mrs. Alladale, "tell me about her. Sugar? … Not sugar," she withdrew the little silver bowl. "What did *she* wear? Not petunia, I'm sure."

"No, it certainly wasn't petunia," said the young man smiling and feeling that after all he had been a success; "it was—something white, I think. I don't remember," he ended lamely.

"Goodness, poor girl, not to be remembered," said Mrs. Alladale mockingly. "How is Lady Moreton?" she briskly added.

"I haven't seen her since July," said George, sipping his coffee; "not since Jack's wedding."

"Oh, were you at the wedding?" asked Mrs. Alladale, sipping too. "Who was there ? How did it go?"

"Oh, there was a most tremendous mob. Jack looked superbly bored as usual."

"Oh, he looked superbly bored as usual did he?" echoed Mrs. Alladale, and her eyes added a sparkle as of wit to George Bingham's plain statement.

"Lady Moreton was magnificent, of course. She was in great feather about it."

"Literally, so I should imagine."

"They were talking of selling Howe, you know."

"Yes, I knew they contemplated that this winter."

"Jack wouldn't have cared if they had—at least so Simon Ellis-Jones was telling me."

"They ought to have sold immediately after the war if they wanted to make money," said Mrs. Alladale.

"Oh, well, he's provided for, for life now," said the young man.

"Yes," said Mrs. Alladale.

"Coal," said George, "a ward in Chancery, 'no encumbrances,' Alice Moffat said. She's pretty, too."

Mrs. Alladale reached for his cup. "More coffee? Is she dark or fair? What a silly question!"

"Fair, at least ..." he paused and laughed, "yes, she certainly is fair. She thinks Jack the cleverest man in the world."

"Don't you think him clever?" asked Mrs. Alladale.

"Well, no," the young man meditated, "clever is too small a word," he finally added.

Mrs. Alladale smiled at something that she thought of, then she said: "Well, she'll be very happy—as long as she thinks that. It's nice to be young and pretty and rich and at the beginning of things—thinking one's husband the cleverest man in the world, you know." She laughed.

George Bingham wondered what she wanted him to say next.

"Jack's hung fire for a long time as a prospective bridegroom," he said. "Lady Moreton was getting desperate, Simon Ellis-Jones told me. She was saying Jack would have to leave the army and look for work …"

Mrs. Alladale did not appear to be listening. She was looking at the square of the open window where, burning dimly against the candlelight, the stars were showing over Florence.

Perhaps she wanted him to begin about Elmer Seton again. "Elmer Seton," he said, but her eyes did not turn from the window and the laughter had gone out of her face.

He put down his coffee cup and stood up. "It's time for me to say good-bye," he said.

Mrs. Alladale rose too.

"It has been so nice, seeing you," she said formally.

This was the Mrs. Alladale whom he had known in London— gracious, beautiful, but remote.

"Good-bye," he said, turning to the door.

"I'll bring a light," said Mrs. Alladale, "or you won't be able to find your hat."

She picked up one of the candles and stood in the doorway.

"When you are back in England," she said, "remember me to everyone, won't you?"

"I will, indeed."

"To Alice Moffat, and the Crouches, and the O'Rourkes, and Jack Moreton, and everybody."

"And Elmer Seton and Lady Moreton?" asked George.

"No," again mockery, a rather sad mockery came into her face, "I don't think you need remember me to Lady Moreton."

George Bingham had an inspiration.

"I'll tell them what a lovely life you live out here."

"Do," said Mrs. Alladale, suddenly bright and laughing again. "Do. Tell them all. Tell everyone. Tell them everything about me. Tell them about the petunia tube thing I wore and about the gold thing tied round my head, and about the bad dinner and the squalid

– 37 –

view, and how Captain Wallace thinks I'll be murdered here some night in my lonely bed."

"I'll tell them," said the young man, confused by the radiance of her image.

"Remember me to them all," cried Mrs. Alladale. "Remember everything. Remember that the jasmine is in flower and how bright the stars are over Florence."

Black Cat for Luck

G. B. STERN

The sea has its enchantment, and the woods have their witchery, and even a meadow full of cows shambling down to drink from the brook is all very well; but there is that about a big city in early June which can surpass all these by a magic of its own: a promise in the flicker of sunshine through the flat leaves, and on the pale, shining, mottled trunks of the plane trees, more exciting than the broadest fulfilment.

London in early June hints that this is going to be the loveliest summer, the only summer, the summer of gay adventures and desires come true.

You can catch these subtle whispers in the very way the awnings flap in the light breeze; in the brilliance of the window-boxes, scarlet and pink geraniums, on the facades in Mayfair; in the hydrangeas and rhododendrons massed bushily about the parks, and seen through the railings of demure private gardens; in the flutter of light chiffon dresses, in the very cadence of a passing voice, in the glimpse of a cool hall through a doorway left open.

London in early June. … Ashamed of the word "enchantment", with its shimmering suggestion of fairy-tale, we continue to say blandly: "The season was in full swing," or perhaps: "The season was not yet in full swing."

At an eighteenth-century house of mellow brick, at the Chelsea end of the Embankment, facing the river, a luncheon-party was just breaking up; a rather formal luncheon-party, if one might judge from the men's clothes; formal, but enjoyable, for most of them were still laughing as they strolled down the steps and along the path to the gate; or if not actually laughing they had that faint smile of happiness on their lips which tells that they have recently said something witty, and that others have laughed at it.

Some of them had cars waiting; others hailed a taxi from the rank near the bridge, casually told the driver, "You might open it," and, while he did so, stood looking down-stream towards the white yachts and launches moored at the opposite bank.

"It was so kind of you to ask me. At such a gifted little party of yours. I was honoured at being present."

Maurice Jodelet's hostess, Mrs. Alec Lindsay, was amused at his choice of the word "gifted". She barely knew this handsome young man; he had been invited late, to fill up a gap, but she had been pleased with what she had seen of him—his animated, slightly cheeky manners, not too fulsome on the one hand, nor too impudent on the other; his deference towards the older, more distinguished guests; his facility at flirtation with whatever was placed near enough at table.

He flirted with both his neighbours, and with the dowager opposite him; he flirted with the salted almonds and with the *omelette surprise*. Yes, distinctly an asset, Maurice Jodelet. She was not quite sure of his profession. Either he was going into the diplomatic service, or he was a young artist; she could not remember which.

"These are very clever—oh, very clever indeed," remarked Maurice, with a nod full of genuine admiration towards the black-and-white caricatures that hung on both sides of the hall, and all the way up the staircase, every one of them by the same man.

"Ah, the Bentleys. Yes. Another time when you come, you must examine them in detail. My husband collects Bentleys. In fact, I think he has the best collection in existence."

"And always adding to it," said Sir Nicholas Broadfoot, joining them on his way out. "Unluckily for Alec's pocket, Bentley's an industrious man."

"Oh, surely not," Maurice Jodelet protested, "he's far too brilliant!"

Broadfoot was amused at this perfectly genuine assumption that brilliance and industry could not go together. "Do you know George Bentley?"

"Oh, you must know him," put in Mrs. Lindsay; "everyone knows the Bentleys, they're such a charming family. The three girls …" She broke off a little absently, for other guests were claiming her to say good-bye.

"No, I don't know them at all. Not even by sight. I wish I did." And he scrutinized again the caricature nearest him, a particularly incisive piece of mockery at a particularly pompous statesman.

"A good investment," said Nicholas Broadfoot, looking over his shoulder, for he was taller than Maurice, but of burlier build, not so slim and supple as young twenty-five. "The value of Bentley's work is going up. Do you collect?"

"I'm beginning to, yes. I believe in buying works of art on one's own judgement. It's a most exciting form of gamble."

They left the house together. "Where are you going now?" Sir Nicholas asked when they reached the pavement. "Can I drop you?" His enormous dark blue car was waiting in the flickering shade.

"Thanks. I'm going to Grosvenor Park, if that's on your way."

"Certainly. What number?"

"Number seventy-five."

Sir Nicholas told the chauffeur seventy-five, Grosvenor Park, and afterwards the Foreign Office. And the car slid away with that aloof air that no smaller car can ever quite achieve.

They drove through radiant London on the best of terms, talking lightly enough of the luncheon-party, of their sweet but extremely vague and inaccurate hostess, of the way that the upper half of the Portland-stone buildings gleamed in the sun, and the lower black-sooted half looked even blacker and more velvety by contrast, of why Berkeley Square had more fascination than any other square in London, and what it was in to-day that was making them both remember Venice, although nothing that they saw could possibly remind them of Venice.

At seventy-five Grosvenor Park the car stopped, and Maurice got out.

He stood for a moment on the pavement, his hat off, very charmingly thanking the older man for the lift. While he was still saying good-bye, the front door of number seventy-five opened and a girl came out, dressed in a thin garden-party frock of yellow and white, fluttering and vivacious as the golden weather. Maurice had his back turned to her, but she smiled at the sight of Nicholas, who said: "Hallo, there's Barbara!"—and immediately he, too, alighted from the car.

Maurice had swung round at the sound of the door closing and Barbara's exclamation. And Sir Nicholas added: "Here's your friend Maurice Jodelet. He wanted to be dropped here on my way to the office."

"And I was on my way to the Kemps' garden-party," explained the girl called Barbara, smiling now at Maurice.

"Am I too late? Have I kept you waiting? What an escort! Ten million apologies. I should never have forgiven myself if I'd arrived only in time to see you drive off there alone. But Sir Nicholas will tell you that our luncheon-party went on for ever."

"It doesn't matter. I do forgive you. Anyhow, you'd have followed me, wouldn't you?"

"Oh, I'd have followed you," fervently from Maurice. "Who wouldn't?"

"Anyhow, I doubt if you'd have seen me drive off. It's such a heavenly day, I was going to walk for a little way. It's so lovely for us that sandal shoes are in fashion."

"Run, then, don't walk," murmured Maurice, looking down passionately at Barbara's delicious feet. "But don't forget to drop the apples …"

"I hate to come in heavy on this sparkling dialogue," interrupted Broadfoot, whom both appeared to have forgotten for the moment, "but it wasn't Atalanta who dropped the apples. It was she who picked them up."

"You never were any good at classics, Maurice, were you? I remember someone told me that when you were at school you always thought that Diogenes and Dionysus were the same person, because they both had barrel associations!"

"I believe"—Maurice was blushing a little—"that I am just not young enough to be overcome by confusion. Nearly, but not quite."

Sir Nicholas was pleased by the semi-confession. "Well, suppose Barbara abandons her walk, and I drive you both to Holland Park? It's rather far, you know, either to walk or to run."

"Weren't you invited, Nicholas? Oh, poor Nick, who never gets invited anywhere."

"On the contrary, I was invited twice. Lady Kemp's a careful woman and wanted to make sure. But I've an important interview at four o'clock, so we mustn't linger."

He followed her into the car, and sat down next to her. Maurice modestly took a seat opposite, and they drove off. Nicholas left them at the gates of the Kemps's, with an injunction not to fall too deeply into the strawberries and cream, and a cordial request to Maurice Jodelet to come and see him at his private address in the Albany that evening between nine and ten, as he had something to talk over with him.

"Good-bye, Barbara, my dear."

"Good-bye, Nick. Thanks for driving us down. I wish you could come in."

"So do I. I don't get nearly enough playtime."

The car slid away again, and the two young people were left alone. Just inside the gate, in the front garden, Barbara faced round on Maurice, her eyes both indignant and puzzled: "Look here, who *are* you?"

"You know. He told you. I'm Maurice Jodelet."

"Yes, he told me. But—what's it all about?"

"I can't thank you enough," exclaimed the young man impulsively. "You were splendid to help me, to play up, not to give me away!"

"Yes, but now—I must know now. Why did you pretend to Nicholas that we had an appointment? That you were coming to fetch me?"

"Well, you see …"

Automatically they had walked under the awning and down the short path by the side of the house; it led into the garden where the hostess stood receiving her guests, and they had to stop, at this breathless climax of revelation, while they were hospitably greeted, introduced to other people, parted, given iced lemonade, escorted separately towards deck-chairs where they did not want to sit, and towards tennis which they wanted neither to watch nor to play.

And throughout the afternoon some fate, mischievous and tricky, arranged matters so that they should not be alone together, except spasmodically, and always for the briefest intervals; so that Barbara only learned in fragments the story of the luncheon-party and its sequel; and had plenty of time, between the young man's half-apologetic, half-impudent presentation of his story, to wonder whether she should accept the apology or smite the impudence.

When he had woken up that morning, Maurice Jodelet had already known that it was to be his lucky day. He was very badly in need of a lucky day. Looking round the shabby, tiresomely utilitarian bedroom where he lodged, in the decayed gentility of a down-at-heel neighbourhood that lay between Earl's Court and Hammersmith, he reflected disconsolately that it had been years since he had been a four-leaved-clover man, a right-end-of-the-wish-bone man, a pick-up-a-horseshoe man.

Maurice was superstitious. He would rather be lucky than good. He explained to Barbara very earnestly, that it made him feel good to be lucky. But last night he had seen the new moon, a clear little silvery boat riding high between two dingy chimney-pots, and for the first time for many months there had been no fatal glass accidentally dividing them.

He had only four single shillings and a half-crown and a sixpence to turn in his pockets, but he fervently did turn these coins in the sight of his distant silver Artemis, and fervently wished that the very next day might fling some new good fortune across his path—something to do with his career, he added quickly, for he was an ambitious young man, and was afraid lest his goddess might believe, in her usual impulsive maiden fashion, that all he most desired was some romantic nonsense to do with love and so forth.

He noticed with pleasure, however, that his means amounted to seven shillings in all, not counting, of course, an overdraft at his bank of several hundred pounds. Yes, the exact sum for which he was indebted to Messrs. Coutts was seven hundred and seven pounds.

And the morrow after the new moon was June the seventh. His lucky number was seven. Also, his age was twenty-five; you add five and two, and they make seven, and there you are ... and there you are! And then:

> ... *"Oh, Barbara darling, don't forget to come and talk to me, before you go, about Thursday. I want your advice so badly about whether we should dine out-of-doors or simply have a buffet under the trees. ... And wouldn't your friend like to play clock-golf?"*

... And then, the next morning, in Pall Mall, he ran into Bobbie Lindsay, who almost embraced him, saying: "You're the very man I want. A couple of guests have let down my mother at the last moment. She's got a luncheon-party, and she told me to bring in any two friends of mine that I could rake up. Not easy, at the last moment like this, especially when they've got to be presentable. You'll do fine, Jodelet. For the Lord's sake, chuck up any other engagement you've got, and help me out. I've managed to hook Ranny Stokes already."

And, of course, Maurice had known at once that this luncheon-party was bound to lead to something significant.

> ... *"But, Barbara, my lamb, you haven't got any strawberries and cream. They've been neglecting you. I'll send Grant over." ...*

It had been a delightful luncheon-party; but, throughout,

Maurice had been a little over-excited, a little breathless, a little conscious of moving about in a not quite real world. For it was to-day or never. If to-day failed him …

But it could not fail him; at any moment might come a revelation, whimsical or dramatic, of the gift that Artemis, that young silver slip of a new moon, had all along intended for him.

> … *"Barbara dear, there are a lot of chairs hidden among the shrubbery. Are you sure you and your friend wouldn't rather sit there in the shade? So warm in the sun, is it not? And my aunt, Mrs. Barrett, has been specially asking for you. Do go to her for a minute. She's over there—the mauve parasol."* …

The luncheon-party came to an end, and still he had not been able to strike where his luck lay; until Sir Nicholas Broadfoot, of the Foreign Office, had offered to give him a lift.

Now Maurice Jodelet's ambitions were clearly defined from his earliest youth. He had inherited from his father all those qualities which only exist in the French language. He had *savoir-faire*, *aplomb*, *insouciance*, *diablerie*, *esprit* and *je ne sais quoi*. Particularly, he insisted now to Barbara, he had *je ne sais quoi*. *Aplomb*, of course, was the result of his Gascon blood. All Gascons had *aplomb*. Look at Cyrano de Bergerac! Look at D'Artagnan! Look at Francois Villon!

"He was a Parisian," interrupted Barbara.

"Yes, well, his grandmother was probably a Gascon; his grandmother on the distaff side. Anyhow …"

Anyhow, he had trained for the diplomatic service, had been sent abroad to learn German and Hungarian and Spanish, and had contrived to steer a way through the necessary exams. And then Destiny had started serving him every number except the lucky seven. His father's sudden severe financial losses; his father's illness, long and exacting, with no one but Maurice to look after him; finally, his father's death.

One effort after another to get some footing which would start him off again on the career he had been obliged to abandon. One disappointment after another; five, six, eight, nine, ten disappointments; eleven, twelve, thirteen disappointments. He reckoned them up on his fingers, chagrin and wit blended in each rapid résumé of how audacity or persuasion had alike failed him and toppled him down again to where he had been at the start.

Till at last, on the seventh day of June, when his overdraft was seven hundred and seven pounds, chance had come his way for the fourteenth time ("Twice seven, you see!"), when he was twenty-five years old ("You add up the figures, five and two, they make seven, you see!"), and had placed him with one foot on the step of Sir Nicholas Broadfoot's Minerva. And Sir Nicholas, a power in the Foreign Office, had asked him courteously where he wished to be driven.

> … *"Can I get you some hock-cup, madam? Or iced coffee? Her ladyship said I was to be sure and look after you, and that you had 'ad nothing to eat. … Strawberries and cream, sir? There are ices, if you'd prefer."* …

Maurice had been going home, but naturally he was not going to say: "It would be very kind if you would take me to five, Lanark Villas, past the Tube station, and just round the corner from the second pub on the left." A good appearance and a good address, these were essentials in a blossoming young diplomat. And readiness of mind, that was an essential too.

But for once readiness of mind could not supply a single authentic address quickly enough for the social emergency. His usually supple brain went stiff. He could think only of the National Gallery, Westminster Abbey, the Army and Navy Stores, Lyons' Corner House, or the Mint.

None of these, obviously, would do. They were not in the style and spirit of the occasion.

Quite simply and naturally, Maurice made up an address, a Mayfair address, the right sort of address. He meant, of course, to seem to sound the bell, to wait till the car had driven on, and then quietly to walk away.

In the meanwhile, during their drive from Chelsea to Mayfair, there would be ample time for Sir Nicholas to have said: "Well, call round and see me, my boy, this evening, if you've nothing better to do; and we'll talk things over. I might be able to help you. There are two or three decent appointments vacant just now, and a word from me. …"

… "Oh, here you are, Barbara! Sitting in the shade? Aren't you cold? You'd better come into uncle's orchid-house and get warmed up. Have you seen his orchids, by the way? You must, before you go. Will you—oh, you've got strawberries and cream" …

"And then I spoiled it," said Barbara, "by coming out of that very address at that very moment."

"Spoiled it?" cried Jodelet, enthusiastically worshipping her. "On the contrary, the whole point is, you angel, that you did not spoil it. You played up; pretended you knew me. What would have become of me if you had been adamant, or, worse still—but how impossible!—if you had been stupid? If you had said: 'Come to see *me*? That young man? But he's a stranger. We none of us know him. I've never seen him before!'"

"Oh, but I had to play up. That look you gave me—that one pleading, rueful look. It would have haunted me all my life if I'd given you away."

"What did it say to you, my look?" Maurice was profoundly interested in her version of the encounter.

"It said: 'I'll die laughing if I must, but need I die at all? It rests with you.'"

Naturally Maurice was enchanted by this free translation.

"Who are you?" he asked. "So that even when I am an ambassador in Paris, New York or Madrid—which may take me two or three years—I shall still be able to remember you in my prayers! Barbara, I know you as, already. Santa Barbara, Saint Barbara of the Broken Barricades ..."

"I'm Barbara Bentley. My father is the artist. Chiefly caricatures, you know. They—what is it?"

For Maurice had let his untouched strawberries and cream slip on to the lawn and mingle with the fallen chestnut petals of dappled red and white.

"Bentley! Oh! Did it have to be Bentley?"

"Why not? What is the matter? You've turned as white as ..."

"To-day after luncheon," Maurice explained in a state of magnificent despair, "I told Sir Nicholas definitely, while we were looking at the Bentley caricatures in the hall, that I did not know the Bentleys; that I had never met any of them; that I wished I had, but I had not. I made it perfectly clear to him."

Upon that disclosure they were parted, maddeningly, for some considerable time. When they accidentally met again, and managed to unite and be alone for a few moments, it was in the humid atmosphere of the orchid-house, closely surrounded by little masterpieces of sinister beauty.

At once Maurice exclaimed, as though they had never been sundered: "So, of course, Sir Nicholas realized from the start that I'd given the address of people I didn't even know. That must have been amusing for him. All the time in the car, when I was being so casual, so light-hearted, really very effective, as I thought, all the time I was making a damn fool of myself. I am in a silly mess!"

But the girl was looking even more troubled than he. "I'm in a worse mess. I thought, during that moment outside our house, that Nicholas imagined we really did know each other, and he'd never find out we didn't, and so it wasn't important and none of it mattered. And audacious people always amuse me. But if he knew that I was lying, knew then even when I was doing it—and for your sake!" She added to herself, not caring to add to Maurice's naïve conceit: "For the sake of an extremely handsome young man whom I'd never met before …"

"What else could you have done?"

"I could have drawn myself up, saying with dignity: 'Nicholas, this young man and I are total strangers.'"

"But that would have been—not you. Besides, you're not answerable to him."

"I am in a way. You see, I happen to be engaged to him."

"*Engaged to him!*" Maurice repeated, scowling at her in bewilderment.

"Oh, it's not official yet; it only happened a week or two ago. I wanted a little while to—oh, just to have fun. To adjust things in my mind. But we are engaged. Maurice, why are you looking at me like that?"

"Like that" was not the anguish of a young man who has suddenly seen his heart's desire dashed away from him by another, but the puzzled stare of a child. "Engaged? You—to Sir Nicholas Broadfoot?"

"Yes. Why not? He's splendid. Everybody says so. He's a very big man in his own line. And besides, he's a darling. And if you don't think him terribly good-looking, well, I do, and ..."

"But he's quite old."

Barbara looked round wildly for something she could smash across Maurice Jodelet's head. There was nothing but orchids, and orchids are rather awe-inspiring. Had they been geraniums, she might easily have seized a flower-pot.

She said icily: "You don't seem to know what you are talking about. I have suspected you were a little mad, once or twice already this afternoon. Sir Nicholas is forty-seven, the perfect age for a man. I happen not to care for boys. I am twenty-eight, and a little bit *passée*, but it is remarkably fortunate for me that he has overlooked that. Anyhow, when people reach any maturity, like Nicholas and, I hope, myself, I hope we have the ah—the—er *savoir-faire* and the *aplomb* and the *je ne sais quoi* not to talk about age at all, ever. It's a most distasteful subject."

Maurice Jodelet sat down, crushed, on the floor.

"Get up," said Barbara quickly. "You can't sit on the floor of a greenhouse."

"Say you forgive me, then."

"Oh, I forgive you," frantically, as the door at the other end of the glass-house was pushed open and a clamour of voices floated down the warm aisles. Jodelet sprang to his feet, nimble as a harlequin, but just a few seconds too late. They stared at him. He perceived that there was another door at his end, seized Barbara's hand, and rushed her out without attempting any explanation.

"And now we're in a worse mess," she gasped breathlessly, when at last he allowed her to pull up between the high yew hedges of a miniature maze. "You didn't notice, but I did, that one of those good ladies was our hostess."

"That," retorted Maurice, with the slightly French idiom of speech that was in his blood, "is a bagatelle. What is not a bagatelle is that my luck has snapped, and there is no seven left in all the Pleiades!"

With widespread arms he gestured his despair. "Only an hour ago, when your wise and handsome and not-at-all-too-old fiancé said, just before he left us, that he wanted to see me this evening, I was already rejoicing in the job he would offer me. 'No wonder,' I thought, 'that he is a great man. He recognizes young talent—or shall I say young genius?' As it is, of course, the appointment was made only so that he could rage at me for compromising you."

"That," said Barbara, "that is a bagatelle. I should say, wouldn't you, that it would be too late for Nicholas to break off his engagement to me to-night? He'll call round and do it to-morrow."

"He hasn't the shadow of an excuse to be such a cad!" Jodelet contended hotly.

"Yes, he has. He has every excuse. He thinks me sly, and a flirt, and a liar, and—and cheaply impressionable. Oh, I knew when I saw the new moon through glass last night, that something horrible was going to happen to me to-day. And I put on a stocking inside out, and actually changed it, when I ought to have worn it like that all day."

Maurice stopped short and faced her. "Barbara, are you superstitious too?"

"Madly."

"Barbara, why did you get engaged to Sir Nicholas Broadfoot?"

"Because I adore him."

"Yes … and because you're ambitious."

"Of course I am. It isn't wrong to be ambitious. My ambition is very proud of him."

"Barbara, why haven't you scolded, me yet for my snobbery in giving him a Grosvenor Park address, instead of my own in Lanark Villas, Earl's Court?"

"Because, clear Prosper," she mocked him, "I should have done the same myself." She called him Prosper because he was reminding her of Prosper Le Gai, of *The Forest Lovers.*

"Barbara, doesn't it occur to you that we were made for each other, you and I? We are both superstitious, both ambitious, both snobs, both young, both good-looking …"

"… and both donkeys. Yes, Prosper, yes."

"And both donkeys. So I suppose we're in love."

"But we're not."

"We must be. We're both superstitious, ambitious …"

"Don't go through the whole list again. I'm not, and I don't believe you are."

"I don't feel much about it," he confessed, "but that's probably because I'm numb. It may be from sitting on the floor of the greenhouse. The stone was rather cold, and it creeps up.… But if we're not in love, it's very odd, don't you think, that we shouldn't be?"

"I shall never care for anyone except Nicholas."

Suddenly he realized that her voice was trembling, and that she had to clench her hands hard to avoid a burst of tears. At once he became serious; that is, as serious as his temperament and personality would allow. He swore that he would put the whole matter right for her at any cost to himself. He would put it right that very evening. There was no further need for her to worry.

"Trust me! Maurice Jodelet has never yet … To-night I will prove to him that you detest me, that you abhor me, that you were acting solely out of courteous consideration for an obnoxious stranger. Barbara, darling little Barbara, please don't worry. Don't give the matter another thought. I have a hundred plans in four different languages. I have trained for this predicament from my very birth. I have passed examinations for no other reason than to get us out of it, than to get you out of it …"

Barbara was half laughing, half crying.

And still Maurice spouted on, inventing fantastic ways of convincing Sir Nicholas. He would tell him that Barbara thought the whole business some sort of diplomatic complication, and that he, Maurice, was royalty in disguise. … That Barbara thought someone, a spy, had been watching, overhearing the conversation on the pavement in Grosvenor Park; and that if it did not appear that she knew and was expecting this young man, M.J. in the dossier, then they were going to assassinate him—or Nicholas—or the King …

"But, Prosper, my sweet, why on earth or heaven should Nicholas ever imagine that I'd think out such incredibly bad melodrama?"

"Well, then." And swiftly, along rattled another inspiration: Let him say that she thought Nicholas was testing her *savoir-faire*, so necessary, so essential in the wife of a diplomat, by suddenly introducing a strange man to her as someone with whom she should be familiar. "That is a situation which every great lady has had to carry off at some time or other."

"But, Prosper, Nicholas knows I would never expect him to be such a—such a whimsical elf as to test me like that, after luncheon, and on my way to a garden-party!"

But Maurice was not to be discouraged. More and more rapidly, and ever more fantastically, he thought out more and more solutions of their difficulty; the last one involving an offer, a promise, to shoot himself in Nicholas's flat, if Nicholas would not believe.

"Prosper, don't be silly! All this is just good Gascon bravado."

At this instant, after more walking than they had realized, they found themselves once more at the entrance to the maze. "And we're just about as far in everything as we were when we started!" Again the forlorn little shake in her voice betrayed that she was feeling more about Nicholas's probable alienation than she cared to let Maurice Jodelet know.

So he said: "I have had an idea. No, a real idea this time. This new idea will work."

And though she pleaded with him to tell her what it was, he refused, saying gravely that the entire episode was his responsibility, and that she must trust him.

"But at five minutes past nine—and if you add five and nine together, Barbara, you will find they make fourteen, which is twice seven!—you will know that everything is as it was between you and Sir Nicholas. I say so, and I am a very strong and also a very silent man. Do you believe me?"

"Yes, Prosper."

"Well, then … will you let me get you some strawberries and cream?"

Actually, Maurice had not the remotest idea of how he was going to put things right with Broadfoot that evening. But as it seemed essential that Barbara's life should not lie about in honey-coloured ruins, where it had so recently been a graceful temple, he left his lodgings, gloomily determined to be at Broadfoot's rooms in the Albany, and ready with some plausible explanation, when the clock was striking nine.

Yet still he could not think of what he would say to Broadfoot.

Suddenly he heard nine striking, and hastened down Bruton Street into Bond Street, queerly shuttered and shadowed, and turned sharply by Atkinson's perfumery shop at the corner of Bond Street and Burlington Gardens. Behind each of its windows stood a vase of flowers, lit by a beam of white light which searched out the intricacies of stamen and tendril. He stood there for a moment, enchanted, looking at it.

And still he did not know what he was to say to Broadfoot.

But when he reached the sedate entrance opposite Savile Row, the heavy ribbed shutter had already been lowered behind the small iron gate. Maurice stared furiously at such callous indifference to his troubles, barely restraining a desire to batter it with both his fists, or an alternative wish to sob his heart out against the bolted door, thrusting at it like Love Locked Out in the picture.

He now had to make the whole detour, pretending he was in no hurry, through Sackville Street into Piccadilly, and round into the Albany courtyard. Perhaps it was all ordained, and perhaps even now, during the last fragment of time allotted him, he might yet be seized with an inspiration of what he should say to Broadfoot, so as to put things right for Barbara.

But nothing came.

The Rope Walk behind the Mansion was ominously silent, dimly lit by its antique square gas-lamps. There was a faint fresh scent from the rhododendrons blossoming in tubs on either side of him, as though they had been watered just after sunset.

Three or four cats were moving about with a certain dignity. One of them, sweep-black, moved indifferently across Maurice's very path, and within a few inches of his feet.

"Black cat for luck," he thought, but even his superstitions hung limply and would not wave with their usual banner bravery. And still he did not know what he was going to say to Broadfoot.

Sir Nicholas received him kindly, with a touch of crispness, like autumn in the air. "Just enough to make the celery good," thought Maurice the irrepressible.

Maurice need not have bothered as to what he was going to say. He was hardly allowed to say anything.

Sir Nicholas said briefly and astonishingly that he had heard that Mr. Jodelet had intended to go into the diplomatic service, and was on the look-out for a job. He was looking for a young man with resource, and it seemed to him—without the flicker of an eyelid—that here *was* a young man with resource.

"So I have a proposition to make to you. In a few months I am going to be married"—again not the least betrayal of consciousness—"and then I shall need a personal secretary to help my London establishment to run smoothly. Because, naturally, we shall entertain a great deal more than I do now, on my own. I already have a couple of secretaries, of course, but they are concerned entirely with the Foreign Office side of my work. This job I am offering you is much more unofficial, or shall we say social?"

"A drawing-room secretary," murmured Maurice.

"Call it that, if you like. Does it appeal to you?"

The young man did not reply, and Sir Nicholas went on: "As a matter of fact, there is another job to which I could help you if you cared for me to use my influence. I didn't mention it first, because it's not very attractive. It involves going out to Chile for five years, to the consulate at Valparaiso. Do you know Portuguese?"

"No."

"It would be a good thing to learn Portuguese and Spanish—oh, you do know Spanish? Good. But it's a long way off from London, and the climate—some people like it in spite of the frequent earthquakes. And a good many don't. Sweating hard work. Of course, a post of that sort has a great many possibilities for the future, even though it may not be at all agreeable in the present. But most young men prefer a job nearer home, and with what they call a personal atmosphere. It gives them a chance to show that they're individuals, and so forth. However, you can choose. Don't be in a hurry. Think it over. Weigh the …"

But Maurice did not stop to weigh anything. Without a second's delay—for he, too, had forgotten all about Barbara—he chose the Chilean job. How could an ambitious young man hesitate between being a tame cat in London, and a chance which would eventually, step by step, lead to ambassadorial appointments in Paris, Madrid or New York? Of course the Chilean job! Five years was nothing. Distance and climate and hard work, these were bagatelles …

"When do I book my passage? I can be ready to start to-morrow, sir, if you wish!"

Sir Nicholas Broadfoot looked at him with a certain grim favour. "It's just as well, young man, that you have made this choice, because, as a matter of fact, the other job, the London job, didn't exist."

"*Tiens!*" remarked Maurice, lapsing into diplomacy's own language. "Then may one ask why …"

"Testing you, that's all."

Maurice suggested, rather naughtily, that Sir Nicholas might have been placed in a somewhat awkward position had he, Maurice, chosen the non-existent post of secretary to Sir Nicholas's future establishment in London.

"No, I didn't take much of a risk. In this game, as you'll learn when you get on, one has to guess. But the best guessing is founded on a knowledge of psychology."

Directly he was alone again, Sir Nicholas rang up his fiancée, according to the promise he had made when she had come to see him three hours before.

"Barbara … You were right."

"Chile?"

"Certainly Chile. Not a moment's hesitation."

"Five years out of London; thousands of miles away. And yet you actually dared to think—oh, Nicholas, apologize at once."

"My darling, I will—I have—I do! But I had a dreadful moment, all the same, waiting to hear which he'd choose. It struck me as a dangerous, entirely feminine solution of the situation."

"Nicholas, there never was a situation, and it was never dangerous. A feminine solution, if you like, brief and brilliant and utterly convincing."

"You're being deliciously arrogant."

"Am I? Three hours ago you were being deliciously idiotic. Youth flies to youth, you said, and every grey hair quivered at the temples as if you'd actually seen me fall in love with Maurice on the pavement in Grosvenor Park."

"That's burlesque, but I couldn't help knowing what's natural. Youth does fly to youth, even in the flash of a first meeting. Look at Pelleas and Melisande. Look at Paolo and Francesca—look at Tristan and Isolde—look at …"

"Me and Maurice Jodelet. And I bet you it hasn't occurred to him, even yet, that accepting the London job would have meant the divine rapture of being near me, in my golden company, answering notes at the same desk, arranging flowers in the same bowl, all day long."

"I must own," remarked Sir Nicholas confidentially, "that he did show quite definite signs of distaste for that sort of thing. You know, Barbara, I'll help that young-man. I like him. I like his cheek, and I like his ambitious spirit. And he's full of resource." … He went on enthusiastically, praising Maurice.

Barbara smiled. Resolved to be the right sort of wife to a diplomat, she did not point out that neither Maurice, budding in that corps, nor Sir Nicholas, its proud and full-blown magnolia, had shown the slightest resource in dealing with to-day's scrape.

If, for instance, she had possessed one fraction of confidence in Maurice's inventive wits, or in Nicholas's sense of proportion about her love for him, she would not have suggested that really quite simple technique by which he could reassure himself of the truth, when she went straight round to see him, that evening after the garden-party.

Seven o'clock had chimed as she swayed down the cool shade of the Rope Walk, and the gardener was just watering the rhododendrons. A black cat …

The Sand Castle

MARY LAVIN

John was the oldest. He had straight black hair and a pale face. Emily came next. She had bright hair. Every summer she got gold freckles, but in the winter they went away. Alexandre was the youngest. His freckles never went away, but Alexandre did not mind. He did not mind about being fat, either, as long as he was getting big, one way or another.

One summer they went to Deever Shallows. Deever Shallows was a small seaside resort. It had a silver bay and a silver sea and a fan of glittering sand. It had a cold white harbour and a bright green boat-slip. There were things to do, every hour of the day, and the nights fell even faster there than they fell at home. You could dig for cockles and go down so deep with the spade that you came to jet-black clay underneath the silver sand. You could skim stones on the shallow waters when the tide was out. When the sea was full and high, you could fish for periwinkles with a string and a pin. You could vault over the old pier stakes that stuck up in the sand like stunted trees. You could sit on the slimy boat-slip and talk to the fishermen as they mended and dried their nets. You could pile up big stones and try to knock them down again with smaller stones. You could walk out to the end of the cold white harbour and look down over the sides at the great green tongues of the sea that licked up the walls. You could do This, and you could do That.

Emily and John quarrelled all day long because they could not decide between This and That. Even Alexandre was independent in his ideas, for a four-and-a-half-year-old.

"What will we play today?" he said, on the second day, as they sat at their lunch in the window-alcove of the hotel.

"You can play what you like," said Emily. "You won't play with us!"

"Why?" said Alexandre. "Why won't I play with you?"

"You're too small," said Emily.

Alexandre accepted this familiar insult. He stared at his plate. The tears began to splash on to the surface of the shining porcelain.

"Alexandre is not as small as you think," said Nurse. "He walked to the end of the pier yesterday afternoon, all by himself." She looked anxiously at Alexandre's tears that were falling on the plate, with the loud, steady fall of the first raindrops that herald a thunderous downpour. "Tell them about your walk, Alexandre!"

Alexandre looked up, with such a jerk that two tears sped from his cheeks into the air on either side of him. He entered upon the narrative with vigour, and a complete faith in the fact that it would vindicate him from future charges of being too small to play with the others.

"I walked to the end of the pier," he said, "all by myself. Nurse sat at the other end. I walked to the very end, and when I got there I sat down on a seat." As he spoke he was impressed by the exactitude of his narrative, but when it was over he became aware of a certain paucity of detail, and moreover, when he looked at his audience, he realized that he had held their attention to no purpose, for the story was ended and his audience clearly expected more.

"Well?" said Emily.

"What happened then?" said John.

Alexandre was humiliated. Desperately he tried to remember further incidents about the walk, but, although he called up a picture of the pier, it was a cold, straight pier, without turns or steps, and all he could see on it was himself, walking along towards the seat at the far end, and a solitary, dull sea bird. Alexandre was forced to fasten upon the sea bird.

"While I was sitting on the seat," he said, taking up the narrative after the most fragmentary and imperceptible pause, "a big bird came along and sat beside me."

"Did you catch him?" said John.

Fearing that evidence of the find might be expected if he answered in the affirmative, Alexandre shook his head in negation.

"Before I had time to catch him," he said, earnestly staring at his listeners, "he ran away."

"You mean he flew away," said Emily, beginning to look somewhat incredulous.

"He ran away," said Alexandre, having learned that it is best to stick to one's first story even if it is a poor one. Emily looked at John.

John fixed Alexandre with a fierce and unblinking stare. "How many legs had he?" said John.

"He had four legs, of course," said Alexandre, indignantly, but as he spoke he began to doubt his statement, and when at that particular moment a sea-gull flew past the window, with no legs visible at all, his doubts became more serious.

"A seagull with four legs!" said John, and he began to laugh.

"I knew he was lying all the time," said Emily.

Nurse looked up. "Emily! That is not a nice way to speak about your little brother."

"Make him tell the truth then!" said Emily.

"Tell the truth, Alexandre," said Nurse.

Alexandre began again but this time his voice was humble and broken by apologetic sniffling. "It's true that I walked to the end of the pier," he said, "but it's not true about the bird. There was a bird, but he just stood on the ground."

"Did you sit on the seat?" said John.

"I did."

"Did the bird come near the seat?"

Alexandre did not reply for a minute, and then he straightened up. "No," he said, "but he looked at me," and proudly, putting his own head to one side and shutting an eye, he showed how the bird looked when it looked at him. "I am going to walk down the pier again today," he said, when he had opened his eye and straightened his neck again.

"You are not," said Emily at once.

"I am," said Alexandre.

"You will do as we say," said Emily.

The tears came into Alexandre's eyes again. Nurse frowned and bit her lip. Nurse was pale, and there was a dark stain under the lashes of her young blue eyes. "Why are you children so difficult?" she said. "Why aren't you like other children? Why are you always quarrelling?" She paused, and then she brightened. "Why don't you build a nice big sand castle?"

"A sand castle!" John was almost speechless with indignation.

"The sand is dirty," said Emily. "I heard a lady say that she saw fleas in it, hopping up and down!"

"Emily!" Nurse looked around hastily to see if there was anyone within earshot. "There are some things that are not discussed at table," she said.

There was silence then for a few minutes, and Nurse looked out between the stiff lace curtains at the far blue sea, and the grey beach lit along its length with bright cockle streams catching the silver sunlight. When she spoke again it was softly, as if to herself. "Very few people can build a good sand castle. It takes skilful planning. It takes a strong steady hand."

Alexandre looked rapidly from Emily to John and from John to Emily, no doubt regretting that he could not look in two directions at one time. Emily and John were looking at Nurse. But Nurse still looked at the sea.

"I could build the best castle that was ever built," said John.

Nurse continued to look at the sea. She said nothing, but she allowed a faint and supercilious smile to fashion itself at the corners of her mouth.

John addressed the smiling mouth. "I'll show you!" he said, angrily, and he beckoned to Emily. "Are you coming?" he said to her, and he strode out of the room. Emily strode after him.

Alexandre had some difficulty descending from his chair, and so he could not stride after them with arrogance, as he would have liked to do, because they were already going through the swinging glass doors of the vestibule, and he would have to run if he was not to be left behind altogether.

Outside the hotel, the air was bright and challenging. The wind shook the red geraniums that stood in glaringly white urns on the terrace and threatened to dash and scatter their petals all over the green grass.

Alexandre caught up with Emily. He drew a deep breath and pulled her by the skirt. "Wait for me!" he said, mysteriously, and disappeared around the corner of the hotel in the direction of the yards. When he came back he carried a rusty, corrugated bucket in his hand. He had seen it some time previously and had been unable to devise a use for it.

"Where did you get that?" said Emily, enviously stretching out her hand for it.

"Finders, keepers!" said Alexandre, retreating a pace or two, and putting the bucket behind his back.

"Oh, keep it!" said Emily, tossing her hair angrily, and she began to run after John.

They caught up with John in the long dune grasses that separated the hotel lawn from the flat sand on the lower shore.

"Here is a good place to build the castle," said Alexandre, setting down his bucket. The soft white sands lifted into streamers on the air. John glanced with contempt at Alexandre.

"Is that all you know about building?" he said, as he strode ahead, his feet sending up branching foam from the sand, as a clipper sends up sea foam.

"What is the matter with this place?" said Alexandre to Emily, in a whisper.

"You have to have wet sand to make the walls firm," said Emily.

"I could get water from the sea to wet the sand." Alexandre held up the bucket, and looked out through the handle at the tempting blue waters with which he would fill it.

"The sea is too far away from here," said Emily.

Alexandre put the bucket on his head, tilted it forward, and put the handle under his chin as a chin strap.

"If we were playing soldiers," he said, with infinite regret, "I could be the General."

"John is always the General," said Emily, scathingly.

Down on the hard, damp, corrugated ripples of the lower shore, John had taken off his coat. Emily sat down with her legs spread out. Alexandre sat on his upturned bucket. For a time John dug in the sand silently, mounting it high. Then he looked up and glanced around at the shell-strewn shore.

"Get me an oyster shell," he said to Emily.

Emily poked Alexandre in the ribs.

"Get him an oyster shell," she said, pointing to the cockle beds that were rippling with shallow water, blown by the wind. Alexandre sped for the shallows. They watched him as he went, and listened with satisfaction to the flat flapping sound that his feet made as he ran through the waters of the cockle stream and reached the far side where shells littered the sand. In a few minutes they saw him bend and pick up something, and then they saw him turn and run back across the flat and empty beach, starting a flurry among the feeding gulls, and splashing water up each side of himself.

"Is this right?" he shouted, holding up a great shell.

John put out his hand and took the shell without speaking.

"Do you want anything else?" said Alexandre, panting.

John did not hear him.

Alexander turned to Emily. "Will I get another shell for him?" he said, politely.

But Emily was sitting with her legs spread out wide, and she was absorbed in the task of taking a lollipop out of her pocket. She had some difficulty because the lollipop had melted and become somewhat stuck to the inside of her pocket. She did not answer. Alexandre, however, had forgotten his question in the intensity of watching the lollipop emerge. His eyes opened wider and wider. As the lollipop came unstuck at last, he clapped his hands.

"Can I have a lick?"

Emily took a long steady lick of the lollipop and said nothing.

"Just one lick?" said Alexandre.

"Go away," said Emily, taking two short licks and one long, defiant one.

"Please!" said Alexandre humbly.

"Don't bother me!" said Emily. "Go away!" and she took up a fistful of sand and threw it at the pleading Alexandre. Alexandre pursed his lips. He made a dive upon the sand to gather a fistful of retaliation, when a more effective method of achieving his object occurred to him. He glanced up at the dunes to see that the setting was right, and seeing, as he hoped, that Nurse was sitting there, within earshot with her book and her striped sunshade, he threw back his head, and putting his hands to his face, gave a long, thin, penetrating wail of anguish.

"There's sand in my eye!" he wailed. "Oh, oh! there's sand in my eye. I'm blinded." And he began to stagger, very blindly, up the beach.

"Come back, Alexandre," said Emily urgently, and she pulled John by the sleeve. "What will I do?" she said. "He'll tell Nurse that I threw it at him."

"You did!" said John, without looking up.

"We'll be kept in after tea!" said Emily, warningly.

John looked up. He saw the lollipop in Emily's hand. He took in the situation. "Give him the lollipop," he directed. "That's what he wants."

Emily looked after Alexandre. He had paused momentarily in his blind stagger forward, and his wailing had lulled, as both of these strenuous efforts interfered somewhat with his hearing. When Emily made no answer, however, he began to lurch ahead once more and threw back his head with a view to louder wailing.

"Alexandre!" Emily stood up. "Alexandre!" she called, running after him. "Will you stop crying if I give you my lollipop?"

Alexandre turned around slowly, and came back with his tear-wet hand outstretched. He took the lollipop and sat down on the sand. Emily sat with her back to him. John resumed his work.

"Now, I am going to dig the moat," said John after a while, and he began to dig around the castle with both hands, throwing up the sand on all sides.

Wildly the sand rose in the air. Lightly it floated downward again. It lay like a fine mist of rain on Emily's bright hair, and it drifted all over Alexandre, but he sat in beatific unconcern of it, although the fastly falling grains settled upon the sticky lollipop and impeded the progress of his bright, industrious tongue, that licked and licked and licked.

"This will be the best castle that was ever built," said John, and he wiped his hand across his mouth leaving a whisker of sand upon his chin.

"Oh," said Alexandre. "John has a beard. John has a beard." And throwing away the lollipop stick, clean as if it had been licked by the briny tongues of the sea, he lifted a fistful of sand and began to decorate his own sticky chin with blond whiskers.

"Stop that," said John, "we have no time to waste." He picked up Alexandre's bucket where it lay on its side forgotten, and he put it into Alexandre's hand. "Get me water for the moat," he said.

"The bucket is leaking," said Emily, disparagingly.

"He can run quick, so the water won't have time to leak out," said John.

Alexandre went off towards the thin sea waves, with his battered bucket swinging in his hand. Every time he let it down to chase a seagull, or to poke his finger into a pool, John called out to him, and the sea birds rose in a flurry, and he picked up the battered bucket again and ran towards the waves with fresh vigour.

In a short while he was racing back, with all the fury of a full-blown wave racing for the shore.

"Is it spilling? Is it spilling?" he shouted, as he ran, not daring to take time to look behind him.

"Hurry! Hurry!" shouted John and Emily together, and they stood up and cheered him, as he dashed through the last cockle stream an inch ahead of the racing drops of water that seemed to be chasing him like a swarm of silver bees.

John rushed forward and caught the bucket from him and dashed the remaining water into the moat. Triumphantly the three of them flung themselves face-down on the sand to lean over the edge of the moat with pride and admiration. But in a few minutes the water had stolen out of sight between the grains of sand, and soon there was a defiant gleam of granite as the sand dried out again to a pale silver colour. Soon there was nothing left of the perilous water but a few iridescent bubbles.

"The water is gone!" said Alexandre, and the statement of this truth seemed to be more bitter than the truth itself, for the tears welled into his eyes.

"What will we do?" said John, looking at Emily.

"We'll think of something," said Emily, and she got down on her knees and inspected the bottom of the moat. "Perhaps, if we put stones along the bottom it might keep the water from leaking away," she said.

Alexandre edged nearer. He sat down on his hunkers and began to root in his pocket. After a minute he produced a ball of silver paper, and began to tear off pieces of the thin tinfoil and lay them along the bottom of the moat.

"Look at the water!" he said, pulling Emily by the sleeve.

"It's just like water," said John, and he got down on his knees. "Give me some, Alexandre," he said. "It's just as good as water. You'd think it was water," and he began to line the moat upon the opposite side from Alexandre until the whole circle of the dyke around the castle shone with fake silver water.

And so, gradually, although at first he wanted to work at the castle alone, John allowed the others to offer suggestions and give him help. When the artist begins to shape his creation he is filled with a pride in himself and cannot bear to think that any hand but his could shape the perfection of the dream behind his brain, but as the dream emerges into tangible form his selfish pride in his own power fades before a pure, unselfish pride in the thing he has created. Then he is willing and anxious to accept help from others, and is even ready, if necessary, to make the tragic abnegation of abandoning his task to other hands if those hands seem better fitted than his own to consummate the task.

Emily pinned back her hair. Alexandre took off his shoes. Sitting with their legs spread out all three of them worked without talking. They patted and dug, they mounded the sand, they smoothed it, and they piled it high. And soon a noble castle, with a noble crenellated tower, rose out of the sand and stood between them and the sun. It rose so high, so proud, so tall, that it cast its own blue shadow on the pale sand.

"What kind of doors will we have?" said John. "We could have real wood for doors."

"We could have real glass in the windows," said Emily.

"I'll get the wood," said Alexandre. "I'll get the glass." And he ran up to a bank of seaweed, higher up on the shore, where broken china, bits of glass, splinters of driftwood, tin, pearl buttons, shells, and empty bottles were tangled in the mesh of seaweed. He ran back with his arms filled and let fall a glittering cascade of treasures.

John began to pick out suitable pieces of glass, but all at once Emily clapped her hands. "I have an idea," she said. "We could have real doors and windows; that you could see through!" and picking up a shell she began to dig a hole in the side of the sturdy wall.

"Be careful," warned John. But the idea gripped him, and picking up another shell he began to tunnel into the castle upon the opposite side from Emily.

"Be careful," he called out, from time to time. "We are nearly meeting!" and indeed, even as he spoke he felt something alive stirring within the castle, and a minute later he felt Emily's hot fingers underneath his own.

"Hurrah!" said John, and throwing himself on his face he peered into the tunnel. "Can you see me?" he yelled in delight as he caught sight of Emily's blue eyes at the other end.

"Can you see me?" screamed Emily.

Alexandre jumped up and down. "Can I have a look? Can I have a look?" he yelled, but without much hope of being heard. He continued to jump up and down.

When at last the furious ecstasy of creation had wasted his strength John sat back and drew a deep breath of renewal.

"What do you think of it, Alexandre?" he said patronizingly.

But Alexandre was speechless. He jumped up and down more

furiously, and all he could say, as he stared at the castle, was "Gosh".
"Gosh," cried Alexandre. "Gosh! Gosh! Gosh!"

But as Alexandre said "Gosh," a faint voice in his ears whispered it back again, slyly: "Gosh".

Alexandre stopped jumping up and down. Emily and John stared at him suspiciously.

"Gosh," said Alexandre, once more, bravely, but while he spoke he put out a hand, edging near to Emily, and caught at her skirt. "Gosh," said the small white voice behind him, "Gosh, gosh, gosh."

They all swung around, with their lips apart, their hands groping out for each other. There, at their feet, were the thin white lips of the cold sea waves, saying over and over again, without even waiting, now, for Alexandre, "Gosh—" and then, "Gosh". "Gosh—" and then, "Gosh—"

John looked at Alexandre, Alexandre's ears were sticking out with excitement. His chin was pulled in tight. He stared at the waves, mesmerized with their words, and forgot the castle behind him. But when John looked at Emily her lips were pressed tightly together. John pressed his own lips together. Stronger than the bitter scent of the sour sea-water that stole into his nostrils, was the first bitter foretaste of human impotence.

"What will we do?" he cried. "Our castle will be destroyed!" But while he spoke a combative spirit woke within him.

"We will fight back the sea!" he cried. "We will rout the enemy. Arm yourselves, my men! Arm yourselves." And taking up stones he led his men. "I am the king of the castle!" he cried, and missile after missile was hurled into the water, breaking the faces of the pale waves but unable to silence their chuckles of triumph or stem their relentless advance. The green regiment outnumbered even the stones on the shore, and soon the defenders had to lay down arms as the castle keep began to collapse with a slow sliding of grain after grain.

Tears shone in John's eyes. Big blue tears ran down Alexandre's red cheeks. But Emily's eyes were tearless, and they seemed to have taken on the angry agate colour of the sea.

"There is one thing left that we can do!" she said, and she bit her lip and looked at the castle. "There is one thing left to do!" She turned around and looked at the boys. "I am queen of the castle!" she said, in a loud voice, and raising her arms like a bird lifting his wings for flight, she leapt into the air, and landed with both feet upon the crenellated tower of the castle, which crumbled to dust around her.

Her feet sank into streaming sand. She raised them heavily, one after another, and rivers of sand ran lightly over the white knobs of her ankles. Her dress belled out like a tulip. Her bright hair blazed.

"Now you can't have our castle!" she cried to the greedy reaching waves.

John and Alexandre looked on uncomprehendingly for a moment. Then they, too, ran forward and, jumping into the air, landed upon the castle, and began to leap up and down. "Gosh!" said Alexandre. "Gosh! Isn't this great? Isn't this the best game ever?"

They jumped and jumped, all three of them, while the waters stole around their feet, with swirling foam, and writhing seaweed, and millions of grains of sand travelling restlessly.

And soon they forgot the reason why they were jumping and they began to see who could jump the highest, and who could make the biggest splashes in the rising water. And as they rose up and down, in their hearts also, there rose and broke, and rose again, and broke, the silent waves of a wild intuition that was carrying them forward, nearer and nearer to the shores of wisdom—those bright shores of silt.

The Shark's Fin

Phyllis Bottome

Dorothy Layton stared at the retreating head of her young husband with incredulous eyes. Was it really Jo walking away from her with that easy, effortless swing, accompanied by the boring young man, tactlessly introduced to them at lunch by an acquaintance, interrupting without a qualm a perfectly good honeymoon?

Dorothy had been mildly annoyed even then, though in her scale of values two young men were generally better than one—but not two young men interested in each other—their eyes and their minds obstinately glued upon imaginary diesel and turbine engines.

Dorothy was five foot three of concentrated easiness to look at; and she knew it. Her hair, the silvery gold of platinum, had never been dyed, her skin was creamy and her colour clear. She used lipstick from habit, but nature would have done as well for her. Her eyes were not quite the blue of the Caribbean Sea, but they sustained the comparison. Had the Medician Venus consented to diet and take P.T. from infancy, she would have had precisely Dorothy's figure. Probably neither the Venus of the Medici nor Dorothy had much heart, but the Venus would at least have pretended to feelings which Dorothy frankly despised. What Dorothy wanted was to have the best of everything on the table on her plate at the same time, and to be helped first; and so far in her nineteen dashing years fate had heard Dorothy's prayer.

Most people get what they live for, but as they do not know what they are living for, they do not always like it. Until her honeymoon Dorothy had often had to put up with shouldering crosses. Her parents for instance—she was an only child—had given way to her all along the line, yet it was evident to Dorothy that they did not always like it. What Dorothy had wanted was to be loved and admired while she was having her own way. She did not want just to have her own way and be criticised for taking it. But when Jo fell in love with her, it was quite evident that whatever she wanted was Heaven itself to Jo. Her whims enchanted him almost, if not quite as much, as they enchanted Dorothy. Everything she did was right for Jo; everything she said was purest wisdom. Everything she wanted became in a flash the purpose of Jo's life to obtain for her. And now, after a sparkling month of unsullied felicity, with no fin of a shark showing like a sinister shadow in the translucent sea of her bliss, came this sudden appalling shock. Jo had walked off with Tony Cootes, down the steps of the promontory on which the hotel stood, to the little white-sanded cove with only one small motor launch, and into this they both got and made off for the Island. Neither man once glanced up at the hotel to see what had become of Dorothy. The centre of the universe had fallen out and they behaved as if nothing had happened. It was true that Jo had told Dorothy to hurry if she wanted to come to the Island because Tony had to get back early. But why should Dorothy hurry? She had never in all her life hurried unless she had wanted to hurry, though she had always hurried when many people—including Jo perhaps—had wished her to keep still.

They had gone to visit the Island with the coconut palms, the feathery waves—perhaps real coral strands—without Dorothy. They simply hadn't waited that one little half-hour which Dorothy had proposed to make them wait.

The Island floated like a leaf on the breast of satiny, untroubled azure. Everything shimmered in the sunny air so that Dorothy could not be quite sure which was Island and which was foam. The sea and the sky were an interchangeable, unsubstantial blue. The little black dot, which was the motor launch, moved swiftly and purposefully towards the landing stage. The engine—it was Tony Coote's launch—worked beautifully. Dorothy's softly curved lips set in a straight line, which would make wrinkles later on if she set it too often.

There were two things she might do to punish Jo; and to punish Jo was her immediate and single-minded aim. The choice was merely in the nature of the punishment. Should she wait till he came back and just explode? She could frighten him out of his wits if she put her mind to it. Or could she think of something less savage but more subtle—something lingering, like boiling oil—which would continue to hurt him whenever he thought of unilateral action again? The trouble with rage is that it seldom keeps. Dorothy could explode now, but in two hours' time—and that would be the soonest she could expect Jo back—she might have mislaid the dynamite. Should she then swim to the Island after him and strike while the iron was hot? This would really punish Jo for, of course, the swim had the element of risk. Besides a mile of perfectly solitary sea with unknown currents, it was the Caribbean Sea. The channel between the Island and the promontory was unprotected from "fish". Sharks are not mentioned in polite society in Jamaica; but Dorothy had never known real danger, and anything that a selfish person has not had happen to them, does not exist. She simply saw the pain she was going to inflict on Jo as Jo's pain.

She quickly slipped off a dawn-pink linen frock and substituted her prettiest bathing dress, a diminutive butterfly wing of a yellow skirt with a frill across her pointed breasts. Her body was the colour of a shell and her finger- and toe-nails a dark crimson. It was a pity to cover her soft yellow curls with a bathing cap, but salt water doesn't suit silky hair, so Dorothy covered hers. No one saw her slip like a ray of honey-coloured light, across the lawn to the steps, and down the steps into the softly lapping sea.

The sea took Dorothy's slim young body caressingly, as if it loved her, not breaking over her, but gently drawing her into its pulseless rhythm.

Dorothy swam a quick crawl to start with, till she felt herself well out into the swinging depth of the channel, then she went in for a steady over-arm stroke, getting her breath quietly to match the rise and fall of the foamless sea. Her anger ebbed away from her and she began to think quite differently of Jo. She longed to see him with that happy anticipation of a lover. Soon she would be with him, and sea and sky and earth would be enriched and sociable again. In her mind's eye she saw Jo's tall, strong body, useful and graceful at the same time, his incredibly kind young eyes, always, when he looked at Dorothy, so full of wondering pride. Well, perhaps after this swim, it wouldn't be pride just at first. He'd be more surprised than pleased to see Dorothy, as indeed she still meant him to be. "You don't mean to say you've *swum* across! Why the hell, girl—don't you know it's not *safe*!" she almost heard him say. "Well, you took the boat, didn't you?" she would answer casually rather than viciously. "There wasn't any other! You went without me, didn't you? You didn't even call up. You knew I wanted to see the old Island, didn't you?" Then of course he'd be right down sorry; and he'd look a fool. He might even be a little angry and bluster a little, as people sometimes do who are in the wrong. She would take it quite calmly because now she felt calm—cool and calm—and she had already swum a third of the way across the channel. "Well," she'd say, "don't run off and leave me alone again Jo—that's all!"

It would be a lesson to Jo—and possibly also to that Tony Cootes—she might have been made out of leather for all the notice he had taken of her at lunch.

Suddenly it occurred to Dorothy in quite a cheerful way, that what looks like a mile of water, doesn't feel like a mile of water when you're swimming across it—it feels rather more. If a current is strong and keeps pulling a swimmer toward rocks, which can't be climbed, instead of towards the one safe landing place, which is his goal, it can seem very much more than a mile. Dorothy was a good swimmer, but she changed her stroke and began to feel extraordinarily alone. The channel was very deep; but depth means nothing to an accustomed swimmer. Still, when Dorothy had swum over deep water before she had always had companions. She could not remember ever having swum alone over an empty sea. Far away the hotel stood glittering up to the sky, and far away the Island moved its palms in idle grace, as sea weed moves in the soft swaying of a summer sea. There was no sound at all. Far off, at the foot of the rocks, white feathery screens of foam rose high and fell back noiselessly into the shining sea. A Johnny crow swooped its slatternly wings high above Dorothy's head. Its chafed red head and evil eyes looked cynically down at her. Of course, Dorothy assured herself, she was perfectly all right. The sea was calm, it was not cold, she was making headway against the current, though not fast. Something, probably a jellyfish or a piece of floating sea-weed, brushed against her thigh. It didn't even sting her; but it did worse. Fear slid from that light touch through Dorothy's whole body. It rushed full tilt into her shallow heart. She remembered sharks—not any longer as a threat to Jo—but as a threat to herself. She was out on this lonely sea at the mercy of whatever was in it. She didn't know what was in it, and if she had known she couldn't get out. She was in an ice-cold predicament. Sheer panic seized her, and she knew she'd go under if she panicked. She drew several long deep breaths and swam on as well as ever; but the fear at her heart remained. What a fool she had been, safe in that clean, comfortable hotel bedroom, with the twin beds so reassuringly promising under pink silk slip covers. All she'd had to do was to read a book or go downstairs and turn on the radio till Jo came back. Jo wouldn't have stayed away from her for long; he'd probably hurry over seeing the Island. Perhaps he hadn't even meant to vex her but had honestly believed that she didn't want to go: he was terribly good-natured and might just not have liked to disappoint Tony Cootes, whose one chance it was to see the Island before he left for Miami that very evening. Jo would just be longing to rejoin her as soon as he decently could, and they'd have their evening game of tennis and a long, leisurely drink. Tony Cootes hadn't really mattered a red cent to Dorothy and except for engines, which happened to be both their jobs, he couldn't have mattered a red cent to Jo either. Dorothy had made a mistake. It was no use blaming Jo for it; besides, he wasn't there to blame.

Dorothy was all alone in the Caribbean Sea with sharks. It was her body that would have to take the punishment, the agony, the helplessness, the panic—all would be hers. Death too; and she'd never even thought of death before, except as something which happened to the old and the infirm—or to other people anyway. There were accidents, of course. You read about death, or you saw it on films—but such accidents only happen to murderers or unpleasant people; and now suddenly death leered at her. Once more she felt a touch on her knee, and she thought it was harder this time—not so much like sea-weed. Dorothy subsided into the old-fashioned breast stroke, she was too frightened to hide her head under the false, smiling water. Just for a moment it flashed through Dorothy that she was to blame—she'd done something not only silly, but cruelly, hideously wrong: not only wrong because she might be torn to pieces in agony, but wrong because it wasn't only her own body she'd carried with her into unknown depths, but Jo's heart.

She had swum out with Jo's heart, to risk it against the teeth of sharks.

Dorothy might die in rending torments but she would soon reach nothingness; Jo would not reach it. Jo would be tied for his life to her brief agony. Love, that Dorothy had played with as a becoming ornament, suddenly pierced her heart as a two-edged sword. "Oh, if I can only *live!*" she cried to Something, Somewhere. "Oh, for Jo's sake let me live!" And then, as if there was a direct answer, though not the least the answer which Dorothy had expected, she began to swim in earnest, not just keeping herself up, but moving decisively and purposefully through the water. She swam as if she were swimming for a prize. She shut her eyes and her mind to fear. She took the sea over her head and face as if she no longer minded the rush and darkness of the water; and she reached the landing safe and sound, though thoroughly exhausted.

Pulling herself out of the water, Dorothy staggered painfully across the hot sand to the shade of a broad-leaved almond tree. The kind, solid earth held its wilful child safe, without her having to move. She closed her eyes and tried not to think—just to live till Jo came. Suddenly she heard hurrying footsteps, a sharp exclamation, and Jo's voice. "There," she thought, "he's found me!" Blinded by her safety, which seemed somehow to be a part of Jo's voice, habit ran back into Dorothy's light, stubborn heart. "It's all his fault," she told herself accusingly. "He shouldn't have gone off like that and left me!" "Dorothy, Dorothy, darling!" Jo cried. "What's—what's happened to you?" She opened her eyes and gazed into his. Jo's eyes were full of horror—not anger, not surprise—just horror. "Nothing's happened," she said quietly, "I just swam across. I—I wanted to see the Island—you'd left me alone!" The horror in Jo's eyes changed under her accusation but it didn't become anger, it was a most peculiar expression—an expression of sick shame. But Jo was not ashamed because he had left her, Dorothy had the sense to see that, he was ashamed because of what Dorothy had done. Tony Cootes stood behind them. "My God!" he irritatingly said, "you swam that channel full of fish! You certainly took some risk, Babe! Didn't I tell you at lunch time—a boatman told me he'd killed a ten-foot shark in the middle of that channel yesterday. Gosh, what a challenge!" "Why did you do it, Dorothy?" Jo asked her in a most curious, grave way, as if he'd just met her for the first time and had to be polite. "Well," she heard herself saying, belligerently, "you'd gone off and left me, hadn't you? I had to pay you back somehow!" Jo looked up at Tony. "You might go down to the launch," he said, "and start up the engine. We'll have to get her back to the hotel as quick as we can." "Well, I guess we all need a drink!" Tony agreed, walking off. "Don't, don't look at me like that, Jo!" Dorothy cried, "and oh, love me! Jo, love me! You don't know what it was like out there alone! I got frightened! I'm not sure, but I think—I think a fish touched me! It was terrible, Jo! You can't think!" She stopped. It was as if Jo still wasn't there. He said slowly, "I'm sorry, Honey, I don't feel so good. I reckon I love you all right but not just now—not till I get over this. You did it—you did this thing—just because we'd gone over to the Island without you? Why—why, I didn't know you *wanted* to go to the Island! I waited half an hour and then I thought you'd just not *be* coming back! Besides, such a little thing—and this!" "But it's over!" Dorothy pleaded. "Oh, Jo darling! It doesn't matter any more, now I'm here!" But even as she said it the sense of her own identity— the lovely deity she was to Jo—slipped away from her. She saw in Jo's eyes a different Dorothy. He would try to get used to this new Dorothy. He would see that she was cared for and protected. He would love her again. Even now his unsteady hands tried to be a lover's hands, but she knew they were not. The Dorothy Jo loved had been given to the sharks.

The Lovely Evening

MARY NORTON

It wasn't lovely, really. But it could have been: all the ingredients were there, pressed down and overflowing.

"… Like a stage set," Brigitta had said, looking about her: the dark lake, the shadowy mountains, the skeins of light below. Over the vines hung a single electric bulb; breeze-swayed shadows trailed across the stone. Little tables, ghost-white cloths, wine in carafes … And music (too loud for Sarah but not, it seemed, for the girls).

"Do you eat out here every night?" asked Miranda.

"Yes, if it doesn't rain."

"Oh, goodness …" Miranda breathed.

Sarah laughed: she had wanted "Italy" to be like this. It wasn't always. There had been windy nights when the tablecloths flew up and napkins slithered away into the shadows: when the gay Campari umbrellas, threshing a little, swayed from their moorings and suddenly took wing; there had been nights of mist—the lake "perspiring": and nights of sudden thunder storms, which blew up without warning—crashing about between the peaks. On such occasions, one ate upstairs in a white-washed dining room, hung with last year's calendars. Then the place looked what it was—a village trattoria run by peasants, clean but second-rate. "It is anything like you imagined?"

"Better," Miranda cried, "a thousand times better. Absolute heaven …"

How lovely their skins were, Sarah thought, marble-smooth with a patina of silvery shadows which slid quicksilver when they laughed or spoke. Miranda was Sarah's daughter; Brigitta—her daughter's friend.

"It isn't a smart place."

"Who wants a smart place? It's heaven!"

"You know," Brigitta went on, wrinkling her nose, "it's like a night club ought to be but isn't."

"Do you go to night clubs?" asked Sarah, surprised. Brigitta was just sixteen.

"No, I don't really," Brigitta admitted, laughing. "But you know what I mean—coffee bar places all done up with moonlight and imitation vine leaves. I mean," again she looked about her, "—this is the whole thing itself."

"It's very quiet up here," Sarah warned them, "you don't think you'll be bored?"

"Bored!" exclaimed Miranda, "darling Mummy, don't be *too* silly …" She laughed delightedly, catching her breath, "How long can we stay?"

"Three weeks."

"Sure you can afford it?"

"Yes, if we stay *here*."

"Tomorrow, may we swim in the lake?"

"Of course, if you don't mind the climb back."

"We've brought our painting things. At least, Brigitta has."

"Good," Sarah hesitated. "No young men, I'm afraid. At least, I don't know any …"

"Young men!" Brigitta gave a little snort: again she wrinkled her nose (really, thought Sarah, she's quite enchanting—that honey-gold skin, that honey-fair hair …). "We've come for a holiday—we want a rest from all that."

All what?—wondered Sarah, amused.

The music stopped and, in the silence, a night-jar sounded its single calling note.

"What's that?"

"A bird."

"Yes," breathed Miranda, "It's deep country: you almost forget." She lifted her eyes to the shadowy mountains, and breathed in the mountain air. "Heaven …" she murmured again.

Brigitta turned her head and gazed across the courtyard at the lighted kitchen door: a young man came out and stood against the lintel. His white shirt gleamed in the dusk, a hint of gold light in the hair; and the pale face, caught sharply by the sideways gleam from the kitchen seemed curiously still.

"Who's that?" Brigitta asked.

Sarah narrowed her eyes: "Luigi, I think. The youngest son, I don't know him. He lives in Bolzano and has just come home for a rest …"

"Who else is there?"

"Candido. And a married daughter with a baby. And a boy called Nino. And Giuseppe …" Nice boys, all of them, she reflected, but a little shy of strangers.

"Do they—" asked Brigitta lightly, "ever come and sit out here or dance or anything?"

"Sometimes. Not often. They're rather serious …"

"Who does dance?" asked Miranda.

"The village boys. On Sunday nights."

Miranda inclined her head towards Luigi: "Isn't he a village boy?"

Sarah laughed, "No, he's a cut above."

"Tonight is Sunday," Brigitta pointed out.

The canned music, relayed from a loud speaker, blared out into the darkness above the lake: the softly moving air, neither hot nor cold, seemed to vibrate with it.

"Get up and dance yourselves," suggested Sarah suddenly.

"Who with?"—they looked appalled.

"With each other. The girls here often do."

"What," exclaimed Brigitta shocked, "me dance with Miranda?"

"Why not?"

"Two girls dancing together?"

"Why not?"

"Good gracious," Miranda exclaimed, "We couldn't. I mean we'd have to practise first ..." But her feet began tapping to the music.

"I will, if you will," said Brigitta, raising her voice (... little animated golden face, pony tail jumping on her shoulders).

"Oh, don't let's," exclaimed Miranda laughing. They both became silent, Brigitta swaying her shoulders, Miranda tapping her foot.

Luigi stirred suddenly and moved towards them across the courtyard. He walked purposefully with a swift, lithe step but he did not (as Sarah hoped) paused beside their table but went on past them to a chair beyond the light. He sank down into it—enfolded in darkness he sat, withdrawn and silent—too far to be with them, too near to be apart.

A party arrived, seven in all: village boys and three girls. The boys wore their best clothes—clean, white shirts and dark trousers: the girls wore blouses and skirts. They ordered white wine in a carafe and grouped themselves about a table.

"*Permesso?*" A tall young man stood at Sarah's side: he was asking to borrow a chair; as he spoke his glance slid quickly from one girl to another. "*Prego*," murmured Sarah politely, trying not to smile: there were chairs and tables to spare at other tables.

"Please, do," cried Brigitta—a little too animated, a little too eager. He stared at her, chair in hand, without speaking, then, bowing, gravely turned, and walked away. It was almost a snub, not quite. Brigitta coloured and Miranda looked down at her plate.

Sarah leaned forward and began to talk (… conceited young ass, she thought); she spoke quickly, comfortingly describing places they must see, expeditions she had done and would do again with them; she told them about the play-suits one could buy beside the lake—and the funny, large straw hats: about the church processions in the village: about the alpine flowers.

They smiled brightly, sweetly, but they did not seem to be listening. They would laugh suddenly at the wrong places for no reason and Brigitta—one ear on the music—beat time with her fork.

The dancing began. Casually, correctly, the couples rose from the further table—one man left sitting alone. The girls' eyes, almost absently slid sideways: they knew good dancing when they saw it—the steady hips, the controlled, bored sway.

Then out of the shadows, a voice spoke. Sarah, startled, turned quickly: she had forgotten about Luigi. "You do not like to dance?"

He was leaning forward in his chair, his hands lightly clasped above his parted knees, his drawn face lifted towards the light.

"I?" stammered Sarah, and gave a little laugh (was the "you" in this case, singular or plural?). "No thank you—" she glanced across at the girls, "but perhaps the *Signorine* …"

He rose immediately and came over to Miranda. She stood up, with a half smile, and glided off in his arms.

Little Brigitta dissolved into laughter: the ice was broken—now all would be well. "He asked *you* to dance," she whispered giggling, "do they always do that?"

Sarah hesitated. "Always do what?" she asked, after a moment.

Brigitta saw her mistake. "I mean—" she began and blushed.

"I know what you mean," exclaimed Sarah, laughing, "I'm not hurt really! Yes, they've got charming manners …"

"I didn't mean—"

"I know you didn't, I know you didn't!" she squeezed Brigitta hand.

"Oh, thank you for having me," exclaimed Brigitta suddenly, and her blue eyes filled with tears.

Miranda danced shyly. Slender, dark-haired, golden-skinned— she seemed more Italianate than the fair boy who guided her. The couple moved softly, cut with trembling shadow; the arc lamp, slung on wires, glared down from above. "Like a scene from a play," said Brigitta again, "like something from opera. And I'm part of it," she added ecstatically on a note of surprise.

You are indeed, thought Sarah: the peasant skirt of white and scarlet, the little, short-sleeved blouse. Strange and charming quirk of fashion which made their clothes so right. Miranda, too, swam into the setting correctly dressed for the part.

The music stopped and, after a moment, the other two came back. Sarah leaned sideways in a gesture of welcome, and pulled up Luigi's chair. He sank into it, making one of the party.

"My feet hurt," he said.

The conversation, stilted but friendly, continued in Italian. How old was Miranda? How old was Brigitta? How old—"How old are you?" Sarah hastened to ask. Luigi was twenty-nine.

"*Permesso*?" Sarah looked up: the odd man out from the other table had emerged again from the shadows. He stood beside them, two paces distant, bowing towards Miranda. Miranda hesitated: it was Brigitta's turn. But Brigitta, beating soft time to the music, seemed lost in thought.

Nobody spoke. Nobody moved. And Miranda glided off. If only, Sarah worried, I could speak better Italian … She glanced at Luigi but Luigi did not look up; he had taken out his pocket-book and thumbing through the leaves; smiling shyly, at last he produced a photograph. "You like to see?" he said.

Sarah stared at the picture without seeing it. Suddenly she

looked. "Oh," she exclaimed and began to laugh. It was a picture of his motorbike, standing up alone.

Luigi looked anxious. "It is funny?"

"No, no. Not in the least." She said in Italian "It's lovely. But …" she hesitated, searching for words, "I thought to see you fiancée—"

"I have no fiancée," he said.

"Or your wife, or your mother …"

He interrupted then, leaning across her, and began to describe the machine. He spoke quickly with a kind of modest pride. When he spoke of the gear box his voice deepened: there was a tenderness in it and something like awe. "You like?" he said, suddenly in English, staring into her face.

"Very much, yes."

"To ride with this on the mountain roads?"

"Well," began Sarah doubtfully just as the music stopped. Miranda returned, then, dropped by her partner, and the picture was passed to her. "You like?" Luigi repeated. Miranda liked very much. They talked awhile of motorbikes and Brigitta did her share. The music then struck up again but none of the party moved. Luigi aired his English, the girls politely helped.

Again the tall stranger approached and again he asked Miranda. "Oh dear," thought Sarah as the couple swept away; there was nothing she could do. Then at last Luigi stood up. Brigitta's lips parted, but he did not look her way. "I change my shoes," he announced and, bowing slightly, he left the table. They watched in silence as he crossed the courtyard.

"His feet hurt," said Sarah at last.

"Oh?" Brigitta said.

"Where's your sketch-book?' Sarah went on brightly (Brigitta's sketch-book she thought suddenly, could lie on the table between them: Luigi would be impressed). But Brigitta merely shrugged. "In my room somewhere," she muttered and went on tapping her fork.

The music stopped, Miranda came back to the table. Gaily, Brigitta looked up, "How was that one?" she asked.

"Not bad. Better than Luigi. Luigi's awful. He doesn't lead … Let's go and look at the lake."

They went out of the gate and into the shadowed lane. They stood against the parapet, looking down. It was still warm from the sun. Luigi joined them as the moon rose above the water. They talked of this and that … of dancing at home, of jazz and jive. "Jive? Show me," Luigi said. And, laughing, they showed him. Dancing together in the dust, flicked here and there by light, wary as fencers, light as flower-petals—it was charming.

Sarah moved away. She crossed the lane, into the courtyard. She went back to the table to fetch her bag. It was not there. Stooping, she felt on the chairs.

"You lose something?"

It was Luigi again. Sarah felt suddenly irritated: why had he left the girls?

"My bag. It's all right, it's here …"

She looked around; Miranda was dancing again. Where was Brigitta? They she saw her, coming towards them. Forlorn and slightly embarrassed—threading her way through the dancers. "Get her, Luigi," urged Sarah. He went forward quickly and brough Brigitta to the table. Politely, he pulled out a chair.

They sat down together—Brigitta and Sarah. Luigi went off to fetch wine.

"Tired, Brigitta?"

"No, not at all."

Miranda came back. Down she flopped, panting a little and looking rather pink. "Gosh—" she exclaimed.

"How was that one?" asked Brigitta.

"Awful. He smelt of something. Not garlic exactly, more like chives …" and she fanned her face with her hand. Comforting Brigitta …

"Oh," said Brigitta. "Poor Miranda …"

"Yes, it was ghastly."

"Ghastly!" Brigitta repeated. They both became silent. Brigitta powdered her nose.

When Luigi came back with the wine he drew up a chair and leaned forward. "I go tomorrow," he said.

"Where?" they asked in chorus.

"Back to Bolzano. My work. A very fine city," he told them, "with mountains around and palms." He took out a diary, "I send you a postcard. Please will you write here the name?" (Who was he addressing? Brigitta or Miranda?) Brigitta turned away; she stooped right down, below the level of the table as though to fasten a shoe.

"Here, Brigitta," said Sarah, pushing the notebook across, "he wants you to write your name."

"My name?" exclaimed Brigitta, as though she had not heard.

"Yes," said Sarah, "to send you a postcard."

"Me?"

"*And* Miranda. A picture of his town."

"Oh," said Brigitta, blushing. "There," she exclaimed, as she laid down the pen. She seemed happy again, at ease …

"Brigeet-ta …" repeated Luigi.

"What time do you go?"

"Early. Tomorrow early. Before you will be awake."

Miranda wrote her name and Sarah, too, wrote hers.

Luigi studied the page. His face seemed drawn again, a little tired. "*Grazie,*" he said, and put away the book.

"You are glad to be back?" asked Sarah.

He shrugged. "Here … there, it is the same." He stared at her, suddenly brooding. "You believe in a future life?"

"In a what?" said Sarah, startled.

He repeated the phrase in Italian.

Sarah floundered. "Yes, of course, I mean, I think so. It depends ..."

"What does he say?" asked Brigitta. Sarah translated.

"Oh," gasped Brigitta delightedly. She leaned forward across the table, grasping her elbows: "You mean life after death?" she said. It was easy to say in Italian: she looked pleased that it rolled off her tongue. "Or," she added to Sarah, in English, "does he mean ghosts?"

"Ghosts?" repeated Luigi.

Out came the pocket vocabulary. They were off: page turning furiously, fingers pointing, snatchings, arguments, laughter ... Miranda joined in and they ran the gamut: premonitions, astral bodies, fortune-telling, astrology and yoga. I could leave them now, Sarah thought—I really could—and slide away to bed. She had done her best—expounded her philosophy and told her one true ghost story; translated Luigi to the girls, and the girls to Luigi. Things, she thought, would run on from here; and without her presence, Luigi might act as host.

She stood up. Luigi stood up, too. He looked a little startled. It's all right, Sarah wanted to say, the girls won't eat you ... She put out her hand: "Goodnight, I'm very tired. And goodbye, too. Are you really going tomorrow?" He looked rather white, his face shrunken ... She wondered if he had been ill. "Perhaps we shall meet again?"

"Perhaps," he said.

"Need we come?" asked Miranda.

"Of course not. Stay and dance." Sarah looked at Luigi. "You'll look after them?' And find a partner for Brigitta? But she did not say it, instead she took his hand: "Goodbye, again. One day, we'll come to Bolzano."

She walked away across the courtyard, threading her way among the dancers. She climbed the stone steps which led to the first floor. From the balcony she looked down. It was a romantic scene—no film studio could have done better—the shadows of the vine leaves, artificial light and moonlight. Brigitta, Miranda and Luigi splashed about the table. The dancing couples, the air alive with music …

In she went, and upstairs to her room: tin basin, toothpaste, peeling shutters … her nightdress laid out. She undressed, unworried. Miranda was all right. Miranda was two years older—Italian village boys meant little to her. But Brigitta—that was different: Brigitta was trying her wings …

One more look, before she went asleep. Across the passage to the girls' room, opposite, the creaking door, the ghostly beds—beds used as tables, covered with half-seen objects: paint-boxes, books, sewing materials … At the window, standing in the darkness, she pulled the lace curtain aside. The same scene—moonlight, lamplight and shadow, revolving couples—but, at the further table, under the arbour, Brigitta sat alone—still, sprawled, silent, the dress like a crumpled rose. Miranda, she saw, was dancing. Not with Luigi. Luigi, she realized had gone. And now what? Nothing she could do.

As she watched Brigitta rose and ran across the courtyard to the house, threading her way through the dancers. "Oh, don't do that," Sarah wanted to cry, "stay a little longer …" But Brigitta now had reached the courtyard steps—up she came, two stairs at a time. Sarah drew back from the window, and quickly ran out of the room. Across the passage she flashed, and shut her bedroom door.

Footsteps, up the stairs, along the passage. Running footsteps. A kind of gasp. A door creaked open. A door slammed shut. And there she would be, thought Sarah, lying across the bed …

Knock on the door and go in? No, she couldn't do that. She must not have seen; she must not have noticed. Sarah began to undress.

More footsteps. Sarah listened. Here now, was Miranda. Running, running—leaving her partners, leaving the dance. How kind they are to each other, Sarah thought. Miranda will make it right. The creak of the door. The slam of the door, Voices, voices.

Sarah climbed into bed. They will talk, she thought, into the small hours.

Next day, Brigitta went sketching. She wanted to be alone. At lunch, she was quiet. At dinner, quieter still. They spoiled her, they paid her compliments, they tried to make her laugh. "It's no good, Mother," explained Miranda when they found themselves alone. "It isn't that. She knows she's pretty. She said last night 'It isn't that I'm not pretty; if I were ugly, I'd understand. What's wrong with me?' she said."

"But there's nothing wrong with her!" Sarah exclaimed hotly. "She's adorable. Just because one stupid boy—"

"Luigi isn't a boy. And he didn't want to dance. His feet really hurt him …"

"Then why," cried Sarah, "did he ask me?"

"Out of politeness, I suppose. I don't know, I mean, he didn't know then this his feet would hurt."

"Nonsense," cried Sarah, "then why did he dance with you?"

"Out of politeness again. You practically asked him to."

"But why you and not Brigitta?"

"Because I was your daughter, I suppose. I tell you, Mother, he didn't really want to dance. He was awfully dull. Perhaps he thought that to dance with me was enough."

"But the others?"

"I think they thought that she just wasn't dancing. I mean, there she was sitting and there was Luigi at the table—"

"I know," said Sarah glumly, "it was all Luigi's fault."

"Luigi liked her. He called her '*bella bamina*'. But he thought her rather young."

"Well, she is young," said Sarah, "what's wrong with that?"

"He thought me young, too," Miranda said, "but not as young."

"Brilliant," remarked Sarah, "considering he'd just asked both your ages."

"He said you looked thirty-five."

"That was kind of him. Look here, Miranda, if he sends you a postcard, don't—"

"Of course, I won't. I'm not so silly. I wouldn't show her. I'd tear it up."

"Perhaps," mused Sarah, "he'll send her one, too."

"He will, I think. He liked her. He liked her just as much as he liked me."

"Yes," cried Sarah, "that's it. That's what she's got to know. Explain to her, too, this thing about the others."

"I did. I have. And she saw the point. And now if we *both* get a postcard—"

"You think it'll be all right?"

"Yes, quite. I know it. As long as it isn't just me—"

"But she did *like* Luigi?" asked Sarah, after a pause.

"Not much. No."

"Did you?"

"No. Not much." At Sarah's expression, Miranda began to laugh. "That isn't the point, at all!"

But neither of the girls got a postcard. Sarah got it: an aerial view of Bolzano, set about with mountains, studded with palm trees. Tactful Luigi, this was a masterstroke. She set about to read it.

"Do show us," complained Miranda laughing. Both of the girls seemed amused.

"Be quiet. It's in Italian—"

"Oh, go on. What does he say?"

"Leave me alone. You're both jealous."

"Go one. Read it aloud."

Sarah frowned. "'*Per ricordo tenero*'," she said, "Really, the writing's awful … '*di una conversazione—*'" she paused, "Oh, I don't know …" she threw down the card, "It does look rather lovely. Look at the palm trees …"

"You're blushing," said Miranda. Idly with two fingers she picked up the postcard. "'*di una conversazione interotta*'," she read aloud. "What does it mean?"

"In memory of a pleasant conversation—something like that." Sarah began to pour out the coffee. "Two lumps, Brigitta?"

"'*Interotta*' doesn't mean pleasant," announced Miranda, squinting sideways at the card.

"Doesn't it?"

"You know it doesn't. It means 'broken' or 'interrupted' or something. What's '*tenero*'?" she asked.

"'*Tenero*'? …" repeated Sarah vaguely, "Here, darling, take your cup and pass the rolls to Brigitta …"

"'*Tenero*' …" repeated Miranda dreamily. 'I know—Maria said it last night—about the veal. She said the veal was, '*molto tenero*'—very tender."

"Oh," said Sarah. She glanced across at Brigitta's face—parted lips, wide, mystified eyes.

"The correct translation of this sentence," announced Miranda deliberately, "is—'in tender memory of an interrupted conversation.'" She looked sideways at her mother, her mouth lifted. "'From one who …'—really, Mummy." There was a moment's silence. "So it was you after all!"

Brigitta began to laugh. Delightedly, happily, she gulped her coffee.

"Careful, Brigitta," said Sarah.

"Honestly," said Miranda. She looked genuinely indignant. "And you made me dance with him."

Brigitta began to choke. Pink in the face, eyes brimming, she was coughing and laughing as well. They patted her on the back. "He asked you to dance," she gasped, when at last she could speak. "Don't you remember? He asked you to dance, first? It was her all the time," she exclaimed again to Miranda. "And neither of us ..." she chanted. She leaned back in her chair, softly clicking her fingers: back and forth she tipped, swaying as though to music. "Neither of us ... neither of us ..."

The Pool

Daphne du Maurier

1

The children ran out on to the lawn. There was space all around them, and light, and air, with the trees indeterminate beyond. The gardener had cut the grass. The lawn was crisp and firm now, because of the hot sun through the day; but near the summer-house where the tall grass stood there were dew-drops like frost clinging to the narrow stems.

The children said nothing. The first moment always took them by surprise. The fact that it waited, thought Deborah, all the time they were away; that day after day while they were at school, or in the Easter holidays with the aunts at Hunstanton being blown to bits, or in the Christmas holidays with their father in London riding on buses and going to theatres—the fact that the garden waited for them was a miracle known only to herself. A year was so long. How did the garden endure the snows clamping down upon it, or the chilly rain that fell in November? Surely sometimes it must mock the slow steps of Grandpapa pacing up and down the terrace in front of the windows, or Grandmama calling to Patch? The garden had to endure month after month of silence, while the children were gone. Even the spring and the days of May and June were wasted, all those mornings of butterflies and darting birds, with no one to watch but Patch gasping for breath on a cool stone slab. So wasted was the garden, so lost.

"You must never think we forget," said Deborah in the silent voice she used to her own possessions. "I remember, even at school, in the middle of French"—but the ache then was unbearable, that it should be the hard grain of a desk under her hands, and not the grass she bent to touch now. The children had had an argument once about whether there was more grass in the world or more sand, and Roger said that of course there must be more sand, because of under the sea; in every ocean all over the world there would be sand, if you looked deep down. But there could be grass too, argued Deborah, a waving grass, a grass that nobody had ever seen, and the colour of that ocean grass would be darker than any grass on the surface of the world, in fields or prairies or people's gardens in America. It would be taller than trees and it would move like corn in a wind.

They had run in to ask somebody adult, "What is there most of in the world, grass or sand?", both children hot and passionate from the argument. But Grandpapa stood there in his old panama hat looking for clippers to trim the hedge—he was rummaging in the drawer full of screws—and he said, "What? What?" impatiently.

The boy turned red—perhaps it was a stupid question—but the girl thought, he doesn't know, they never know, and she made a face at her brother to show that she was on his side. Later they asked their grandmother, and she, being practical, said briskly, "I should think sand. Think of all the grains," and Roger turned in triumph, "I told you so!" The grains. Deborah had not considered the grains. The magic of millions and millions of grains clinging together in the world and under the oceans made her sick. Let Roger win, it did not matter. It was better to be in the minority of the waving grass.

Now, on this first evening of summer holiday, she knelt and then lay full-length on the lawn, and stretched her hands out on either side like Jesus on the Cross, only face downwards, and murmured over and over again the words she had memorized from Confirmation preparation. "A full, perfect and sufficient sacrifice … a full, perfect and sufficient sacrifice … satisfaction, and oblation, for the sins of the whole world." To offer herself to the earth, to the garden, the garden that had waited patiently all these months since last summer, surely this must be her first gesture.

"Come on," said Roger, rousing himself from his appreciation of how Willis the gardener had mown the lawn to just the right closeness for cricket, and without waiting for his sister's answer he ran to the summer-house and made a dive at the long box in the corner where the stumps were kept. He smiled as he lifted the lid. The familiarity of the smell was satisfying. Old varnish and chipped paint, and surely that must be the same spider and the same cobweb? He drew out the stumps one by one, and the bails, and there was the ball—it had not been lost after all, as he had feared. It was worn, though, a greyish red—he smelt it and bit it, to taste the shabby leather. Then he gathered the things in his arms and went out to set up the stumps.

"Come and help me measure the pitch," he called to his sister, and looking at her, squatting in the grass with her face hidden, his heart sank, because it meant that she was in one of her absent moods and would not concentrate on the cricket.

"Deb?" he called anxiously. "You are going to play?"

Deborah heard his voice through the multitude of earth sounds, the heartbeat and the pulse. If she listened with her ear to the ground there was a humming much deeper than anything that bees did, or the sea at Hunstanton. The nearest to it was the wind, but the wind was reckless. The humming of the earth was patient. Deborah sat up, and her heart sank just as her brother's had done, for the same reason in reverse. The monotony of the game ahead would be like a great chunk torn out of privacy.

"How long shall we have to be?" she called.

The lack of enthusiasm damped the boy. It was not going to be any fun at all if she made a favour of it. He must be firm, though. Any concession on his part she snatched and turned to her advantage.

"Half-an-hour," he said, and then, for encouragement's sake, "You can bat first."

Deborah smelt her knees. They had not yet got the country smell, but if she rubbed them in the grass, and in the earth too, the white London look would go.

"All right," she said, "but no longer than half-an-hour."

He nodded quickly, and so as not to lose time measured out the pitch and then began ramming the stumps in the ground. Deborah went into the summer-house to get the bats. The familiarity of the little wooden hut pleased her as it had her brother. It was a long time now, many years, since they had played in the summer house, making yet another house inside this one with the help of broken deck-chairs; but, just as the garden waited for them a whole year, so did the summer-house, the windows on either side, cobweb-wrapped and stained, gazing out like eyes. Deborah did her ritual of bowing twice. If she should forget this, on her first entrance, it spelt ill-luck.

She picked out the two bats from the corner, where they were stacked with old croquet-hoops, and she knew at once that Roger would choose the one with the rubber handle, even though they could not bat at the same time, and for the whole of the holidays she must make do with the smaller one, that had half the whipping off. There was a croquet clip lying on the floor. She picked it up and put it on her nose and stood a moment, wondering how it would be if forever more she had to live thus, nostrils pinched, making her voice like Punch. Would people pity her?

"Hurry," shouted Roger, and she threw the clip into the corner, then quickly returned when she was halfway to the pitch, because she knew the clip was lying apart from its fellows, and she might wake in the night and remember it. The clip would turn malevolent, and haunt her. She replaced him on the floor with two others, and now she was absolved and the summer-house at peace.

"Don't get out too soon," warned Roger as she stood in the crease he had marked for her, and with a tremendous effort of concentration Deborah forced her eyes to his retreating figure and watched him roll up his sleeves and pace the required length for his run-up. Down came the ball and she lunged out, smacking it in the air in an easy catch. The impact of ball on bat stung her hands. Roger missed the catch on purpose. Neither of them said anything.

"Who shall I be?" called Deborah.

The game could only be endured, and concentration kept, if Roger gave her a part to play. Not an individual, but a country.

"You're India," he said, and Deborah felt herself grow dark and lean. Part of her was tiger, part of her was sacred cow, the long grass fringing the lawn was jungle, the roof of the summer-house a minaret.

Even so, the half-hour dragged, and, when her turn came to bowl, the ball she threw fell wider every time, so that Roger, flushed and self-conscious because their grandfather had come out on to the terrace and was watching them, called angrily, "Do try."

Once again the effort of concentration, the figure of their grandfather—a source of apprehension to the boy, for he might criticize them—acting as a spur to his sister. Grandpapa was an Indian God, and tribute must be paid to him, a golden apple. The apple must be flung to slay his enemies. Deborah muttered a prayer, and the ball she bowled came fast and true and hit Roger's off-stump. In the moment of delivery their grandfather had turned away and pottered back again through the french windows of the drawing-room.

Roger looked round swiftly. His disgrace had not been seen. "Jolly good ball," he said. "It's your turn to bat again."

But his time was up. The stable clock chimed six. Solemnly Roger drew stumps.

"What shall we do now?" he asked.

Deborah wanted to be alone, but if she said so, on this first evening of the holiday, he would be offended.

"Go to the orchard and see how the apples are coming on," she suggested, "and then round by the kitchen-garden in case the raspberries haven't all been picked. But you have to do it all without meeting anyone. If you see Willis or anyone, even the cat, you lose a mark."

It was these sudden inventions that saved her. She knew her brother would be stimulated at the thought of outwitting the gardener. The aimless wander round the orchard would turn into a stalking exercise.

"Will you come too?" he asked.

"No," she said, "you have to test your skill."

He seemed satisfied with this and ran off towards the orchard, stopping on the way to cut himself a switch from the bamboo.

As soon as he had disappeared Deborah made for the trees fringing the lawn, and once in the shrouded wood felt herself safe. She walked softly along the alley-way to the pool. The late sun sent shafts of light between the trees and on to the alley-way, and a myriad insects webbed their way in the beams, ascending and descending like angels on Jacob's ladder. But were they insects, wondered Deborah, or particles of dust, or even split fragments of light itself, beaten out and scattered by the sun?

It was very quiet. The woods were made for secrecy. They did not recognize her as the garden did. They did not care that for a whole year she could be at school, or at Hunstanton, or in London. The woods would never miss her: they had their own dark, passionate life.

Deborah came to the opening where the pool lay, with the five alley-ways branching from it, and she stood a moment before advancing to the brink, because this was holy ground and required atonement. She crossed her hands on her breast and shut her eyes. Then she kicked off her shoes. "Mother of all things wild, do with me what you will," she said aloud. The sound of her own voice gave her a slight shock. Then she went down on her knees and touched the ground three times with her forehead.

The first part of her atonement was accomplished, but the pool demanded sacrifice, and Deborah had come prepared. There was a stub of pencil she had carried in her pocket throughout the school term which she called her luck. It had teeth marks on it, and a chewed piece of rubber at one end. This treasure must be given to the pool just as other treasures had been given in the past, a miniature jug, a crested button, a china pig. Deborah felt for the stub of pencil and kissed it. She had carried and caressed it for so many lonely months, and now the moment of parting had come. The pool must not be denied. She flung out her right hand, her eyes still shut, and heard the faint plop as the stub of pencil struck the water. Then she opened her eyes, and saw in mid-pool a ripple. The pencil had gone, but the ripple moved, gently shaking the water-lilies. The movement symbolized acceptance.

Deborah, still on her knees and crossing her hands once more, edged her way to the brink of the pool and then, crouching there beside it, looked down into the water. Her reflection wavered up at her, and it was not the face she knew, not even the looking-glass face which anyway was false, but a disturbed image, dark-skinned and ghostly. The crossed hands were like the petals of the water-lilies themselves, and the colour was not waxen white but phantom green. The hair too was not the live clump she brushed every day and tied back with ribbon, but a canopy, a shroud. When the image smiled it became more distorted still. Uncrossing her hands, Deborah leant forward, took a twig, and drew a circle three times on the smooth surface. The water shook in ever widening ripples, and her reflection, broken into fragments, heaved and danced, a sort of monster, and the eyes were there no longer, nor the mouth.

Presently the water became still. Insects, long-legged flies and beetles with spread wings hummed upon it. A dragon-fly had all the magnificence of a lily leaf to himself. He hovered there, rejoicing. But when Deborah took her eyes off him for a moment he was gone. At the far end of the pool, beyond the clustering lilies, green scum had formed, and beneath the scum were rooted, tangled weeds. They were so thick, and had lain in the pool so long, that if a man walked into them from the bank he would be held and choked. A fly, though, or a beetle, could sit upon the surface, and to him the pale green scum would not be treacherous at all, but a resting-place, a haven. And if someone threw a stone, so that the ripples formed, eventually they came to the scum, and rocked it, and the whole of the mossy surface moved in rhythm, a dancing-floor for those who played upon it.

There was a dead tree standing by the far end of the pool. He could have been fir or pine, or even larch, for time had stripped him of identity. He had no distinguishing mark upon his person, but with grotesque limbs straddled the sky. A cap of ivy crowned his raked head. Last winter a dangling branch had broken loose, and this now lay in the pool half-submerged, the green scum dripping from the withered twigs. The soggy branch made a vantage-point for birds, and as Deborah watched a nestling suddenly flew from the undergrowth enveloping the dead tree, and perched for an instant on the mossy filigree. He was lost in terror. The parent bird cried warningly from some dark safety, and the nestling, pricking to the cry, took off from the branch that had offered him temporary salvation. He swerved across the pool, his flight mistimed, yet reached security. The chitter from the undergrowth told of his scolding. When he had gone silence returned to the pool.

It was, so Deborah thought, the time for prayer. The water-lilies were folding upon themselves. The ripples ceased. And that dark hollow in the centre of the pool, that black stillness where the water was deepest, was surely a funnel to the kingdom that lay below. Down that funnel had travelled the discarded treasures. The stub of pencil had lately plunged the depths. He had now been received as an equal among his fellows. This was the single law of the pool, for there were no other commandments. Once it was over, that first cold headlong flight, Deborah knew that the softness of the welcoming water took away all fear. It lapped the face and cleansed the eyes, and the plunge was not into darkness at all but into light. It did not become blacker as the pool was penetrated, but paler, more golden-green, and the mud that people told themselves was there was only a defence against strangers. Those who belonged, who knew, went to the source at once, and there were caverns and fountains and rainbow-coloured seas. There were shores of the whitest sand. There was soundless music.

Once again Deborah closed her eyes and bent lower to the pool. Her lips nearly touched the water. This was the great silence, when she had no thoughts, and was accepted by the pool. Waves of quiet ringed themselves about her, and slowly she lost all feeling, and had no knowledge of her legs, or of her kneeling body, or of her cold, clasped hands. There was nothing but the intensity of peace. It was a deeper acceptance than listening to the earth, because the earth was of the world, the earth was a throbbing pulse, but the acceptance of the pool meant another kind of hearing, a closing in of the waters, and just as the lilies folded so did the soul submerge.

"Deborah …? Deborah …?" Oh, no! Not now, don't let them call me back now! It was as though someone had hit her on the back, or jumped out at her from behind a corner, the sharp and sudden clamour of another life destroying the silence, the secrecy. And then came the tinkle of the cowbells. It was the signal from their grandmother that the time had come to go in. Not imperious and ugly with authority, like the clanging bell at school summoning those at play to lessons or chapel, but a reminder, nevertheless, that Time was all-important, that life was ruled to order, that even here, in the holiday home the children loved, the adult reigned supreme.

"All right, all right," muttered Deborah, standing up and thrusting her numbed feet into her shoes. This time the rather raised tone of "Deborah?", and the more hurried clanging of the cowbells, brought long ago from Switzerland, suggested a more imperious Grandmama than the tolerant one who seldom questioned. It must mean their supper was already laid, soup perhaps getting cold, and the farce of washing hands, of tidying, of combing hair, must first be gone through.

"Come on, Deb," and now the shout was close, was right at hand, privacy lost forever, for her brother came running down the alley-way swishing his bamboo stick in the air.

"What *have* you been doing?" The question was an intrusion and a threat. She would never have asked him what he had been doing, had he wandered away wanting to be alone, but Roger, alas, did not claim privacy. He liked companionship, and his question now, asked half in irritation, half in resentment, came really from the fear that he might lose her.

"Nothing," said Deborah.

Roger eyed her suspiciously. She was in that morning mood. And it meant, when they went to bed, that she would not talk. One of the best things, in the holidays, was having the two adjoining rooms and calling through to Deb, making her talk.

"Come on," he said, "they've rung," and the making of their grandmother into "they", turning a loved individual into something impersonal, showed Deborah that even if he did not understand he was on her side. He had been called from play, just as she had.

They ran from the woods to the lawn, and on to the terrace. Their grandmother had gone inside, but the cowbells hanging by the french window were still jangling.

The custom was for the children to have their supper first, at seven, and it was laid for them in the dining-room on a hot-plate. They served themselves. At a quarter-to-eight their grandparents had dinner. It was called dinner, but this was a concession to their status. They ate the same as the children, though Grandpapa had a savoury which was not served to the children. If the children were late for supper then it put out Time, as well as Agnes, who cooked for both generations, and it might mean five minutes' delay before Grandpapa had his soup. This shook routine.

The children ran up to the bathroom to wash, then downstairs to the dining-room. Their grandfather was standing in the hall. Deborah sometimes thought that he would have enjoyed sitting with them while they ate their supper, but he never suggested it. Grandmama had warned them, too, never to be a nuisance, or indeed to shout, if Grandpapa was near. This was not because he was nervous, but because he liked to shout himself.

"There's going to be a heat-wave," he said. He had been listening to the news.

"That will mean lunch outside tomorrow," said Roger swiftly. Lunch was the meal they took in common with the grandparents, and it was the moment of the day he disliked. He was nervous that his grandfather would ask him how he was getting on at school.

"Not for me, thank you," said Grandpapa. "Too many wasps."

Roger was at once relieved. This meant that he and Deborah would have the little round garden-table to themselves. But Deborah felt sorry for her grandfather as he went back into the drawing-room. Lunch on the terrace could be gay, and would liven him up. When people grew old they had so few treats.

"What do you look forward to most in the day?" she once asked her grandmother.

"Going to bed," was the reply, "and filling my two hot water bottles." Why work through being young, thought Deborah, to this?

Back in the dining-room the children discussed what they should do during the heat-wave. It would be too hot, Deborah said, for cricket. But they might make a house, suggested Roger, in the trees by the paddock. If he got a few old boards from Willis, and nailed them together like a platform, and borrowed the orchard ladder, then they could take fruit and bottles of orange squash and keep them up there, and it would be a camp from which they could spy on Willis afterwards.

Deborah's first instinct was to say she did not want to play, but she checked herself in time. Finding the boards and fixing them would take Roger a whole morning. It would keep him employed. "Yes, it's a good idea," she said, and to foster his spirit of adventure she looked at his notebook, as they were drinking their soup, and approved of items necessary for the camp while he jotted them down. It was all part of the day-long deceit she practised to express understanding of his way of life.

When they had finished supper they took their trays to the kitchen and watched Agnes, for a moment, as she prepared the second meal for the grandparents. The soup was the same, but garnished. Little croutons of toasted bread were added to it. And the butter was made into pats, not cut in a slab. The savoury tonight was to be cheese straws. The children finished the ones that Agnes had burnt. Then they went through to the drawing-room to say good night. The older people had both changed. Grandpapa was in a smoking-jacket, and wore soft slippers. Grandmama had a dress that she had worn several years ago in London. She had a cardigan round her shoulders like a cape.

"Go carefully with the bath-water," she said. "We'll be short if there's no rain."

They kissed her smooth, soft skin. It smelt of rose leaves. Grandpapa's chin was sharp and bony. He did not kiss Roger.

"Be quiet overhead," whispered their grandmother. The children nodded. The dining-room was underneath their rooms, and any jumping about or laughter would make a disturbance.

Deborah felt a wave of affection for the two old people. Their lives must be empty and sad. "We *are* glad to be here," she said. Grandmama smiled. This was how she lived, thought Deborah, on little crumbs of comfort.

Once out of the room their spirits soared, and to show relief Roger chased Deborah upstairs, both laughing for no reason. Undressing, they forgot the instructions about the bath, and when they went into the bathroom—Deborah was to have first go—the water was gurgling into the overflow. They tore out the plug in a panic, and listened to the waste roaring down the pipe to the drain below. If Agnes did not have the wireless on she would hear it.

The children were too old now for boats or play, but the bathroom was a place for confidences, for a sharing of those few tastes they agreed upon, or, after quarrelling, for moody silence. The one who broke silence first would then lose face.

"Willis has a new bicycle," said Roger. "I saw it propped against the shed. I couldn't try it because he was there. But I shall tomorrow. It's a Raleigh."

He liked all practical things, and the trying of the gardener's bicycle would give an added interest to the morning of next day. Willis had a bag of tools in a leather pouch behind the saddle. These could all be felt and the spanners, smelling of oil, tested for shape and usefulness.

"If Willis died," said Deborah, "I wonder what age he would be."

It was the kind of remark that Roger resented always. What had death to do with bicycles? "He's sixty-five," he said, "so he'd be sixty-five."

"No," said Deborah, "what age when he got *there.*"

Roger did not want to discuss it. "I bet I can ride it round the stables if I lower the seat," he said. "I bet I don't fall off."

But if Roger would not rise to death, Deborah would not rise to the wager. "Who cares?" she said.

The sudden streak of cruelty stung the brother. Who cared indeed. ... The horror of an empty world encompassed him, and to give himself confidence he seized the wet sponge and flung it out of the window. They heard it splosh on the terrace below.

"Grandpapa will step on it, and slip," said Deborah, aghast.

The image seized them, and choking back laughter they covered their faces. Hysteria doubled them up. Roger rolled over and over on the bathroom floor. Deborah, the first to recover, wondered why laughter was so near to pain, why Roger's face, twisted now in merriment, was yet the same crumpled thing when his heart was breaking.

"Hurry up," she said briefly, "let's dry the floor," and as they wiped the linoleum with their towels the action sobered them both.

Back in their bedrooms, the door open between them, they watched the light slowly fading. But the air was warm like day. Their grandfather and the people who said what the weather was going to be were right. The heat-wave was on its way. Deborah, leaning out of the open window, fancied she could see it in the sky, a dull haze where the sun had been before; and the trees beyond the lawn, day-coloured when they were having their supper in the dining-room, had turned into night-birds with outstretched wings. The garden knew about the promised heat-wave, and rejoiced: the lack of rain was of no consequence yet, for the warm air was a trap, lulling it into a drowsy contentment.

The dull murmur of their grandparents' voices came from the dining-room below. What did they discuss, wondered Deborah. Did they make those sounds to reassure the children, or were their voices part of their unreal world? Presently the voices ceased, and then there was a scraping of chairs, and voices from a different quarter, the drawing-room now, and a faint smell of their grandfather's cigarette.

Deborah called softly to her brother but he did not answer. She went through to his room, and he was asleep. He must have fallen asleep suddenly, in the midst of talking. She was relieved. Now she could be alone again, and not have to keep up the pretence of sharing conversation. Dusk was everywhere, the sky a deepening black. "When they've gone up to bed," thought Deborah, "then I'll be truly alone." She knew what she was going to do. She waited there, by the open window, and the deepening sky lost the veil that covered it, the haze disintegrated, and the stars broke through. Where there had been nothing was life, dusty and bright, and the waiting earth gave off a scent of knowledge. Dew rose from the pores. The lawn was white.

Patch, the old dog, who slept at the end of Grandpapa's bed on a plaid rug, came out on to the terrace and barked hoarsely. Deborah leant out and threw a piece of creeper on to him. He shook his back. Then he waddled slowly to the flower-tub above the steps and cocked his leg. It was his nightly routine. He barked once more, staring blindly at the hostile trees, and went back into the drawing-room. Soon afterwards, someone came to close the windows—Grandmama, thought Deborah, for the touch was light. "They are shutting out the best," said the child to herself, "all the meaning, and all the point." Patch, being an animal, should know better. He ought to be in a kennel where he could watch, but instead, grown fat and soft, he preferred the bumpiness of her grandfather's bed. He had forgotten the secrets. So had they, the old people.

Deborah heard her grandparents come upstairs. First her grandmother, the quicker of the two, and then her grandfather, more laboured, saying a word or two to Patch as the little dog wheezed his way up. There was a general clicking of lights and shutting of doors. Then silence. How remote, the world of the grandparents, undressing with curtains closed. A pattern of life unchanged for so many years. What went on without would never be known. "He that has ears to hear, let him hear," said Deborah, and she thought of the callousness of Jesus which no priest could explain. Let the dead bury their dead. All the people in the world, undressing now, or sleeping, not just in the village but in cities and capitals, they were shutting out the truth, they were burying their dead. They wasted silence.

The stable clock struck eleven. Deborah pulled on her clothes. Not the cotton frock of the day, but her old jeans that Grandmama disliked, rolled up above her knees. And a jersey. Sandshoes with a hole that did not matter. She was cunning enough to go down by the back stairs. Patch would bark if she tried the front stairs, close to the grandparents' rooms. The backstairs led past Agnes' room, which smelt of apples though she never ate fruit. Deborah could hear her snoring. She would not even wake on Judgement Day. And this led her to wonder on the truth of that fable too, for there might be so many millions by then who liked their graves—Grandpapa, for instance, fond of his routine, and irritated at the sudden riot of trumpets.

Deborah crept past the pantry and the servants' hall—it was only a tiny sitting-room for Agnes, but long usage had given it the dignity of the name—and unlatched and unbolted the heavy back door. Then she stepped outside, on to the gravel, and took the long way round by the front of the house so as not to tread on the terrace, fronting the lawns and the garden.

The warm night claimed her. In a moment it was part of her. She walked on the grass, and her shoes were instantly soaked. She flung up her arms to the sky. Power ran to her fingertips. Excitement was communicated from the waiting trees, and the orchard, and the paddock; the intensity of their secret life caught at her and made her run. It was nothing like the excitement of ordinary looking forward, of birthday presents, of Christmas stockings, but the pull of a magnet—her grandfather had shown her once how it worked, little needles springing to the jaws—and now night and the sky above were a vast magnet, and the things that waited below were needles, caught up in the great demand.

Deborah went to the summer-house, and it was not sleeping like the house fronting the terrace but open to understanding, sharing complicity. Even the dusty windows caught the light, and the cobwebs shone. She rummaged for the old lilo and the moth-eaten car rug that Grandmama had thrown out two summers ago, and bearing them over her shoulder she made her way to the pool. The alley-way was ghostly, and Deborah knew, for all her mounting tension, that the test was hard. Part of her was still body-bound, and afraid of shadows. If anything stirred she would jump and know true terror. She must show defiance, though. The woods expected it. Like old wise lamas they expected courage.

She sensed approval as she ran the gauntlet, the tall trees watching. Any sign of turning back, of panic, and they would crowd upon her in a choking mass, smothering protest. Branches would become arms, gnarled and knotty, ready to strangle, and the leaves of the higher trees fold in and close like the sudden furling of giant umbrellas. The smaller undergrowth, obedient to the will, would become a briary of a million thorns where animals of no known world crouched snarling, their eyes on fire. To show fear was to show misunderstanding. The woods were merciless.

Deborah walked the alley-way to the pool, her left hand holding the lilo and the rug on her shoulder, her right hand raised in salutation. This was a gesture of respect. Then she paused before the pool and laid down her burden beside it. The lilo was to be her bed, the rug her cover. She took off her shoes, also in respect, and lay down upon the lilo. Then, drawing the rug to her chin, she lay flat, her eyes upon the sky. The gauntlet of the alley-way over, she had no more fear. The woods had accepted her, and the pool was the final resting-place, the doorway, the key.

"I shan't sleep," thought Deborah. "I shall just lie awake here all the night and wait for morning, but it will be a kind of introduction to life, like being confirmed."

The stars were thicker now than they had been before. No space in the sky without a prick of light, each star a sun. Some, she thought, were newly born, white-hot, and others wise and colder, nearing completion. The law encompassed them, fixing the riotous path, but how they fell and tumbled depended upon themselves. Such peace, such stillness, such sudden quietude, excitement gone. The trees were no longer menacing but guardians, and the pool was primeval water, the first, the last.

Then Deborah stood at the wicket-gate, the boundary, and there was a woman with outstretched hand, demanding tickets. "Pass through," she said when Deborah reached her. "We saw you coming." The wicket-gate became a turnstile. Deborah pushed against it and there was no resistance, she was through.

"What is it?" she asked. "Am I really here at last? Is this the bottom of the pool?"

"It could be," smiled the woman. "There are so many ways. You just happened to choose this one."

Other people were pressing to come through. They had no faces, they were only shadows. Deborah stood aside to let them by, and in a moment they had gone, all phantoms.

"Why only now, tonight?" asked Deborah. "Why not in the afternoon, when I came to the pool?"

"It's a trick," said the woman. "You seize on the moment in time. We were here this afternoon. We're always here. Our life goes on around you, but nobody knows it. The trick's easier by night, that's all."

"Am I dreaming, then?" asked Deborah.

"No," said the woman, "this isn't a dream. And it isn't death, either. It's the secret world."

The secret world. … It was something Deborah had always known, and now the pattern was complete. The memory of it, and the relief, were so tremendous that something seemed to burst inside her heart.

"Of course …" she said, "of course …" and everything that had ever been fell into place. There was no disharmony. The joy was indescribable, and the surge of feeling, like wings about her in the air, lifted her away from the turnstile and the woman, and she had all knowledge. That was it—the invasion of knowledge.

"I'm not myself, then, after all," she thought. "I knew I wasn't. It was only the task given," and, looking down, she saw a little child who was blind trying to find her way. Pity seized her. She bent down and put her hands on the child's eyes, and they opened, and the child was herself at two years old. The incident came back. It was when her mother died and Roger was born.

"It doesn't matter after all," she told the child. "You are not lost. You don't have to go on crying." Then the child that had been herself melted, and became absorbed in the water and the sky, and the joy of the invading flood intensified so that there was no body at all but only being. No words, only movements. And the beating of wings. This above all, the beating of wings.

"Don't let me go!" It was a pulse in her ear, and a cry, and she saw the woman at the turnstile put up her hands to hold her. Then there was such darkness, such dragging, terrible darkness, and the beginning of pain all over again, the leaden heart, the tears, the misunderstanding. The voice saying "No!" was her own harsh, worldly voice, and she was staring at the restless trees, black and ominous against the sky. One hand trailed in the water of the pool.

Deborah sat up, sobbing. The hand that had been in the pool was wet and cold. She dried it on the rug. And suddenly she was seized with such fear that her body took possession, and throwing aside the rug she began to run along the alley-way, the dark trees mocking and the welcome of the woman at the turnstile turned to treachery. Safety lay in the house behind the closed curtains, security was with the grandparents sleeping in their beds, and like a leaf driven before a whirlwind Deborah was out of the woods and across the silver soaking lawn, up the steps beyond the terrace and through the garden-gate to the back door.

The slumbering solid house received her. It was like an old staid person who, surviving many trials, had learnt experience. "Don't take any notice of them," it seemed to say, jerking its head—did a house have a head?—towards the woods beyond. "They've made no contribution to civilization. I'm man-made and different. This is where you belong, dear child. Now settle down."

Deborah went back again upstairs and into her bedroom. Nothing had changed. It was still the same. Going to the open window she saw that the woods and the lawn seemed unaltered from the moment, how long back she did not know, when she had stood there, deciding upon the visit to the pool. The only difference now was in herself. The excitement had gone, the tension too. Even the terror of those last moments, when her flying feet had brought her to the house, seemed unreal.

She drew the curtains, just as her grandmother might have done, and climbed into bed. Her mind was now preoccupied with practical difficulties, like explaining the presence of the lilo and the rug beside the pool. Willis might find them, and tell her grandfather. The feel of her own pillow, and of her own blankets, reassured her. Both were familiar. And being tired was familiar too, it was a solid bodily ache, like the tiredness after too much jumping or cricket. The thing was, though—and the last remaining conscious thread of thought decided to postpone conclusion until the morning—which was real? This safety of the house, or the secret world?

2

When Deborah woke next morning she knew at once that her mood was bad. It would last her for the day. Her eyes ached, and her neck was stiff, and there was a taste in her mouth like magnesia. Immediately Roger came running into her room, his face refreshed and smiling from some dreamless sleep, and jumped on her bed.

"It's come," he said, "the heat-wave's come. It's going to be ninety in the shade."

Deborah considered how best she could damp his day. "It can go to a hundred for all I care," she said. "I'm going to read all morning."

His face fell. A look of bewilderment came into his eyes. "But the house?" he said. "We'd decided to have a house in the trees, don't you remember? I was going to get some planks from Willis."

Deborah turned over in bed and humped her knees. "You can, if you like," she said. "I think it's a silly game."

She shut her eyes, feigning sleep, and presently she heard his feet patter slowly back to his own room, and then the thud of a ball against the wall. If he goes on doing that, she thought maliciously, Grandpapa will ring his bell, and Agnes will come panting up the stairs. She hoped for destruction, for grumbling and snapping, and everyone falling out, not speaking. That was the way of the world.

The kitchen, where the children breakfasted, faced west, so it did not get the morning sun. Agnes had hung up fly-papers to catch wasps. The cereal, puffed wheat, was soggy. Deborah complained, mashing the mess with her spoon.

"It's a new packet," said Agnes. "You're mighty particular all of a sudden."

"Deb's got out of bed the wrong side," said Roger.

The two remarks fused to make a challenge. Deborah seized the nearest weapon, a knife, and threw it at her brother. It narrowly missed his eye, but cut his cheek. Surprised, he put his hand to his face and felt the blood. Hurt, not by the knife but by his sister's action, his face turned red and his lower lip quivered. Deborah ran out of the kitchen and slammed the door. Her own violence distressed her, but the power of the mood was too strong. Going on to the terrace, she saw that the worst had happened. Willis had found the lilo and the rug, and had put them to dry in the sun. He was talking to her grandmother. Deborah tried to slip back into the house, but it was too late.

"Deborah, how very thoughtless of you," said Grandmama. "I tell you children every summer that I don't mind your taking the things from the hut into the garden if only you'll put them back."

Deborah knew she should apologize, but the mood forbade it. "That old rug is full of moth," she said contemptuously, "and the lilo has a rainproof back. It doesn't hurt them."

They both stared at her, and her grandmother flushed, just as Roger had done when she had thrown the knife at him. Then her grandmother turned her back and continued giving some instructions to the gardener.

Deborah stalked along the terrace, pretending that nothing had happened, and skirting the lawn she made her way towards the orchard and so to the fields beyond. She picked up a windfall, but as soon as her teeth bit into it the taste was green. She threw it away. She went and sat on a gate and stared in front of her, looking at nothing. Such deception everywhere. Such sour sadness. It was like Adam and Eve being locked out of paradise. The Garden of Eden was no more. Somewhere, very close, the woman at the turnstile waited to let her in, the secret world was all about her, but the key was gone. Why had she ever come back? What had brought her?

People were going about their business. The old man who came three days a week to help Willis was sharpening his scythe behind the toolshed. Beyond the field where the lane ran towards the main road she could see the top of the postman's head. He was pedalling his bicycle towards the village. She heard Roger calling, "Deb? Deb …?", which meant that he had forgiven her, but still the mood held sway and she did not answer. Her own dullness made her own punishment. Presently a knocking sound told her that he had got the planks from Willis and had embarked on the building of his house. He was like his grandfather; he kept to the routine set for himself.

Deborah was consumed with pity. Not for the sullen self humped upon the gate, but for all of them going about their business in the world who did not hold the key. The key was hers, and she had lost it. Perhaps if she worked her way through the long day the magic would return with evening and she would find it once again. Or even now, by the pool, there might be a clue, a vision.

Deborah slid off the gate and went the long way round. By skirting the fields, parched under the sun, she could reach the other side of the wood and meet no one. The husky wheat was stiff. She had to keep close to the hedge to avoid brushing it, and the hedge was tangled. Foxgloves had grown too tall and were bending with empty sockets, their flowers gone. There were nettles everywhere. There was no gate into the wood, and she had to climb the pricking hedge with the barbed wire tearing her knickers. Once in the wood some measure of peace returned, but the alley-ways this side had not been scythed, and the grass was long. She had to wade through it like a sea, brushing it aside with her hands.

She came upon the pool from behind the monster tree, the hybrid whose naked arms were like a dead man's stumps, projecting at all angles. This side, on the lip of the pool, the scum was carpet-thick, and all the lilies, coaxed by the risen sun, had opened wide. They basked as lizards bask on hot stone walls. But here, with stems in water, they swung in grace, cluster upon cluster, pink and waxen white. "They're asleep," thought Deborah. "So is the wood. The morning is not their time," and it seemed to her beyond possibility that the turnstile was at hand and the woman waiting, smiling. "She said they were always there, even in the day, but the truth is that being a child I'm blinded in the day. I don't know how to see."

She dipped her hands in the pool, and the water was tepid brown. She tasted her fingers, and the taste was rank. Brackish water, stagnant from long stillness. Yet beneath … beneath, she knew, by night the woman waited, and not only the woman but the whole secret world. Deborah began to pray. "Let it happen again," she whispered. "Let it happen again. Tonight. I won't be afraid."

The sluggish pool made no acknowledgement, but the very silence seemed a testimony of faith, of acceptance. Beside the pool, where the imprint of the lilo had marked the moss, Deborah found a kirby-grip, fallen from her hair during the night. It was proof of visitation. She threw it into the pool as part of the treasury. Then she walked back into the ordinary day and the heat-wave, and her black mood was softened. She went to find Roger in the orchard. He was busy with the platform. Three of the boards were fixed, and the noisy hammering was something that had to be borne. He saw her coming, and as always, after trouble, sensed that her mood had changed and mention must never be made of it. Had he called, "Feeling better?", it would have revived the antagonism, and she might not play with him all the day. Instead, he took no notice. She must be the first to speak.

Deborah waited at the foot of the tree, then bent, and handed him up an apple. It was green, but the offering meant peace. He ate it manfully. "Thanks," he said. She climbed into the tree beside him and reached for the box of nails. Contact had been renewed. All was well between them.

3

The hot day spun itself out like a web. The heat haze stretched across the sky, dun-coloured and opaque. Crouching on the burning boards of the apple-tree, the children drank ginger-beer and fanned themselves with dock-leaves. They grew hotter still. When the cowbells summoned them for lunch they found that their grandmother had drawn the curtains of all the rooms downstairs, and the drawing-room was a vault and strangely cool. They flung themselves into chairs. No one was hungry. Patch lay under the piano, his soft mouth dripping saliva. Grandmama had changed into a sleeveless linen dress never before seen, and Grandpapa, in a dented panama, carried a fly-whisk used years ago in Egypt.

"Ninety-one," he said grimly, "on the Air Ministry roof. It was on the one o'clock news."

Deborah thought of the men who must measure heat, toiling up and down on this Ministry roof with rods and tapes and odd-shaped instruments. Did anyone care but Grandpapa?

"Can we take our lunch outside?" asked Roger.

His grandmother nodded. Speech was too much effort, and she sank languidly into her chair at the foot of the dining-room table. The roses she had picked last night had wilted.

The children carried chicken drumsticks to the summer-house. It was too hot to sit inside, but they sprawled in the shadow it cast, their heads on faded cushions shedding kapok. Somewhere, far above their heads, an aeroplane climbed like a small silver fish, and was lost in space.

"A Meteor," said Roger. "Grandpapa says they're obsolete."

Deborah thought of Icarus, soaring towards the sun. Did he know when his wings began to melt? How did he feel? She stretched out her arms and thought of them as wings. The fingertips would be the first to curl, and then turn cloggy soft, and useless. What terror in the sudden loss of height, the drooping power …

Roger, watching her, hoped it was some game. He threw his picked drumstick into a flower-bed and jumped to his feet.

"Look," he said, "I'm a Javelin," and he too stretched his arms and ran in circles, banking. Jet noises came from his clenched teeth. Deborah dropped her arms and looked at the drumstick. What had been clean and white from Roger's teeth was now earth-brown. Was it offended to be chucked away? Years later, when everyone was dead, it would be found, moulded like a fossil. Nobody would care.

"Come on," said Roger.

"Where to?" she asked.

"To fetch the raspberries," he said.

"You go," she told him.

Roger did not like going into the dining-room alone. He was self-conscious. Deborah made a shield from the adult eyes. In the end he consented to fetch the raspberries without her on condition that she played cricket after tea. After tea was a long way off.

She watched him return, walking very slowly, bearing the plates of raspberries and clotted cream. She was seized with sudden pity, that same pity which, earlier, she had felt for all people other than herself. How absorbed he was, how intent on the moment that held him. But tomorrow he would be some old man far away, the garden forgotten, and this day long past.

"Grandmama says it can't go on," he announced. "There'll have to be a storm."

But why? Why not forever? Why not breathe a spell so that all of them could stay locked and dreaming like the courtiers in the *Sleeping Beauty*, never knowing, never waking, cobwebs in their hair and on their hands, tendrils imprisoning the house itself?

"Race me," said Roger, and to please him she plunged her spoon into the mush of raspberries but finished last, to his delight.

No one moved during the long afternoon. Grandmama went upstairs to her room. The children saw her at her window in her petticoat drawing the curtains close. Grandpapa put his feet up in the drawing-room, a handkerchief over his face. Patch did not stir from his place under the piano. Roger, undefeated, found employment still. He first helped Agnes to shell peas for supper, squatting on the back-door step while she relaxed on a lop-sided basket chair dragged from the servants' hall. This task finished, he discovered a tin-bath, put away in the cellar, in which Patch had been washed in younger days. He carried it to the lawn and filled it with water. Then he stripped to bathing-trunks and sat in it solemnly, an umbrella over his head to keep off the sun.

Deborah lay on her back behind the summer-house, wondering what would happen if Jesus and Buddha met. Would there be discussion, courtesy, an exchange of views like politicians at summit talks? Or were they after all the same person, born at separate times? The queer thing was that this topic, interesting now, meant nothing in the secret world. Last night, through the turnstile, all problems disappeared. They were non-existent. There was only the knowledge and the joy.

She must have slept, because when she opened her eyes she saw to her dismay that Roger was no longer in the bath but was hammering the cricket-stumps into the lawn. It was a quarter-to-five.

"Hurry up," he called, when he saw her move. "I've had tea."

She got up and dragged herself into the house, sleepy still, and giddy. The grandparents were in the drawing-room, refreshed from the long repose of the afternoon. Grandpapa smelt of eau-de-cologne. Even Patch had come to and was lapping his saucer of cold tea.

"You look tired," said Grandmama critically. "Are you feeling all right?"

Deborah was not sure. Her head was heavy. It must have been sleeping in the afternoon, a thing she never did.

"I think so," she answered, "but if anyone gave me roast pork I know I'd be sick."

"No one suggested you should eat roast pork," said her grandmother, surprised. "Have a cucumber sandwich, they're cool enough."

Grandpapa was lying in wait for a wasp. He watched it hover over his tea, grim, expectant. Suddenly he slammed at the air with his whisk. "Got the brute," he said in triumph. He ground it into the carpet with his heel. It made Deborah think of Jehovah.

"Don't rush around in the heat," said Grandmama. "It isn't wise. Can't you and Roger play some nice, quiet game?"

"What sort of game?" asked Deborah.

But her grandmother was without invention. The croquet mallets were all broken. "We might pretend to be dwarfs and use the heads," said Deborah, and she toyed for a moment with the idea of squatting to croquet. Their knees would stiffen, though, it would be too difficult.

"I'll read aloud to you, if you like," said Grandmama.

Deborah seized upon the suggestion. It delayed cricket. She ran out on to the lawn and padded the idea to make it acceptable to Roger.

"I'll play afterwards," she said, "and that ice-cream that Agnes has in the fridge, you can eat all of it. I'll talk tonight in bed."

Roger hesitated. Everything must be weighed. Three goods to balance evil.

"You know that stick of sealing-wax Daddy gave you?" he said.

"Yes."

"Can I have it?"

The balance for Deborah too. The quiet of the moment in opposition to the loss of the long thick stick so brightly red.

"All right," she grudged.

Roger left the cricket stumps and they went into the drawing-room. Grandpapa, at the first suggestion of reading aloud, had disappeared, taking Patch with him. Grandmama had cleared away the tea. She found her spectacles and the book. It was *Black Beauty*. Grandmama kept no modern children's books, and this made common ground for the three of them. She read the terrible chapter where the stable-lad lets Beauty get overheated and gives him a cold drink and does not put on his blanket. The story was suited to the day. Even Roger listened entranced. And Deborah, watching her grandmother's calm face and hearing her careful voice reading the sentences, thought how strange it was that Grandmama could turn herself into Beauty with such ease. She *was* a horse, suffering there with pneumonia in the stable, being saved by the wise coachman.

After the reading, cricket was anti-climax, but Deborah must keep her bargain. She kept thinking of Black Beauty writing the book. It showed how good the story was, Grandmama said, because no child had ever yet questioned the practical side of it, or posed the picture of a horse with a pen in its hoof.

"A modern horse would have a typewriter," thought Deborah, and she began to bowl to Roger, smiling to herself as she did so because of the twentieth-century Beauty clacking with both hoofs at a machine.

This evening, because of the heat-wave, the routine was changed. They had their baths first, before their supper, for they were hot and exhausted from the cricket. Then, putting on pyjamas and cardigans, they ate their supper on the terrace. For once Grandmama was indulgent. It was still so hot that they could not take chill, and the dew had not yet risen. It made a small excitement, being in pyjamas on the terrace. Like people abroad, said Roger. Or natives in the South Seas, said Deborah. Or beachcombers who had lost caste. Grandpapa, changed into a white tropical jacket, had not lost caste.

"He's a white trader," whispered Deborah. "He's made a fortune out of pearls."

Roger choked. Any joke about his grandfather, whom he feared, had all the sweet agony of danger.

"What's the thermometer say?" asked Deborah.

Her grandfather, pleased at her interest, went to inspect it.

"Still above eighty," he said with relish.

Deborah, when she cleaned her teeth later, thought how pale her face looked in the mirror above the wash-basin. It was not brown, like Roger's, from the day in the sun, but wan and yellow. She tied back her hair with a ribbon, and the nose and chin were peaky sharp. She yawned largely, as Agnes did in the kitchen on Sunday afternoons.

"Don't forget you promised to talk," said Roger quickly.

Talk. ... That was the burden. She was so tired she longed for the white smoothness of her pillow, all blankets thrown aside, bearing only a single sheet. But Roger, wakeful on his bed, the door between them wide, would not relent. Laughter was the one solution, and to make him hysterical, and so exhaust him sooner, she fabricated a day in the life of Willis, from his first morning kipper to his final glass of beer at the village inn. The adventures in between would have tried Gulliver. Roger's delight drew protests from the adult world below. There was the sound of a bell, and then Agnes came up the stairs and put her head round the corner of Deborah's door.

"Your Granny says you're not to make so much noise," she said.

Deborah, spent with invention, lay back and closed her eyes. She could go no further. The children called good night to each other, both speaking at the same time, from age-long custom, beginning with their names and addresses and ending with the world, the universe, and space. Then the final main "Good night", after which neither must ever speak, on pain of unknown calamity.

"I must try and keep awake," thought Deborah, but the power was not in her. Sleep was too compelling, and it was hours later that she opened her eyes and saw her curtains blowing and the forked flash light the ceiling, and heard the trees tossing and sobbing against the sky. She was out of bed in an instant. Chaos had come. There were no stars, and the night was sulphurous. A great crack split the heavens and tore them in two. The garden groaned. If the rain would only fall there might be mercy, and the trees, imploring, bowed themselves this way and that, while the vivid lawn, bright in expectation, lay like a sheet of metal exposed to flame. Let the waters break. Bring down the rain.

Suddenly the lightning forked again, and standing there, alive yet immobile, was the woman by the turnstile. She stared up at the windows of the house, and Deborah recognized her. The turnstile was there, inviting entry, and already the phantom figures, passing through it, crowded towards the trees beyond the lawn. The secret world was waiting. Through the long day, while the storm was brewing, it had hovered there unseen beyond her reach, but now that night had come, and the thunder with it, the barriers were down. Another crack, mighty in its summons, the turnstile yawned, and the woman with her hand upon it smiled and beckoned.

Deborah ran out of the room and down the stairs. Somewhere somebody called—Roger, perhaps, it did not matter -and Patch was barking; but caring nothing for concealment she went through the dark drawing-room and opened the french window on to the terrace. The lightning searched the terrace and lit the paving, and Deborah ran down the steps on to the lawn where the turnstile gleamed.

Haste was imperative. If she did not run the turnstile might be closed, the woman vanish, and all the wonder of the sacred world be taken from her. She was in time. The woman was still waiting. She held out her hand for tickets, but Deborah shook her head. "I have none." The woman, laughing, brushed her through into the secret world where there were no laws, no rules, and all the faceless phantoms ran before her to the woods, blown by the rising wind. Then the rain came. The sky, deep brown as the lightning pierced it, opened, and the water hissed to the ground, rebounding from the earth in bubbles. There was no order now in the alley-way. The ferns had turned to trees, the trees to Titans. All moved in ecstasy, with sweeping limbs, but the rhythm was broken up, tumultuous, so that some of them were bent backwards, torn by the sky, and others dashed their heads to the undergrowth where they were caught and beaten.

In the world behind, laughed Deborah as she ran, this would be punishment, but here in the secret world it was a tribute. The phantoms who ran beside her were like waves. They were linked one with another, and they were, each one of them, and Deborah too, part of the night force that made the sobbing and the laughter. The lightning forked where they willed it, and the thunder cracked as they looked upwards to the sky.

The pool had come alive. The water-lilies had turned to hands, with palms upraised, and in the far corner, usually so still under the green scum, bubbles sucked at the surface, steaming and multiplying as the torrents fell. Everyone crowded to the pool. The phantoms bowed and crouched by the water's edge, and now the woman had set up her turnstile in the middle of the pool, beckoning them once more. Some remnant of a sense of social order rose in Deborah and protested.

"But we've already paid," she shouted, and remembered a second later that she had passed through free. Must there be duplication?

Was the secret world a rainbow, always repeating itself, alighting on another hill when you believed yourself beneath it? No time to think. The phantoms had gone through. The lightning, streaky white, lit the old dead monster tree with his crown of ivy, and because he had no spring now in his joints he could not sway in tribute with the trees and ferns, but had to remain there, rigid, like a crucifix.

"And now … and now … and now …" called Deborah.

The triumph was that she was not afraid, was filled with such wild acceptance. … She ran into the pool. Her living feet felt the mud and the broken sticks and all the tangle of old weeds, and the water was up to her armpits and her chin. The lilies held her. The rain blinded her. The woman and the turnstile were no more.

"Take me too," cried the child. "Don't leave me behind!" In her heart was a savage disenchantment. They had broken their promise, they had left her in the world. The pool that claimed her now was not the pool of secrecy, but dank, dark, brackish water choked with scum.

4

"Grandpapa says he's going to have it fenced round," said Roger. "It should have been done years ago. A proper fence, then nothing can ever happen. But barrow-loads of shingle tipped in it first. Then it won't be a pool, but just a dewpond. Dewponds aren't dangerous."

He was looking at her over the edge of her bed. He had risen in status, being the only one of them downstairs, the bearer of tidings good or ill, the go-between. Deborah had been ordered two days in bed.

"I should think by Wednesday," he went on, "you'd be able to play cricket. It's not as if you're hurt. People who walk in their sleep are just a bit potty."

"I did not walk in my sleep," said Deborah.

"Grandpapa said you must have done," said Roger. "It was a good thing that Patch woke him up and he saw you going across the lawn …" Then, to show his release from tension, he stood on his hands.

Deborah could see the sky from her bed. It was flat and dull. The day was a summer day that had worked through storm. Agnes came into the room with junket on a tray. She looked important.

"Now run off," she said to Roger. "Deborah doesn't want to talk to you. She's supposed to rest."

Surprisingly, Roger obeyed, and Agnes placed the junket on the table beside the bed. "You don't feel hungry, I expect," she said. "Never mind, you can eat this later, when you fancy it. Have you got a pain? It's usual, the first time."

"No," said Deborah.

What had happened to her was personal. They had prepared her for it at school, but nevertheless it was a shock, not to be discussed with Agnes. The woman hovered a moment, in case the child asked questions; but, seeing that none came, she turned and left the room.

Deborah, her cheek on her hand, stared at the empty sky. The heaviness of knowledge lay upon her, a strange, deep sorrow.

"I won't come back," she thought. "I've lost the key." The hidden world, like ripples on the pool so soon to be filled in and fenced, was out of her reach for ever.

In a Different Light

Elizabeth Taylor

The boat brought people and took others away. In summer it came three times a week to the island, and the sisters, sitting outside the waterfront café, would watch it appearing round the point. It came with the most beautiful inevitability—however late. Quayside life would begin to stir and, as the deep sound of the ship's hooter came across the bay, little boats would put out from the shore. They were low on the water, with packed and standing people holding aloft baskets, trying to wave goodbye. The same boats, on their return journey, were watched more critically. Exposed and bewildered, and perhaps sick and tired as well, the newcomers stepped on to the broken marble of the waterfront and looked about them, shading their eyes from the sun and the fierce brightness of the white buildings. Their baggage would be seized by old men or young boys with handcarts and donkeys, and they would follow it on foot as if dazed with the suddenness of their arrival, wiping away sweat and trying to smack down flies.

After a time, the scene was peaceful again, the empty boats hardly moving on the water and, looking out to sea, Jane and Barbara would watch the ship making its wide curve before disappearing round the headland.

Then they would go to a *taverna* and choose their fish (except on Sundays, the boat came at about noon), and when it was cooked and eaten, they would walk slowly up the hillside track, through the herb-scented scrub, to Jane's cottage.

"I shall never go home to England now. I feel it in my bones," Jane said once. "Every time the boat goes back to Athens, I think that."

"But you still say 'home'," her sister said.

"I didn't mean to. *This* is my home. The other's Blighty—I can't imagine it any more. Do they still have those double-decker buses?"

Her husband—an expatriate painter, as Barbara's husband, Leonard, always referred to him—had died that spring and Barbara had come from England to be with her sister for a time and eventually take her home—for she believed that what Jane had written in letters could soon be reasoned away; and so she had sent the children to their grandmother, drawn all her savings from the bank and arrived on the island ready to clasp her younger sister in her arms and soon restore her to her proper place.

"There is nothing to keep you," she had pleaded on her first evening on the island. There had been a sudden, brilliant sunset and afterwards it was dark and warm. The streets smelt of honeysuckle and carnations. Their sandals slapped quietly on the flagstones. They spoke in low voices and were greeted softly by passers-by. "There is nothing to keep you," Barbara repeated.

The next day, they climbed the hillside to Alan's grave in the cluttered little cemetery above the sea; but even standing there, Jane did not weep or seem particularly moved. She turned, instead, to look downwards at the sea and she took a deep breath—almost a satisfied, a triumphant breath, thought Barbara.

"I'm afraid I have come all this way for nothing," she wrote to Leonard. "But I will stay on a little longer as you suggest."

Day by day, she lost her usual pallor and became almost as brown as Jane, and she slept long and deeply at night. Her letters were insincere, for she could only write of how much money she had wasted on the journey and how many people she had inconvenienced at home.

On one of their usual mornings at the café, they waited to see the boat come in from Athens. They had bought a basket of artichokes and some paraffin oil, and now sat under a bamboo awning drinking coffee. The boat appeared far out; it rounded the headland and they watched it curving in towards the harbour. A few people collected by the water's edge with the baggage—baskets of cheese, chickens and bunches of flowers.

Barbara sipped her glass of ice-cold water to take away the bitter taste the coffee had.

"The flowers are always dead by the time they get to Athens," Jane said.

Two rowing boats put out across the water towards the anchored ship and later, when they were returning, Jane said: "I never watch them without thinking of the day Alan and I came. The houses seemed to rise higher and higher as we rowed into the harbour, and I felt alien and self-conscious when I stepped ashore—all the village out watching, taking note of my London clothes. My shirt was far too bright for here, but luckily it soon faded." (She had worn it ever since Barbara's arrival, washing it sometimes at night, but never ironing it and never mending the tear in the sleeve. "In London, I couldn't have just one shirt," she had said. "And that is all I care to have.") "When we came ashore that day, I had no idea what impression we were making. We were the only visitors—which is how we thought of ourselves then, not knowing that we were here for ever."

"What will you live on?" Barbara asked. She had given up persuasion at last, convinced now of her sister's obstinacy, of her determination to stay exactly where she was—among people whose language she spoke indifferently—wearing her one shirt till it was threadbare.

"I've got Mother's money."

"It isn't enough. Mine hardly keeps me in cigarettes."

Jane put on her sunglasses and turned her chair to look across the bright water and the approaching boats. She said: "Don't fuss so much. I can always take summer visitors. You could send them out to me from Blighty. I should like some nice, bewildered-looking visitors like this one. I would take them under my wing."

There was only one bewildered-looking person on the boat. He was dressed in khaki drill and carried a rucksack which—when he had jumped ashore—he set down so that he could give his hand to an old woman, who was swathed in black and proudly carried a Pan-American travel bag. When he had her safely on land, he bowed and said, "*Khérete*." She drew her head veil across her mouth and nodded.

"One of our fellow-countrymen," said Jane, glancing at him without enthusiasm.

He stood looking about him, smilingly refusing to hire a donkey or rent a room or have his rucksack taken from him. Then he appeared to make a great decision and he came over to the café and sat down.

"*Kali méra*," he said self-consciously.

"Good-morning," the waiter replied. That, however, was the extent of his English, and confusion arose about what sort of coffee he should order.

Jane, over her shoulder, off-handedly explained.

"You wouldn't *like* having visitors," Barbara said softly. "And you wouldn't take them under your wing."

"I should like their money. That is what would appeal to me about them."

"You would resent them."

"Let's go." Jane jumped up and went inside the café to pay, then she took up the oilcan and handed the artichokes to her sister. As they were passing the Englishman's table, she relented. She stopped to ask him when he had left home.

"A fortnight ago," he said, pushing the table as he stood up, slopping his glass of water.

"And it was raining, I suppose."

"Pouring down. It was like another world. And still is, my wife writes to say."

"You are badly sunburned," Jane said in a stern voice. "Spyros will give you some yoghourt to soothe it if you ask." She nodded towards the café. "Are you staying at the Amphitryon?"

There was only one hotel on the island—on the other side of the bay from her cottage. She pointed it out to him and gave careful instructions how to reach it, up flights of steps and between orchards of lemon trees.

He watched them walking away, carrying their artichokes and the oilcan, marked out by these as inhabitants, he thought. It was not the kind of shopping that visitors would do.

When Spyros came outside again, he asked him for yoghourt, but was not understood. He shouldered his rucksack and made for the hotel, soon taking a wrong flight of steps and getting lost between the close-packed houses. The sun beat down and the whitewashed walls dazzled him; his shirt under the rucksack was soaked with sweat. He took a map from his pocket and unfolded it and held it up as a screen between the blazing sun and his peeling face. From dark doorways shy children stared at him; old women, shelling peas or spinning, inclined their heads graciously towards him. "*Kali méra*," he repeated gallantly as he passed the open doorways. "*Kali méra sas.*" The children smiled and turned aside their heads.

"It is quite wonderful," he told himself. "I am here. It is true." His wife was miles away in a dark world underneath the clouds. He was sorry for her; he told himself he missed her; he forgot her. "Hibiscus," he murmured, looking up at a wall. He recognised it from pictures. When he reached the hotel, he would describe everything in his diary—the sea, the boat, the two Englishwomen

– 136 –

at the café, the flowers. He had climbed to one of the higher streets and could look down through the leaves of some lemon trees at the harbour. The waterfront was deserted now, for everyone had gone in out of the heat and there was complete human silence over the island—bees buzzed, crickets chirped, a church bell chimed—but there were no voices. At the end of one of the deserted streets, he saw the word "Amphitryon" written on a board over a doorway and he went towards it in triumph.

Jane and Barbara, at lunch, discussed him—Jane, with an almost Greek sharpness of curiosity and detachment, her sister thought. It was very much like the way she was eating her artichoke—the deft stripping away of leaves, the certainty of the hidden heart being there for the reaching. Licking oil from her fingers, Jane said: "So his wife writes to tell him about the rain. Complainingly, I dare say. He thinks he is glad to get her letters, but he is gladder to put them out of this mind."

"This you know," said Barbara.

"This I know. And he also thinks he is glad to be in Greece. He has to be. I expect he has waited twenty years or more to come here and how can he afford, now that he's here, to dwell on his sunburn and his blistered feet and mosquito bites? I bet he gets frightful diarrhoea, too, poor old thing."

"Is everyone who comes on the boat such a matter of conjecture?"

"Everyone. Luckily one doesn't know till later, or who could dare to brave it? You noticed the crowds when *you* arrived? Although you were expected and known about, so there was a more critical turnout for you."

"I thought they were meeting people off the boat, or going back in it themselves."

"Well, you know better now."

In the afternoon—as on every afternoon—Jane lay down on the big brass bedstead in her room and went to sleep. Barbara, unused to this habit and scorning it, wrote to her children and then took the track down the hillside to the village to post her letter. In the hot, quiet afternoon the smell of wild sage was overpowering as she brushed against it along the path.

The post office was dark and cool, and inside it sat the Englishman. He had come to buy stamps and had been requested to draw up a chair and have some conversation with the clerk, who had a married sister living in Bermondsey. A boy came in from the café, carrying a swinging tray, with coffee and glasses of water. Barbara stood by while the Englishman was handed his cup and glass. He had risen when she entered, but was curtly motioned to sit down by the clerk, who got up to tear off stamps for Barbara and give her change.

"Roland Bagueley," the Englishman said slowly and loudly in answer to an earlier question. He took the pad he was offered and wrote his name in capitals.

"From London? Swindon? Falmouth?" asked the clerk.

Barbara, sticking on stamps, lingered. The buckle of her sandal was given some attention.

"London," said Roland Bagueley. "A part of London."

"Hampstead, for instance," Barbara thought. She picked up her change, put it in her purse and, smiling in his direction, went out. As he once more jumped to his feet, she heard him shouting, "Hampstead—a part of London called Hampstead."

She stopped at the café for cigarettes and on her way home printed his name on the packet lest she should forget it. "Roland Bagueley from Hampstead," she would tell Jane. She wondered if in the end her sister would go mad, living alone, nourished on such trifles.

In the evening, they met him again. He was sitting outside

a waterside *taverna* where they went for dinner. Jane looked disconcerted when he stood up and offered them chairs. She liked conjecture about strangers rather than facts about acquaintances.

They sat down and ordered drinks. "So you're not visitors here," he said to Barbara, as Jane was speaking in Greek to the waiter.

"I am, but my sister lives here—Jane Bailey. And I am Barbara Fennell."

To know their names seemed to gratify him enormously.

"I heard it in the post office this afternoon," Barbara said when he had introduced himself.

"The clerk knows a little English and hoped to practise it on me. His sister lives in Bermondsey and he supposed that I must know her."

"And you live in Hampstead. I heard that, too."

"Yes, I am an architect."

Jane returning her attention, nodded as if this much she had already guessed. "And have you been to Greece before?" she asked.

"No. It is a dream realised after many, many years."

She put out her foot and tapped Barbara's. "And are you disappointed in it?" Here questions were peremptory and put him out. She was a small, dark, darting person, often intimidating—even to her sister.

He shook his head, looking puzzled; but what he was puzzled about was not his reactions to Greece, Barbara realised suddenly, but the sight of his name written on the cigarette packet which was lying on the table. Unlike Jane, she was liable to blush and, doing so, puzzled him more.

"*Yassoo*," he said painstakingly, lifting his glass.

"Oh, good luck," said Jane, who had just put hers down.

Barbara took the cigarette packet and in rather an affected voice said: "How amusing! When I heard your name in the post office I wrote it down on this so that I could remember to tell Jane."

"But why?"

"I thought she would admire my sharpness. No one arrives on this island without being scrutinised, you see; and I am falling into the habit."

"Wasn't it your wife's lifelong ambition to come to Greece, too?" asked Jane.

"No, Iris likes to spend her holidays with her sister in Buxton."

"Well, I expect that's very nice, too."

They went into the *taverna* to choose their fish and when they came outside again the sun was dropping fast into the pinkish water. They watched it go and it was suddenly dark and the air seemed warmer and more still. "I really wanted to be alone here," Roland was thinking. The brisk, dark little woman was in no way part of what he had come all this distance for and awaited so long, and about the place itself she seemed imperious and possessive, describing to him how she had chosen it for life. She had traded it for a great deal, he thought—for she was a young woman to make such a decision— and under the influence of ouzo, he began to make a list for her of what she lacked.

"But I have friends here," she said, dropping a fish's head to a pleading cat and wiping her fingers on a piece of bread.

"Not you own kind."

"I never found my own kind anywhere—only in my husband."

"Even everyday things—comfort we take for granted."

"Like the Underground at rush hours; fog and rain; cocktail parties; wearing hats."

"There is no water at my hotel—one carafe in my room for drinking, which I'm too nervous to do. I have paid extra for a shower, but nothing comes out of it."

"Oh, well, the sea is warm now."

"I wasn't complaining," he said quickly, wondering if there had been impatience in her voice—even, perhaps, contempt. In fact, he had wanted—and still wanted—everything to be quite different from at home, and had already written almost boastingly to tell his wife about the shower.

"I know that the man who understands how to work the pumps has gone to Athens to have his chest X-rayed," Jane said. "He will be back on the boat the day after tomorrow and then you'll be all right."

"I wasn't complaining," he said again, thinking, "Two more days!"

"Can't you imagine England now?" Barbara asked. "A long light evening and the sound of mowing-machines." The children would be going to bed; she tried to visualise them—pink faces, fair hair, blue dressing-gowns—and they remained unreal. A barefooted boy, no older than her son, was driving a donkey along the sea front, whacking its rump and making kissing noises at it. Other children were playing in boats under the harbour wall, their voices conspiratorial above the sound of the water peacefully slapping the stone wall.

"I could *sleep* … I could sleep," she said, and covered her face with her hands and yawned. But Jane was perfectly alert—had hardly begun the second half of her waking day.

"It's the air perhaps," said Roland, trying not to yawn, too.

"It's trying to keep going all day in the heat," said Jane. "The air is perfectly invigorating."

When they had said good-night to Roland and seen him going off in the opposite direction to his waterless hotel, the sisters began the steep climb up the hillside. Pausing for breath and looking back at the harbour lights, Barbara said: "I'll have to go home soon, I suppose. Next week, perhaps."

"Well you are not to think of me. I'm quite all right now. You must do whatever you must. I expect you are missing the children."

"A little." All the way along the track, she was treading on the thyme or brushing against sage bushes, freeing the scent of the herbs upon the air. I don't really miss the children, she thought. Each day, I miss them less, not more.

When they reached the cottage, Jane lit two oil-lamps. She gave one to Barbara to take upstairs to bed with her, and sat beside the other to read until two or three o'clock. As she kicked off her sandals and settled down, she said, "In the morning, I might get out Alan's paints and make a start. I'll teach myself and surprise you all." Although she had said this before, and in a tone of great decision and determination, nothing had been done.

Barbara went to her bedroom and leant out of the window, breathing the scented air. She was beginning to understand her sister and even to foresee difficulties for herself lying ahead, and imagined herself back home, unsettled by her experience, deprived of the dazzling light, and the deep silence.

There were fewer boats now down in the harbour. She got into bed. Her sunburned body was fiery between the coarse sheets; she felt wonderfully lulled and, turning her cheek at once to the pillow, she let out a long breath like a contented sigh, and fell asleep.

They saw a great deal of Roland, as it was natural to do in that small village—meeting at the *taverna*, the café, the bathing-place below the rocks. Sometimes, on afternoons when Jane was sleeping, Barbara went on excursions with him—to one of the bays to swim and, once, by mules, to a convent at the highest point on the island. There, among lemon trees, they tied up their mules and Roland sat down on the hillside, while Barbara went into the courtyard. It was filled with stocks and roses and the sound of bees. The Reverend Mother came to meet her. She led her into a cool dark room and gave her a spoonful of jam and a glass of water on a tray. She was a plump lively woman with gold teeth and a great smell of garlic.

Although they had no words in common, they had plenty of nods and smiles and Barbara had admiring sounds as well—at the *ikons* and the ugly little chapel, at a piece of sacred bone in a box, at the view, and the arum lilies in the courtyard. She bought a lace-edged handkerchief and was given a bunch of stocks. When she took the old nun's hand, it was as hard as leather, and creased; for she had worked in the fields like any peasant. As Barbara left, she heard whispering and giggling above her and, looking up, glimpsed two nuns peeping from a high window. She lifted her flowers to wave; but, as soon as she had turned, they had drawn back out of sight.

Under a lemon tree lay Roland, fast asleep. Not liking to wake him, she sat down a little way off, smelt her bunch of stocks, gazed down at the dark sea with the pale outlines of other islands circling it. He slept on and soon she felt drowsy, too, and stretched herself out among the rock-roses and wild larkspur and dozed a little.

When they awoke, both suddenly stirring at the same moment, it seemed much later, but they had no idea of the time. They pumped some water for the mules in the convent yard and mounted them. It was an odd, holiday companionship they shared, founded on nothing but what had happened in the last few days—the mistakes they had made from not understanding the language, their delight in their new experience and, now, the hazards of riding their mules down a rocky, dried-up river bed. Half-way down it, with a guilty backward glance towards the now hidden convent, Barbara threw away the stocks, which had died in the sun.

When they reached the cottage, they found Jane rummaging among some canvases, as if about to make a start at last. She had washed her hair and it hung straight and wet close to her head and dripped on to her shoulders. She smiled when Barbara told her that they had fallen asleep up on the hillside.

Barbara and Roland began to count the days they had left. She had chosen a date haphazardly and despairingly. She knew that she ought to go early and she wanted to go later and, between conscience and desire, must find a compromise. Roland's return to England was already arranged, and as it grew nearer he began to sacrifice other projects he had had in mind—Mycenae, Delphi, Perachora. "I shall go to Perachora next time," he explained. "Perhaps in two years' time." He wondered if his wife had been happy with her sister in Buxton and hoped devoutly that she had been.

Meanwhile, he stayed on the island, sitting lingeringly outside the café talking to the sisters, who could not help wondering, when they were alone, how it was that they could find him both amiable and boring. One day, he brought a photograph of his wife to show them, and they looked at it carefully and said "Awfully pretty". An insipid face, they decided.

"You must miss her," Barbara said.

"She would love it here," he said and then added, "Yes, in many ways she'd love it. Then things go wrong and I'm glad, after all, that I'm on my own. The frustrations and misunderstandings about the language. And sometimes the food … and having no water all the time."

"Well, it's all put right now," said Jane. She was really making a start that morning and had brought a sketching-block and a box of watercolours down to the café and was now washing in a grey sky above the tiers of white houses. For the first day, there was no sun. It was hot, though, and a glare came off the sea.

Spyros, bringing them more coffee, looked over Jane's shoulder and said something angrily and rapidly in Greek. She shrugged and pointed at the sky with her brush. He protested, set down their coffee, slopped water over the table, then shrugged too—but crossly, not indifferently—and pushed his way back through the chairs, banging the tray angrily against his knee as he went.

"What was that about?" asked Barbara.

Still washing in grey, Jane said; "He wanted me to paint a blue sky. Over this island, he says, the sky is always blue. When I pointed out that today it was not it was today's sky I was painting, he said that people from other islands would misunderstand."

"Day after day, there are the same illogical arguments," Barbara said.

"Trivial, silly things happen in Blighty, too."

Roland, who had been fidgeting with his wife's photograph, flipping it to and fro, glanced at it again and slipped it into his pocket. He was leaving the next day. His holiday was almost over and he felt lost and disconsolate. Dreams had come true, but merely to give birth to others. He had overcome discomfort, his skin was now at terms with the sun as his digestion was with the food, and he had formed new habits, such as sleeping in the afternoon and eating late at night. It was life in Hampstead that had the look of strangeness about it now—the little dinner parties with the lace mats set out on the polished table, coming back from his office to those, or to an evening's gardening or listening to records while he stuck his holiday photographs in an album. He was an intensely patriotic man and dearly loved the English landscape. "I could never live anywhere else," he told himself. He thought it very strange that Jane could, but there was almost nothing about her that he could understand. She was hard, he thought—unlike her sister, whom he found rather girlish and sentimental. He was not greatly drawn to either of them; but they had been part of his holiday and because of that he must feel disturbed at saying good-bye to them.

The cloud at last drifted out to sea and the sun shone in a clear blue sky. Spyros ran out from the café, pointing upwards, smiling triumphantly at Jane.

"Now I can finish my spool of photographs," Roland said. He took out his camera and began fussing with it. "If I may; if you will both look up." He studied the light meter. "My wife's the photographer, I'm afraid. She has endless patience over everything. I don't understand the gadget."

So his wife took a positive role occasionally, Barbara thought. From her photograph this was not to be guessed.

"There … and now if you would …"

Obediently they took off their sunglasses and looked up at him and smiled—Jane holding a paint brush and Barbara a coffee-cup.

He left next day on the morning boat. They waited for it at the café. He thought of it as an enemy vessel coming malignly round the headland; making directly for him, he felt.

He and Barbara had exchanged addresses, for they would meet in England—husbands and wives would be introduced and, in her case, children. There would also be the photographs to be sent on.

They stood on the waterside and watched him stepping into the rowing-boat. He had his rucksack and a large sponge as a present for Iris. Barbara had tears in her eyes—for she could not bear any good-byes, and departures by boat were especially poignant to her. She was also reminded of her own going away in two days' time.

Roland, steadying himself, standing up in the crowded boat, turned to wave. They waved back and called good-bye, as he was rowed out across the harbour. To him, the shape of the island changed as he went farther out from it—the hills spread out and the coast line was seen to be dotted with windmills.

"Well," Jane began, as they turned away. "You may be invited once to Hampstead; then you'll have to ask them back, and you'll wish you hadn't to—and Leonard will, even more. 'My friend I met in Greece,'" she said mockingly. "After that, you'll send Christmas cards for a year or two—especially if you can find any with a Greek flavour, which I should think would be unlikely."

"I know all that. People are different in different surroundings."
Barbara, under her sunglasses, wiped her eyes. "I cry too easily," she
explained. "Just as I'm sick too easily."

"It's a good thing to be easily sick," said Jane.

It was another kind of poignancy Barbara felt when it was time to
go herself. As she left the harbour, she was surprised to see Jane
turn and walk away almost at once. She was not the type to stand
waving until the boat was out of sight, but her turning away seemed
impatient and abrupt. She was soon too far away to be seen and the
whole of that little world where she was seemed to lock itself closer
and closer together until the expansive waterfront of life, with its
comings and goings—its landings of fish and sponges, it trotting
donkeys, its desultory spectators—could hardly be imagined any
more.

Leaning on the rails, she watched until all she could see was the
little village against the golden hills and a white speck at the summit
of one of them—which was the convent to which she and Roland
had ridden on the mules.

Soon the whole island was lost on the horizon; but all the time
other islands were coming up on either side—some close, so that
she could see more white villages, more blue-domed churches; some
distant, misty shapes.

This journey to Athens was the first stage of her journey, which
would end next day in England. "Blighty!" she thought, and she
leant over the rails and stared down into the brilliant, wrinkled sea,
feeling very strange, both sick and tearful.

Jane went for a walk along the cliffs and after a while noticed a strange dog pacing along with her—sometimes a little in front as if to guide her, and then at her heels as if to comfort her. He had an air of obedience about him, and might have been ordered to keep her company now that her sister had gone. When she sat down to rest, he sat down in front of her and gave her anxious looks.

She felt painfully unsettled. Barbara's visit has made her first loss so much worse. She had come too soon and her departure added the second loss to the earlier one, a second kind of silence to grow used to. "Which can be done," she thought.

She looked out to sea, but the boat was out of sight and nothing was left but its faint trail across the water. She made her way back to the cottage and when she reached it, she thanked the dog for his company and shut the door on him. Then she went and lay down on her bed, for it was siesta time.

Sometimes there were holes in the clouds and through these Barbara could peer down from the plane and see a green landscape crossed by slate grey roads. It looked neat and dark and alienating. She had no feeling of coming home and could not believe that she was here. They flew over reservoirs and gravel pits filled with milky water, and then over the Thames itself—a broad reach lined with houseboats and launches and fringed with willows—a very sedate-looking river. Coming to land, she saw the houses tip suddenly sideways and the fields scudding past, and she imagined her husband somewhere down there, waiting for her.

When at last she saw him, standing outside the customs office—looking pale, she thought—his pleasure at having her back affected her deeply. They drove home slowly and from time to time he took her hand, as if to reassure himself that she was with him again.

"So Jane decided to stay?" he asked.

"I went all that way for nothing."

"You had to go. And it has done you good."

"Is everything all right at home?"

"There have been one or two upsets, but never mind now."

"But I *must* know."

Gradually she learnt the list of calamities—the children with chicken-pox at their grandmother's; the cat who had disappeared (from loneliness? from neglect? she wondered), the tree that had blown down in a gale and the daily help who had given in her notice. She was filled with despair and guilt. "You should have told me," she said again and again.

"I wanted you to have your holiday. And I wish I hadn't to tell you now."

It was a dull, warm night. While she had been away, the summer had come and the trees had grown dark and weighty. All along the lanes was a bitter smell of dusty leaves. They turned into their own drive and she looked about her with a despondent curiosity. The lilac had bloomed and faded in her absence. As they went into the hall together, she put her arms round him, blinded again with tears. "Oh, thank you, my darling, for managing," she said.

No letter came from Jane, although Barbara, after her first letter, wrote a second, then a third. Her tan faded in the mild, dark weather, but images of the island stayed vividly in her mind. She fretted for some word from it and about it, feeling—where she now was—less than half alive. Jane's water-colour sketch—of the harbour and the grey sky—which she had brought home with her, was propped up on her desk—a lack-lustre little painting, but all she had.

Her home seemed lack-lustre, too, and she could no longer see what strangers—exclaiming at its beauty—must see, and the gentle view from upstairs windows—the blue-and-grey Thames valley which she had always loved—was tame and vapid now.

Leonard thought her merely unsettled by travelling, or else worried about Jane. The children—returning spoiled by their grandmother's indulgence—sense her inattentiveness and continued their misbehaviour. Serena, who had never lived up to her name, gave way to even more spectacular tantrums. Robert, her brother, simply did damage. Each day he left the mark of destruction on the house. "It's like having a poltergeist among us," Barbara said, gathering up the fragments of a lustre jug.

She wondered why she had the strange belief that if only Jane would write, she could find her old contentment and see the island in the right perspective—as merely a place where dwelling was primitive, the weather fairer than at home, and life uncluttered—with no fine china to be broken, no cupboards full of clothes to be looked after and no telephone to keep on ringing. Jane's letter, when it came, would reconcile her, she felt, to all these frustrations and annoyances; Serena would stop casting herself down on the floor howling; Robert would go more carefully about the house, and she would find herself once more enchanted with her surroundings. How any letter could accomplish all this she did not ask herself; but she knew that without it she was left in the air, her visit abroad not finally rounded off. And then the letter came at last and there was news of the island, but no reference to Barbara's ever having been on it. This made it seem more remote to her—a different place.

Sometimes, increasingly, she wondered about Roland Bagueley and how he was faring in Hampstead. His association with the island, the fact of his coming so much into her recollections of it, began to give him an illusory charm; but he, too, was lost in silence—had failed even to send the promised photographs. On an impulse, she wrote to invite him and his wife to lunch on Sunday.

This she very soon regretted having done and she began to await his arrival in a state of nervous agitation.

"I wish I hadn't asked them," she told Leonard at breakfast. "I don't know why I did. He's boring, really."

"They won't be here for ever," he said.

"But why on earth should I inflict such tedium on you?"

"An hour or two of tedium can't hurt anybody."

He was equable, she thought; so good-natured. However disastrously things turned out, he would never blame her.

On Sunday, Roland and Iris got out of their car at a quarter to one, just as Robert had shut Serena's fingers in a door and was shouting guilty disclaimers while she was hysterical on the floor. Barbara, with her face hot from the oven and from embarrassment, too, opened the door while Leonard carried the shrieking child to the bathroom.

At first, there was too much to say all at once—introductions, greetings, explanations, apologies—and then, suddenly, standing in the hall with the door shut, there was nothing at all.

"Poor little girl," said Roland, glancing upstairs.

Only curiosity quietened Serena. Feeling that she was missing something, she allowed her screams to die down into a tremulous whimpering; she freed herself from her father and appeared on the staircase, with tears over her face and her lips quivering.

"Poor little girl," said Roland again—and he held out his arms to her as she descended the stairs slowly and suspiciously. She was far from being a shy child, but decided to feign timidity. She skirted the visitors widely and hid her face against Barbara, refusing to be coaxed away from her.

Leonard came downstairs, wearing a jovial and anticipatory look, which even Iris Bagueley's gushing voice did not diminish. "Delightful!" she kept exclaiming, "Your *garden*. 'Oh,' I said to Rollo,

– 151 –

'the garden, Rollo! The irises. What a *show*.' Oh, she's a *shy* girl, is she? Who's lost her tongue?"

"I hope she won't talk like this to Robert," Barbara thought fearfully.

"Have you any animals?" Iris suddenly asked in a low and confidential voice.

"Only guinea-pigs," Barbara said hesitantly.

"Then have you any objection if Chummy comes in? We take him everywhere and he's such an unhappy boy when he's left in the car. Girlie see doggie?"

Chummy was an evil-looking chow with a curled tail, a rather matted coat, and tongue hanging loose in a wicked wolf's mouth. He was brought through the hall, looking balefully about him. He panted, his ears pricked at every sound, claws pitter-pattered on the parquet floor as he restlessly and scornfully explored the room. Serena clung closer to her mother and her whimpering gathered force.

"Aren't you a Mummy's girl?" asked Iris brightly, tapping her on the head with her gloves.

"Go away!" Serena muttered angrily into her mother's skirt.

Robert, who had been comforting himself with a long drink, sidled in, his faced stained with purple juice.

"And here's the son and heir," said Iris.

She seemed to twinkle at him—her spectacles, ear-rings, necklace and her shiny straw hat—and Robert backed away, scowling.

So far, Roland had said very little, except to demur about the dog's being brought in, and ignored. Now—with a glass of sherry in his hand—he looked across at Barbara and said: "*Yassoo!*"

She smiled self-consciously and glanced at him—for the first time, she realised—and saw how utterly unfamiliar he looked in his dark suit—a different person, a different *kind* of person.

"Oh, Rolla and his Greek," said Iris, laughingly. "Cheers, my dears.

You see, I can only say it in English. Before he went away, I thought I should go mad—he was everlastingly going about the house, practising sentences out of his phrase book, quite determined to be able to talk to the natives when he got there. Weren't you, Rollo?"

The nickname, thought Barbara, did not seem to attach itself to him, however constantly it was used; it glanced off him.

He had blushed when his wife spoke of his attempts to learn Greek and said that he had simply wasted his time, and Barbara— with Serena still clinging to her skirt—went on one of her little trips to the kitchen to lift saucepan lids and look in the oven. She had been drinking rather hastily, from nervousness, and felt hot and confused. The thought of finishing off the cooking, dishing-up, the gathering together of them all at the table, oppressed her unbearably.

"*You* didn't feel drawn towards Greece?" Leonard asked Iris when they were in the dining-room at last. It was late. The potatoes had taken so long to brown that Barbara despaired, and several times Iris had peeped at her watch. She had refused a second drink. Then—just when everything was ready—Chummy had wanted to go out and had to be taken and waited for.

Leonard now clashed the carving knife against the steel and Barbara watched anxiously, as he cut off the first slice of beef and, from habit, laid it aside on the dish for himself.

"No," said Iris. "I was never taken with the idea. An aunt of mine went deaf from typhoid on the island of Rhodes."

"A long time ago," said Roland.

"'Don't drink the water and don't eat the salads,' I told Rollo before he went. No, do serve the kiddies first, I implore you."

"Stop kicking your chair," said Barbara to Robert, who ignored her. She blushed, hearing in her mind what Iris must be thinking— "Such behaviour! What spoilt kiddies!" "You lost your tan," she said to Roland.

"And you."

"No, I think 'abroad', as I call it, it terribly over-rated," Iris told them. "Perhaps we haven't been awfully lucky. Goodness, don't you remember when we went to the Costa Brava, Rollo? The people there. They really were rather ... well ..."

"Mixed," Roland said quickly. It was the best he could think of in a hurry and doubtless had staved off worse.

"Yes, *mixed*." She smiled at him gratefully. "And the *food*." She closed her eyes.

When she opened them, she seemed encouraged to see the plate of decent English food in front of her, even though she could not have felt proud of the potatoes if *she* had cooked them. "Delicious," she said, in a faint and trailing-off voice as she took up her knife and fork.

She may have been pretty when she was younger, Barbara thought in her mind, she brightened the hair, took off the spectacles, smoothed out the lines of discontent and eye-strain, and was just able to imagine Roland—a shy and unpractised young man—allowing himself to be carried away. In Greece, she had known that he had nothing but solid worth to recommend him. He had been dogged—even about his holiday, until staying on the island—out of the world, out of context—he had achieved an undreamt of air of negligence. They had ridden up to the convent, she reminded herself. Sweating, sunburned, untidy, he had stretched himself out under a tree and fallen asleep, spread-eagled in the dappled light. It was a different man, she thought, glancing at the trim, anxious one who was listening to his wife with an attentiveness he must have wisely acquired to make up for everyone else's lack of it.

These weeks, since his return from the island, must have been worse than hers, she realised—as the rest of his life would be worse. His experience must have been deeper, his brief escape desperately planned and wearily paid for. It was something for her—for Iris—to deride along with the other things. Once he had liked music, he had told Jane in answer to one of her off-hand enquiries: later the sisters had laughed about it, but Barbara could not have laughed now. She could see too clearly the history of discarded interests.

It would have been better to have asked them to dinner, with the children safely in bed, she thought, slipping a clean plate under the wine-stained table-cloth. Robert had knocked over the glass of wine and water, which plainly Iris thought he should not have been given.

"And who is a little bit tipsy?" she was saying.

"Are you?" Robert asked.

Her laughter, her effusive ways with them, revealed her hatred of all children—and these particularly. They were what she did not want to be reminded of.

"Robert," said Leonard, warningly.

Ignoring his father, staring at Iris, Robert said, with contempt in his voice: "You aren't really laughing. I know."

"I am," said Serena. She threw back her head and half closed her eyes and gave a passable imitation of Iris's trilling laugh.

Affecting not to notice exactly what the child was doing, Barbara said: "Any more silliness from either of you, and you will be sent upstairs to rest until you're sensible again."

"*You* would *like* that, wouldn't you?" Robert said in a low voice, with a glance at Iris.

"Well, then it is no use," Barbara said. "You must go upstairs this minute, Robert." She was very nervous lest he should refuse to, and wondered how she would deal with so much loss of face if he did. To her relief, he slid down at once from his chair, walked round the table, and as he went out of the door was heard to say how glad he was to go. "Horrible old gooseberry tart," he chanted loudly, as he stamped upstairs. "Horrible, beastly old cream."

"I'm sorry," Barbara said.

"Goodness, only a very silly person would take offence at anything a child says," said Iris.

– 155 –

"And that is what we are all afraid of one doing," Leonard thought.

When they had finished lunch, Roland gave Barbara his holiday photographs. "They're really no good," he apologised. "I think the light was too strong."

"I told you to allow for that," said Iris. "You had the meter."

Barbara's hands trembled with eagerness when she took the photographs from him, and her disappointment was great as she looked at one after another. She and Jane—standing beside donkeys or lemon trees or the masts of fishing-boats—were blurred albino figures, their pale lips parted; or marble statues bleached in moonlight. The curving waterfront, the white village was like a heap of rice.

"I think the light was far too strong," he said again.

She could distinguish the café with all the chairs outside, and Spyros's apron like a trail of ectoplasm among them. "Don't you remember ..." she began. She looked up from the photograph and saw that his expression, though gentle, was forbidding.

He was right, of course, she realised. There could be no resurrection of those days—even the photographs had failed.

"Would you like to walk round the garden?" Leonard suggested.

Watched malignly from an upstairs window by Robert, Iris and Roland were shown the garden, flowers picked for them, Chummy was called off the herbaceous border and shooed away from the guinea-pigs. Soon after three they went away.

"Oh dear," said Iris, as they drove through the Sunday afternoon traffic, "my *head*." She pressed her hands to her forehead. Chummy, sitting up in the back of the car, panted loudly, his tongue lolling out of his mouth. "Those *children*," Iris said.

"I must admit they were rather out of hand. What did you think of Barbara?"

"Quite frankly," said Iris, "I wasn't terribly impressed."

Barbara took tea on to the lawn. There was no sun, but it was warm. Robert, having been freed and forgiven, lovingly ate cold gooseberry tart and cream. It was a peaceful tea-time. At the end, Serena, getting up from the grass, asked: "Can we get down?"

For a little while, she and Robert played amicably together and Barbara and Leonard watched them contentedly.

"I wonder if they're back in Hampstead yet?" she asked. "I'd like to know what they are doing at this moment. They must have finished talking about us by now. I'm sorry about the awful fiasco. I let you in for it."

"He was quite a decent sort of fellow."

"But *she*!"

"Yes, she certainly *was* rather …"

"Mixed."

They laughed, and the children, swinging in a hammock, looked across at them. To hear their parents laughing together was a sound they loved very much. Hearing it, they thought they would be good for ever, so that it would never stop. The world then became settled, a serene place to be in.

"Oh, darling! I'm so glad I have you," Barbara told Leonard.

In and Out of
Never-Never Land

Maeve Brennan

In East Hampton, it was the Fourth of July, the hour just before dawn—very early-morning teatime. Mary Ann Whitty looked into the brown eyes of her dog, Bluebell, and she thought, The dog is kind and good, but the cats have style…. She was sitting in her living room, which was remarkable to her because it was hers alone, and because it contained her furniture, her books, her dog, and her cats. The furniture was shabby, the books were worn and showed the signs of long storage, the cats all wore mixed furs, and Bluebell, the black Labrador retriever, was not as serene as a dog of her age and nature ought to be. Bluebell had spent too much time in too many different kennels.

Mary Ann did not care that her household was a trifle bedraggled. What mattered to her was that all her possessions were collected together in one place. She admired the room she had made for herself, and she admired everything in it. She was so pleased with herself and her possessions and arrangements that she even admired the lacks in her house. For example, a simple example, she had no dining-room table. She knew she should have a proper table, a proper place for eating, and that without it her life was makeshift, but she thought that makeshift ways were very well suited to this strange little house, which wore such a temporary air that the first time she walked into it she said to herself that it was not a real house but an impossibility, not a house at all, and that she must rent it immediately, because it might very well not be there when she looked for it again. Not that the house looked as though it might fall down or be blown away. It had a solid look; there was nothing at all fragile about it. But it did not look as though it belonged where it was, by the edge of the sea.

Mary Ann had a friend who rejoiced when he first saw it. "This is not a house by the sea," he said. "It is certainly not a house in East Hampton. It is somewhere else. It is a town house. No, it is a house in the middle of a forest. The Black Forest, I think. It is a *folie* Whatever it is, it is not real—not a real house, at any rate. And why did they put it sideways?"

Instead of facing the ocean, which was so close that the waves made themselves heard all day and all night, the little house faced its lawn—really only a strip cut from the huge lawn that swept down from the great house on the dunes where the seven children lived, all of them Bluebell's friends. Alongside Mary Ann's house, hidden from her by a tall hedge, there was a lovely, simple flower garden that slanted away from a small apple orchard and into a field of long grass. Bluebell wandered among the apple trees without permission, and without permission the cats had taken the wild field for their hunting ground. On Mary Ann's side of the hedge the flower bed that stretched the length of her lawn was strikingly neglected, but the daffodils and roses and hollyhocks that had been planted there long ago still bloomed at their appointed times, as if to show what they once had been and still might be if somebody would give them a little help.

Sometimes Mary Ann walked from her front door to the grove of pine trees that separated her lawn from the golf course, and as she walked she inspected the tangle of weeds and withered vines that smothered the beds, and she thought, It is a disgrace. But the word disgrace came tranquilly into her mind and caused no uneasiness there. She excused herself from gardening as she did from sewing, simply by announcing she had not the gift for it. She was inclined to be mulish about the things she did not do—not drive a car, not garden, not sew—and it was in something of the same spirit that she congratulated herself as sincerely on what her house lacked as she did on what it held. But in spite of all it lacked, and for all its temporary air, the little house had an air of gaiety about it, and even of welcome. It is the high ceiling, Mary Ann thought, and the books, and the big fireplace, and the mauve rug casts a cheerful light. And in any case, she thought, the house, like me, is good-hearted in spite of itself.

It was absurd, the little house with its baronial front door and its towering diamond-paned windows that had more wood than glass in them, and its lofty black beams that were not very old and not at all necessary, and its scalloped black-iron hasps, and handles, and hinges on all the doors—even on the bathroom door. The hinges were always flying off the doors and landing at Mary Ann's feet with a noisy clank, and she was constantly on her hands and knees searching for the long black spikes that would hold them back on the door until the next fit of humor took them, but she did not mind. The house was always losing bits of itself, and she spent hours trying to find lost pieces of paper—letters, bills, lists, old checkbooks that might tell her where the money had gone, but she persevered just as the house did, and she thought, As long as nobody asks me any questions, everything will come out all right.

Her house was closely related to the house on the dunes where the seven children lived. The children's house was really enormous —hundreds of rooms pressed into the shape of a cottage and covered with a deep shingled roof. It had been put up shortly after the First World War, and at the foot of its majestic lawn its miniature, Mary

Ann's house, had been built for the caretaker. The people who had lived in the big house and employed a caretaker had all gone away long ago, and the seven children had been in possession there for years now.

Mary Ann, the newcomer, did not know exactly when Bluebell and the children had discovered each other. She imagined Bluebell on the grass in the sun one morning, or one afternoon, raising her big head to see a pair of bare legs, several pairs of bare legs, standing at a safe distance and on their own side of the driveway that separated them from Bluebell's private ground. The children must have been on their toes, ready to fly if the strange dog turned fierce. Bluebell was very black, and her ample body was covered with shining flat fur, a handsome coat of it, but her muzzle was gray, and she had a comical look. Comical or not, she had long sharp teeth and great paws that could hold her prey to the ground if she chose to find prey. The children must have wondered about her. Bluebell would not have bothered to wonder. What she saw was what she always saw—not children or birds or cats or mice but interesting new manifestations of the friendliness she believed existed for her in all that lived. If it lived, it moved, and whether it moved by creeping or running or walking or flying or hopping or simply by blowing like torn paper about the lawn, Bluebell wanted it. This new apparition, so near to her and quite unknown, must have struck her with joy. Fourteen legs, seven faces, and a variety of voices, all there just waiting to be claimed. She would have begun her campaign at once, beating a vigorous overture on the ground with her heavy tail.

Mary Ann could only imagine all that. What was certain was that Bluebell no longer decorated the front of the house for hours in the morning and during the afternoon. Now she was always away, off somewhere, following the children into their house and out of it again, and travelling with them along the beach and over the golf course and even into the village. Bluebell had another secret now to lay on top of the eternal secret that was guarded, or imprisoned, by her animal silence. She had a new world of her own that was free of the cats and free of Mary Ann, but she showed her independence of them only at the moment of her departure from the house and the moment of her return to it. These days, when she went out in the morning, she was purposeful, and her eyes turned at once to the house on the dunes to see if anyone was out and about. And when she came back and her own door was opened to her, she burst in, breathless, and threw herself on the floor, unable to speak for exhaustion and importance. While she panted, her tail hammered on the floor and her eyes roved wildly around the room, reclaiming everything she saw, but most of all reclaiming Mary Ann. "I choose you," Bluebell's eyes said to Mary Ann, "you, you," and her gaze turned fervently to the kitchen, where her dinner waited.

The cats showed a faint, lazy interest in all this commotion. The biggest of them, the bright orange, sat up and then stood up and stretched, and lay down again, wrapping himself up in his own coat. "I am ignoring you," each cat said, opening its eyes just enough to show a gleam of light, and then, closing its eyes again, each cat said, as always, "I choose myself."

But the moment had arrived when East Hampton, with its waves and sand and its wide golf course and its ponds of wild water birds and its fine main street and its hilly green graveyard, was about to be revealed all over again by the new light. Mary Ann heard the first birds, the smallest ones, who sing suddenly at the end of darkness. She listened to their sweet voices, and then she stood up and went to open the front door. It was still night out, but the darkness had retreated into the bushes and trees. She could see the sky shifting. It was the moment she liked, because it proved she was right and that nothing was real. It was also the moment when the cats went out to kill. She looked around the room and saw the big orange, the little black favorite, the longhaired wild one, and the quiet calico.

Only Tom, the secret hunter, was absent. Tom hunted alone and far away and never, thank God, brought his little victims into the house. Mary Ann walked through the empty blue-floored room that led to her small kitchen and heated a saucepan of milk and gave it to the cats, hoping to lull them back to sleep and sloth. She turned out the light in the kitchen and saw the dim blue world outside. It was nearly time for the sea gulls to start their march inland. She would have liked to go outside to watch them, but the one morning she had gone out, her long white robe had startled them, and they had risen up in outrage and gone away screeching that their day was ruined.

She went upstairs and stood at her bedroom window, which faced the sea. The sea gulls were just appearing, coming in from the beach and lining up along the top of the long rise that banked the road going down to the sea. They began to walk at once, taking their usual path, which brought them at an angle across the golf course and down the children's lawn to Mary Ann's house. Now the golf course was ghostly with them, and they continued to advance, white birds that whitened and grew bigger as they drew closer. They all walked. The few that flew up descended to the ground at once and started walking again. Some sailed while they walked, showing their wings. They came this way every morning, sometimes more of them and sometimes fewer, and the leaders always stopped at the far edge of the narrow driveway that separated her lawn from the children's. A few steps more would have brought the sea gulls to the walls of her house, but they never took the last few steps, and no matter how close they came they always seemed to be very far away. They walked like emperors, or like jockeys, or like stoics. They knew the ocean, and kept vigil by it in regimental rows, and they screamed against patience, and walked for their health on expensive grass, and Mary Ann thought they knew themselves and she was baffled by them. They were indomitable. There was no need to fear for them or pity them. In her imagination they were living stones that had found wings to save themselves during some long and drastic fall in forgotten times.

Now the leaders reached the edge of the driveway, the limit of their walk, and paused, and there was a general pause all the way back across the lawn and the golf course, and then they all rose up and flew back to the sea. To watch the sea gulls go was like watching the snow stop falling. You couldn't say when the last flake fell, and you could not mark the last sea gull. Mary Ann turned from the window and looked at her bed, which was very large and took up most of the room. She had closed the bedroom door after her, but Bluebell had slipped in with her and was now curled humbly on a corner of the pink quilt. "All right, Bluebell," Mary Ann said, "as long as you're here," and she lay down and pulled the quilt over her and fell asleep, knowing unrepentantly that the sun had risen.

Late in the morning, wide awake and dressed at last, she heard the children on her front lawn, and she went out to wish them a happy Fourth of July. The children were going to the big fireworks display in the evening. Mary Ann was not going. The children teased Bluebell while they talked to Mary Ann, and as they talked they straggled irresolutely toward the driveway. They were on their way to the pond to take a boat out, but they were delaying. They were taking their time. Like Mary Ann, they had all the time in the world today. It was the Fourth of July, and the hours were turning in slow motion. There was nothing to do that had to be done, except wait for the fireworks to begin, and the children were finding time for long farewells to Bluebell, who could not go in the boat with them because she was too heavy. "Too heavy and too slippery," the eldest boy said. One time they had taken her in the boat, and she rocked them all around the pond.

The youngest girl, Linnet, spoke up. "Bluebell might have drowned us all," she said.

Linnet was only six. When the others walked, she dawdled behind them or ran after them, and when they stood as they were standing now, she stood in front of them, or at the side, apart from them. She was kneeling at the moment, in the grass beside Bluebell, who sat with her front feet apart and her gaze fixed worshipfully on the eldest boy, the leader in everything but particularly in this boating expedition from which she understood she was to be excluded. She had heard the ban (Bluebell is to *stay*), and she was determined to shame him into changing his mind. But the eldest boy was looking at Linnet, who had announced that Bluebell might have drowned them all. "Listen to her," he said scornfully. "She wasn't even there."

The second boy came out of the reverie in which he spent most of his time. "She's talking through her hat," he said with finality.

Linnet's elder sister, Alice, who was eight and very responsible, looked tolerantly at Linnet. "She wasn't even there," Alice said. "I wasn't there, either," she added sensibly.

"I only said *might* have," Linnet said, and went on stroking Bluebell's anxious, unresponsive neck.

Mary Ann looked at Bluebell, who might have been a murderess. "Bluebell only wanted to drown you so that she could save you," she said.

The second boy emerged from his reverie for the second time, this time in a seizure of decisiveness. "Let's go," he said, so abruptly that Mary Ann thought they would all start running, but they still delayed, moving their feet in anticipation.

Bluebell accepted her fate with dignity. She sank to the ground, composed her paws, and began to gaze coldly past the children's legs at something they couldn't see even if they tried.

Linnet stood up. "I wish it was time to go to the fireworks now," she said. "I have matches. I found them in the road." She put her hand into the pocket of her dress and took out a battered white match folder.

Mary Ann took it from her and opened it. The heads of the matches were crumbling, they had been rained on, and they were quite useless. She handed the folder back to Linnet, who returned it carefully to her pocket. "I hope your mother knows you have those matches, Linnet," Mary Ann said. "You know matches are forbidden."

"But they're for the fireworks," Linnet said, and her face took on the dull expression of one who remembers this argument from other times, and the frustration of it, and sees more frustration ahead.

The boys were moving off, laughing unkindly. "She thinks they're going to run out of matches at the fireworks," the eldest boy said, and the youngest boy doubled up in noisy mirth.

Even Alice, who was so serious, had to smile. "Linnet, you know those matches were run over by a car and *everything,*"she said.

Linnet's faith in her matches was evident in the bitter look she gave them all. But she had her triumph in her pocket, and she was stubborn. She could afford to wait for vindication, and enjoy the last laugh.

The boys set off backwards and gradually turned until they were really walking off. "See you later," they called to Mary Ann.

One of them called, "Goodbye, Bluebell," and poor Bluebell betrayed herself, starting to attention and staring after them, so tense and ready that for an instant she looked like the royal hunting dog she might have been and sometimes thought she was, in her sleep, when she stirred and seemed to run, while her gruff baying showed the course and splendor of her dreams.

"Stay, Bluebell, good dog," Mary Ann said.

"Come on, Linnet," Alice said, and ran off after her brothers.

"No, wait a minute, Linnet," Mary Ann said. She wanted to tell Linnet the truth, that the matches were no good, and to prove to her that they were no good, but instead she said feebly, "You know, you shouldn't have those matches, Linnet."

"But I found them on the road," Linnet said.

"All right, well, I hope you have a nice boat ride."

"I will," Linnet said, keeping her hand in her precious pocket. "Goodbye, Miss Whitty," she said politely, and she ran off.

Mary Ann watched her running, going more and more slowly as she drew near to the little group waiting impatiently for her by the edge of the road. The road was busy with cars driving down to the beach and driving away from it. The golf course was dotted with figures that moved gravely and then stood still, gravely considering the next move. It is not a very funny game, Mary Ann thought. She wished she had had the courage to show Linnet that her hopes were not only all false but all wrong, considering that they were based on matches that were strictly forbidden. I should have told her, Mary Ann thought sadly. No matter how you look at it, I should have made her see. I don't think they light fireworks with matches, and even if they do they won't run out of them, and even if they run out, Linnet will be much too far out in the crowd to help and even if she got a chance to offer the matches, the matches are no good. One way or another, she is going to be disappointed. But false hope feels the same as real hope, and she is going to have a nice day dreaming. She's not going to have a chance at the fireworks, but that doesn't alter the fact that I should have given her a lecture on obedience and a demonstration of what happens to matches that have been lying out on the road in the rain.

Mary Ann went into her house and let the screen door bang behind her. Bluebell dreamed of rescuing people from drowning, and Linnet dreamed of saving the fireworks extravaganza from disaster, and Mary Ann dreamed of being able to persuade a proud six-year-old girl that when the choice must be made between being a heroine and being a good child, one always chooses to be a good child. Well, I'll see Linnet again before the display, Mary Ann thought, and I'll tell her about the matches. She'll be so excited by that time that she won't care. I'll make a point of seeing her. But I should have told her. I should never have let her go off like that. Linnet and the matches went out of her mind. What came into her mind was the house she stood in, which seemed now like a beached ship, stuck in the middle of the summer weather that only Bluebell was really at home in. The little house was very quiet. Buttoned up in its diamonds, with its shingled roof pulled down about its ears and its left shoulder turned to the ocean, the house seemed to enjoy the summer sun cautiously, as though it knew it wasn't a summer house, and not a seaside house, and, in fact, not a real house. And it wasn't a real house. It wasn't a bit real. The living room, where Mary Ann stood, had been copied from the set of some opera or operetta—*Hansel and Gretel*, Mary Ann had heard, although she would have guessed *Lilac Time*. Whatever it was, and operetta or not, the performance must have depended on a good deal of coming and going, people appearing and disappearing and hurrying through from right to left and from left to right, or looking in, talking, perhaps singing, through the enormous windows in the back wall. A small flight of steps led up and off to the right and another small flight to the left. The living room had five ways out—five exits. Eight, if you counted the diamond-paned windows, which were big enough for two people to vault, scramble, or leap through at one time. Nine exits, if you allowed the fireplace, which was roomy enough to walk around in and had a chimney that was as big around as a barrel and went straight up through the roof like a tunnel. Mary Ann thought the chimney probably *was* a tunnel, mislaid from another stage set in another house someplace else. *Journey's End?* As a chimney the tunnel did very well. She had no complaints about the fireplace. As a matter of fact, she had no complaints at all, but she could not help wondering what had been going on in the mind of the architect when he made his scale drawing for this room. He had got in all that the action of the operetta called for. There never was so much big detail in a room. Doors and windows and fireplace all stood out in their full theatrical size, all surrounded with big frames of blackened wood, so that you could see from a mile away what you were looking at. Only, there was no room left for walls. The architect forgot about the walls.

Mary Ann didn't care. It didn't matter. The room pleased her. She had grown fond of it. It was improbable and impermanent, and anyway it was only a stage designed for dialogue and gestures, with two small rooms right and left that were also full of doors and windows, and that were good only for lingering in, because they were anterooms, and as anterooms they resisted furniture the way a cat will resist a collar. Mary Ann had tried several arrangements, but at the moment both rooms were empty. The room with the mauve floor was empty, and the one with the shining dark-blue floor that led to the kitchen was empty. Anterooms were new in Mary Ann's life, and she wanted to have them always. She had not known that rooms could be so content with themselves. But she wondered what the original caretaker had thought when he first stepped into his brand-new living room, with its operatic humility and its need to be explained and its obvious falseness and its meager fate; because it did not even represent a dream but was only the echo of somebody's memory of romantic escape—to a hunting lodge, a mountain hideaway in Austria, or a secret place in Switzerland. It was a wistful conceit, and it stood here only because this site had presented itself and a house was needed here, for the caretaker. Someone must have thought, Since I cannot have that place at all, I might as well have it here, where I can at least look at it. The little house was not real. It was only a facade that stood at the end of somebody's lawn, and Mary Ann thought it did wonderfully for a person who wanted to live by the Atlantic Ocean but who only wanted to live there for a while.

Late in the afternoon, Mary Ann went upstairs to sleep for a half hour, and she slept so late that she was awakened by the first of the explosions from the fireworks display. It was dusk outside her window, and a few minutes later, standing on the high ground of the children's lawn, where she had a good view of the aerial lights, she felt that the night was cold. A cool, quick wind blew in from the sea. She would build herself a fire when she went back into the house. Bluebell, dutiful, sat beside her, and stared as she did into the distance, where they saw the sky brighten after explosions they heard but could not see, and then they saw shooting stars, streams of brilliance, and dazzling ribbons of color that turned into balloons and garlands and cornucopias as they ascended, to hang for an instant at their highest point and then vanish in glory.

Nearer to Mary Ann, on the beach below the children's house, some people were having a private display, a very minor one. A few arrows of light shot up, and then again, more arrows. Someone was walking on the beach, throwing sparklers as he went. Lawbreakers, Mary Ann thought, disobedient people; everyone is committing sins today.

It had grown very dark, and she had had enough of the fireworks, the legal ones and the illegal ones. Time to go home and make a fire, but instead she went inside and made a Martini. She tasted it. It was delicious, but she had made it too soon, and she left it in the freezing compartment while she virtuously washed string-beans and lettuce and turned up the heat in the oven. All the time she was working, she enjoyed the attention of six pairs of animal eyes, five pairs solemn and the sixth pair, Bluebell's, devotional. Every night, Mary Ann gave her cooking demonstration, providing the cats and Bluebell with their favorite entertainment, and every night, as she chopped and peeled and arranged her saucepans on top of the stove, she wondered if it was better to go to a restaurant and have a plate of food brought to you and know that the vegetables will be dreadful or to cook for yourself. While making up her mind, she had become an expert in very small plain dinners, and it was with some complacency that she left her work in progress, retrieved her Martini, and returned through her blue-floored anteroom to her living room, where she proceeded to build a big fire. The flames blazed up, filling the room with shadows, and as she stood back to watch them she heard the fire alarm sound far away. Somebody's house going up, she thought; it always happens on the Fourth of July.

She was quite wrong. It was not *somebody's* house that the alarm was sounding for but the seven children's house, and if Mary Ann had left her front door open, as she often did, even in the winter time, she would have seen the air outside filled with smoke that was billowing down in great clouds from the big house on the dunes. Great excitement was gathering at her windows, and she missed it all. She missed seeing the first engine come hurtling across the flat green and watery landscaped land that stretched from her right all the way back to the sky. On a dark night like this, with all its lights going, the engine must have been a wonderful sight. All lighted up, racing to the rescue, and followed by a second engine and then by a third. Mary Ann missed it all, and she missed seeing the swarm of small cars that flew after the engines and turned with them into her narrow driveway, which was full of holes and long deep ruts like trenches, so that they were all slowed up, coming along one after the other so close together that they might have been sections of a caterpillar. It was a very long, narrow driveway. At the best of times there was room only for one ordinary car. The driveway turned at a right angle from the road that led to the sea and came straight through the golf course and between the lawns to Mary Ann's house, where it made a sharp right turn and disappeared between two dense walls of trees and bushes that led up to the children's house and the sea. Those trees were full of pheasants, and if you walked up that dark curving avenue on a summer night, the wild beating of indignant wings drowned out the sound of the waves that beat out their slower measure on the beach below the children's house. What the pheasants must have thought on this night on the Fourth of July was unimaginable. First they were enveloped in clouds of thick smoke, and then came the invasion by heavy machinery. And all Mary Ann was thinking about was whether or not to put the screen back in front of the fire she had made, or leave the fireplace open and risk sparks on the rug. She was putting the screen back when she heard the first of the engines come lurching and rumbling past her house, and she thought, What a big oil truck. But then came more rumbling and grinding, and she thought, Armored cars.

She ran to the door and opened it and ran out on her lawn, to find that the lawn had vanished. She was hostess to a long line of cars that had pulled in and parked in a neat row with their noses turned toward the big house, and the driveway was so jammed with firefighting cars and apparatus that she could not have crossed over to the children's lawn even if she had wanted to. The smoke was thick, but the children's house was visible, standing up against the night sky with all its lights on. If the lights are on, perhaps things are not so bad, Mary Ann thought, and she saw the miles of floor boards up there, and the deep shingled roof that would blaze up like a torch if a spark caught it. The smoke now seemed to be coming from behind the house. Perhaps it was only a grass fire.

She walked over to the nearest of the cars that were parked by her house and said foolishly, "What's going on?"

The driver glanced at her and then looked back at the house. "Fire up there," he said. The car was full of children, and they all stared out at Mary Ann. She walked away from them, and called Bluebell to follow her. She thought, There is that man has driven in here, tripping up the Fire Department, and now he's trapped here with all those children, and they may not get out until morning.

The avenue of trees that hid the approach to the big house ended just short of the house and to the side of it and out from the shadows up there a small fire car appeared and careered wildly down the children's lawn and across the golf course and was gone. It was followed immediately by another, and then Mary Ann saw that her driveway had been cleared from the pine grove back to the sea road and that the cars lined up in front of her were starting, tentatively, to edge their way back, going out backwards. A tall man in a helmet appeared and ordered the cars parked on Mary Ann's lawn to leave. He was very short with them and she was very glad. She would say to him, "But I live here," she thought, and then she wondered if he would order her to go into her house. Would he be within his rights, ordering her into the house? She began to worry about what she would do if he pointed to her house and said to her, "You get in there and shut that door." She had the right to stand on her own lawn, she knew that, but on the other hand it was hardly the moment to have an argument with a fireman. His colleagues on wheels were making desperate attempts to extricate themselves from the driveway and from one another. Backwards and forwards they went, and none of them moved. It was all the fault of the cars that had joined them for fun, and tied them up. Mary Ann thought of the confusion that must exist on the shrouded avenue leading up to the house. Then, away up at the house, one of the big engines appeared and tore down the lawn and away. The fire was really over. But the cars nearest to her were still stuck, and she thought that in a minute they would all start barking in frustration. The man in the helmet had cleared her lawn and he did not appear to have seen her. All the same, taking no chances, Mary Ann spoke to Bluebell and they both retreated into the house and shut the door. Then Mary Ann looked out through the smallest diamond-paned window. What with the thickness of the window frame and the darkness outside and the angle she was looking from, she couldn't see much, but she had already seen enough to know what was going on. Another big engine shot into sight and out again, vanishing on the far side of the pine grove. A little more to the left and he would have gone down in one of those deep sand craters on the golf course. He could have struggled all night without getting out. The other cars were getting out as best they could, and then they were all gone, but disorder still hung in the air. Over the well-cut lawns that surrounded the golf course, and over the polite undulations of the course itself, and over the clubhouse that sat in wary hospitality on its eminence high above the dunes—over all of these particular human arrangements, Chaos stirred, and smiled, and went back to sleep. What a Fourth of July, Mary Ann thought, and wondered why the firemen had cut their sirens off.

In the morning she was awakened by the sea gulls, who were making more noise than usual because, she thought, they were coming closer to the house than usual. But when she got to the window she saw that they had already turned and were flying back to the sea, protesting all the way against everything. There was mist out and they vanished into it. It had rained in the night, and the holes in the driveway were filled with silver water. Last night the fire engines had bumped in and out of those holes, today the birds would bathe in them. She wondered if the lawns had been much damaged by the traffic. There were car marks on her lawn, nothing serious, and the children's lawn, when she got downstairs, looked all right. The house looked all right, too, and there was Linnet, in her white nightgown, running wildly down the lawn. "Linnet," Mary Ann said, "come into the house at once. Put this shawl around you. Do you know what time it is? It's not six o'clock yet. I saw the fire engines. Was there much damage to the house?"

"I called them," Linnet said. "I was the only one that thought of the telephone."

"That's wonderful, Linnet."

"It was only a grass fire," Linnet said.

"Even so," Mary Ann said. "You saved the house. That is really marvelous. That's wonderful, Linnet."

Linnet had been first to the telephone. While the rest of the family stood transfixed with horror, staring at the grass, she had rushed to the phone and called the fire brigade. What had happened was that something, perhaps a spark from the stray fireworks Mary Ann had seen, had caught the brush below the house and suddenly it had all flared up. They had just arrived home from the fireworks, and they had all gone onto their terrace overlooking the sea, and while the others stared at the sheet of flame that suddenly rose up and became a wall and rose higher as they watched it, Linnet called for help. "Then you saved the house," Mary Ann said. Linnet nodded modestly. "And now you're going to have a glass of milk," Mary Ann said, "and you're going to go straight home and back to bed, before your mother finds out that you're gone. You must go home at once."

"Bluebell has nice paws," Linnet said.

"I know," Mary Ann said. "Now don't sit down, Linnet. You really must come outside, and I'll watch you up to the house. Go in the front door, so that I can see you safely home. Keep the shawl around you."

When they were outside, Mary Ann said, "That's wonderful that you saved the house, Linnet. It's really great." The hem of her robe was wet from the wet grass, and there was Linnet in her bare feet. "Now you *must* hurry home," she said.

"May I come back to see you?" Linnet asked.

Mary Ann looked at her. Linnet was small and friendly, and Mary Ann, who feared trustfulness, had often rebuffed her, but now she put her hands out and tightened the shawl around the little shoulders. "Yes," she said, "but right now, this minute, you must run home. Your mother will be frightened if she finds you not in your bed. Then come back later and tell me everything about the fire. I'll have questions ready. All right?"

"All right," Linnet said, and she started off. When she had crossed to her own lawn, she turned and waved, and Mary Ann waved back. She watched the child running and walking and then running again. It was a long way up that lawn. Mary Ann thought, I had a chance to do the right thing yesterday and I am very glad I failed, and I hope the same chance does not come my way again for a long time. She thought of a joke. "Never put off till tomorrow what you should have done yesterday," she said to herself, and she went placidly into the house to put on the water for her coffee.

Afternoon in Summer

Sylvia Townsend Warner

He became aware that Sally had emerged from her book and was about to say something.

"Murder is an occupational risk for prostitutes."

"Hmmm," said he, clinging to the thread of his calculations. They grew so engrossing that when next she spoke it took him by surprise.

"And for wives, too—though not so much."

Inwardly assenting, Willie asked, "What on earth are you reading now?"

"A book about all the murders committed in the last thirty years. I got it from the public library."

"Is it interesting?"

"Yes. In rather a stark way. Just facts and sentences."

"Sounds enthralling."

"But murder is not so much of an occupational risk for murderers. I mean, they mostly aren't hanged. Of course, that's a good thing."

He looked at Sally's sleek flaxen hear, now bent over her book again. Though he was still young, still a student, he was a year older than she and found her artless sophistications touching. It was as though the mental processes beneath that hood of silken hair were as sleek, as smoothly disposed, as childishly combed and clean.

He worked on. She read. The alarm clock ticked. After an hour had passed he realised that it was two-thirty and that he was unfed.

"Are there any cases in your nice book about husbands who ate their wives? I'd like to know their sentences."

"Oh, Willie, are you hungry?"

Her gaze rested on him, calmly attentive, as if this were another interesting social phenomenon. She put a marker in the book and closed it. He cleared his papers off the table and laid them on the floor. The dwelling they had rented for the summer vacation was advertised as "self-contained". It was so self-contained that the only place for their bicycles was in the bathroom-kitchenette. Skirting the bicycles, Sally now opened a small refrigerator, and considered its contents: a heel of cheese, some rye biscuit, one tomato. She put these on a tray and after further consideration added salt.

The tomato was scrupulously shared between them. It seemed of an Oriental richness and succulence.

"I had a shopping list. But when I was halfway there this morning I remembered the bloody grocer shuts on Thursdays."

"May Hell be hot for him," said Willie, mildly. "Never mind, I'll tell you what we'll do. We'll cycle along the road towards Cowfold, and have an enormous tea at The Goat."

"That inn we passed with the roses?"

"*And* the check curtains."

"*And* the frogs."

"*And* the milking stool."

There was no such adventitious rusticity about the dacha they had rented from Miss Hobson, professor of Lit. Hum. at Willie's red-brick university. Plain as a packing case, with an air of having lost all interest in going further, it stood at the end of a long flinty track across flinty fields of sugar beet. "Wonderful views of the sky," Miss Hobson had remarked.

With only one puncture, they reached the crossroads and turned towards Cowfold. The sun beat on their backs, midges stuck to their faces. Strong Indian tea and strawberries and cream, thought Sally. Strong Indian tea, plum cake, and ham sandwiches, thought Willie. The Goat appeared in the heavens, motionless on its signpost against a glaring blue sky. There were roses, there was a lily pond, with concrete frogs. They dismounted. Swaying with hunger and heat-stroke, they walked up the crazy-paving path. On the doors was a notice: "NO TEAS".

Sally moaned and sank down on the milking stool.

Willie looked at his watch. "Twenty to five," he said. "They're legally bound to open at six. We'll kill time till then. Think of those poor wretches who go to the moon."

"And there'll be a church somewhere. We haven't passed one, so we shall come to one. Churches are cool."

When they had soaked their handkerchiefs in the lily pond and washed off the midges, they rode on, came to the church, went in, sat down. Its proportions were ideal: it was larger than Miss Hobson's packing case, not so large as the face of nature. And somewhere about it a bell was ringing in a calm liturgical way.

"I can't understand why people don't make more use of their churches."

"Sectarianism," said Willie. "I don't suppose anyone will come near this place till Harvest Festival."

"Which is phallic, isn't it?"

At that moment an approaching voice remarked, "We brought nothing into this world, and it is certain we can carry nothing out. The Lord gave and the Lord hath taken away; blessed be the name of the Lord."

It was also certain that they could not escape; for a surpliced clergyman came in, preceding the coffin borne on the shoulders of six heated men in black cloth suits, and followed by a small group of partially blackened mourners. The coffin was put down on trestles and its wreaths adjusted, the mourners, stumbling over hassocks, filed into the front pews, the clergyman glided into the reading desk and began: "I said, I will take heed of my ways: that I offend not in my tongue," to which the clerk responded hastily, "I will keep my mouth as it were with a bridle, while the ungodly is in my sight."

It seemed to Sally that the clerk's glance aimed these words at her bare head and her blue slacks; in fact, Mr Hicks was scanning the congregation with a professional eye for mourners whose grief might get out of hand. The corpse had been bad enough. At no time did the Reverend favour long-departed parishioners being brought back to take up room that the churchyard could ill spare, to cause upheavals in family graves that the course of time had flattened into an easy surface for the grass-cutter, to bring nearer the dreaded day of an extension encroaching on the rectory kitchen garden. The least they could do was to be punctual; and Charles Joliffe was almost three hours overdue, the hearse breaking down and none of them rightly knowing the way. *I became dumb and opened not ... When thou with rebukes dost chasten* ... Me to the life, thought Mr Hicks—the responses snatched from his lips before he'd half finished them. He would have his work cut out to keep up with Reverend, crackling ahead like a gorse fire. And if Reverend was like this in a verse and verse psalm, what wouldn't he be in the Epistle, with the reins thrown over his neck and the smell of his stable, which in this case was his tea, not to say his dry martini, firing his heels through the Fifteenth Corinthians?

... forasmuch-as-ye-know-that-your-labour-is-not-in-vain-in-the--Lord.

The coffin was lifted; its direction was reversed in a peculiar dance by the bearers. Preceded by the clergyman, followed by the mourners, it loomed down the aisle, it went past. One of the mourners paused beside Sally and Willie. "Thank you so much for coming," she said. "It was so kind of you." She hurried after the rest.

"That was a near thing," said Willie. Sally nodded. He got up and began to read the pamphlets displayed on a table near the entrance. Presently he went to the door and peered out. "Still at it," he mouthed; and wandered off to read mural tablets in the chancel. There was a sound of cars being started up. Running down the aisle where the coffin had gone so cumbrously, he whisked her into the porch just as the clergyman came in by a side door, pulling off his surplice.

"Do you think he's a vicar or a rector?" said Sally, averting her eyes from the raw earth, the tumbled wreaths. "They ought to wear some distinguishing badge, like pips in the Army. And, of course, there are curates." Her brave conversational voice snapped like a fiddle string. "Oh Willie, Willie! It's so awful." She burst into tears and clung to him. He patted her shoulder, smoothed her burrowing head, and started at a smart new headstone. *Helena. Beloved Wife of Hubert Wilkins. Aged 71. At Rest.*

It only left Sally fifty more.

"So awful. Why can't one just be cremated without having to die?"

It seemed a quite rational aspiration.

"The chances of a sudden death must be going up by leaps and bounds," he said. "Come, my darling, let's get out of this blackmailing churchyard."

They found a lane and wandered along it till they came to a gate into a meadow. In the meadow was a large sycamore. They lay down in its shade. Forgetting that they were mortal, forgetting that they were hungry, not noticing that they were lying above an ants' nest, they began to make love. He licked the delicious salt off her cheeks, she nibbled his nose. They fell asleep, and woke, vaguely wondering why they were there, and made love again. He cut an "S" and a "W" on the bole of the tree and framed them in a heart and finished off the heart with an arrow; and when they had vowed to come back every year on the seventeenth of July, they bicycled to The Goat and drank dog's-nose and ate small porkpies of the meanest possible description with such abstracted greed that, as the barman said later to the waitress, it was plain to see what those two had been up to.

The Fortune Teller

MURIEL SPARK

The château lay among woodlands in a wide valley in the heart of the old Troubadour country of France. It was about ten years ago at the end of summer.

We were a party of three, Raymond, his wife Sylvia, and me, Lucy. The marriage between Raymond and Sylvia was already going bad, which made me very uncomfortable. I had already decided after the third day of our travels that I would never again go on holiday alone with a married couple, and I never have since.

I had begun to wonder why they had asked me to join them and I fairly guessed that they were trying to prove, by the evidence of my single state, that they were truly a couple. We arrived at the château after a week in France, by which time I was on the point of getting on a train to the nearest airport and so back to London.

But I changed my mind precisely at the château. Sylvia asked for rooms. Mme Dessain, thin, tall, work-worn and elegant, who had come round the side of the house with a bucket of pig-swill in her hand to greet us, declined to answer Sylvia. She addressed me, saying very politely that yes, she had a double room for me and my husband and a small room for Mlle on the maids' floor at the top of the house. Raymond intervened to explain the relationships aright. She gave a sort of smile by which it was plain she had understood perfectly well. I supposed that Sylvia, who spoke French better than I did, had nevertheless lacked the required respect; she had taken Mme Dessain for one of the hired hands, and had selected her tone accordingly. This was a habit of Sylvia's; I always marvelled at the trouble she must have put into harbouring such a range of initial attitudes as she had for different people, when one alone would serve for all. She was, of course, a follower of Lenin who was class-conscious by profession. Raymond was fairly neutral about the incident. He was big hearted and bearded, a television producer; and he was intelligent. But he was vain enough, and perhaps sufficiently at the point of exasperation with his marriage to show himself pleased with the proprietor's mistake, if mistake it was. Madame did not apologize; she merely told us the price of the rooms and asked if we wanted demi-pension. Sylvia, when angry, had a leer. Her teeth protruded and for some reason she dyed her hair bright red. In spite of this she had a handsome look. But, leering, she looked, to me, morally low, very low, and stupid although in fact she was a rodent-biologist of some distinction.

Mme Dessain put down the bucket and again addressed me. She asked me if I would like to see the rooms. Plainly, she was not too grand to be catty and she had taken against Sylvia.

"Have we decided to stay?" Sylvia said to Raymond. "Do you like the place?" "It looks lovely," he said, "I would like to see the room anyway, because I would like to stay."

Mme Dessain led the way upstairs. I followed with my two clever friends behind me. The rooms were fine and we all decided to stay. Strangely enough I wasn't put in a maid's room upstairs, but in a large room on the same floor as my friends. Madame—it turned out that she was in fact a marquise—ran down to get on with her jobs, leaving us to cope with our luggage. I thought she looked well over fifty when I had first seen her but watching her trip so easily downstairs I could see she was younger, not much over forty. She had obviously taken a dislike to Sylvia, but I didn't care. Already

I felt free of the embarrassing couple. I am curious way Mme Dessain had released me. She had held out a straw. I clutched it and miraculously it held me up. It struck me she was highly intuitive, as indeed are so many in the hotel business.

I was delighted with my room. It had windows on two sides. The furniture was French Provincial, plainly belonging to the eighteenth-century château and by no means brought in for hotel guests. It was much the same all over the house. There were two drawing-rooms, the yellow one and the green, and these were by no means rustic, but in the great high style of eighteenth-century France. There was an Oriental room with a Chinese part and an Egyptian part, full of those furnishings and treasures brought back from the travels of nineteenth-century ancestors, which are too good for the use of ordinary tourists yet not too rare for everyday accommodation. It was a satisfaction to feel we had been taken in as guests, since plainly Mme Dessain had to be discriminate.

Few of the guests used the Oriental room, or the other priceless-seeming rooms with their Sèvres ornaments and plates behind glass cabinets. There was a more serviceable library in general use, with a television set, tables, and plenty of worn, cretonne-covered sofas and chairs.

It was there that a few evenings later I offered to tell Mme Dessain's fortune by cards. People were grouped around, after dinner, some just talking, others playing various card games and a couple in a far corner were playing chess. Outside it was pelting with heavy thick rain; it had been raining all day. A small, stout, elderly man was Mme Dessain's husband; a surprising couple. He sat by her side while I told her fortune. Sylvia and Raymond, bored with my fortune-telling, had moved away.

I must explain that when I find myself in a country or seaside establishment of the residential sort on any of my many travels, if I see someone lonely or ill at ease, and obviously not enjoying their stay, I always offer to tell their fortune by my cards. I've never been refused. On the contrary, it tends to have a hypnotic effect on the other guests, and candidates for my fortune-telling are never wanting; they even come up to me and ask me what I charge, and when I explain that I do it for free, they are slightly embarrassed, but want their fortune just the same, and politely accept being put off when I've had too much or for some reason don't want to do it.

My peculiar method for fortune-telling follows no tradition of occult sciences; I follow rules, but they are my own secret ones, varying quite a lot in their application and to each individual. They are my own secret rules but they arise from deep conviction. They cannot be formulated, they are as sincere and indescribable as are the primary colours; they are not of a science but of an art. Very often I make a mistake, but I know it; at such moments I'm thinking my way, talking through dense fog, shining the torch of my intuition here and there until it hits on some object which may or may not prove to be what I say it is. Sometimes my predictions are wildly astray as they pertain to the present time and environment, but I have known them to become surprisingly true much later in life, in a different place, and presume that this may happen, too, in some cases when I lose sight of the person whose fortune I have told.

For the actual selection of the cards I have a precise system. I should never reveal it in detail, except to say that it is based on sevens and fives. Sevens and fives; and if you should ask me any more about this initial stage of the proceedings I should tell you a falsehood; indeed the whole of the process is most precious-fragile to me, and I wouldn't give it away lest I should lose my powers. I mean what Yeats meant:

I have spread my dreams under your feet;
Tread softly because you tread on my dreams.

To tell the cards I begin by asking my client to shuffle them. Then I deal according to my seven and five system; a varying number of cards which emerge from this process are set apart and I ask my client to shuffle again. Again I deal and set apart, and a third time, three cycles in all. The client then shuffles the cards which have been set aside; these are the cards of his fortune. At the same time the client is asked to make a silent wish, and mightily concentrate on it.

Now, I take these cards and again deal them. You mustn't think that because I take my gifts seriously, I take them solemnly. It is all an airy dream of mine, unsinkable because it is light. I don't play the eerie fortune-teller at all; I don't play anything when I tell the cards; I am simply myself.

Well, I take the cards that have fallen to my client's lot and deal them under the following headings: (1) the secret self; (2) the known self (by which I mean, the more limited aspect of the person as he is observable by others); (3) the client's hopes; (4) the client's degree of self-ignorance; (5) his present destination (I don't say his "destiny" for this reason, that any destiny I might take from the cards would be prematurely conceived and would fail to allow for a client's probable divergence from his present destination. Circumstances change. There can be a change of heart. Human nature is essentially unpredictable in the long run. But "destination" none the less often answers for destiny. No clairvoyant, believe me, can say more); (6) affairs of the heart, which means the prevailing love; that is, of any object, including, from time to time, that of money; (7) the wish— will it or won't it come true?

Again I see Mme Dessain in the friendly library of her house leaning over the table, those many years ago, with her husband by her side as I began to tell her cards.

While she was shuffling I saw that she was extremely punctilious about the performance. While I dealt and discarded according to my secret method she watched me with an intensity that meant, to me, a decided confidence in my powers. Her wish was evidently of critical importance. She seemed absorbed by the cards that fell to constitute her fortune, but I advised her light-heartedly not to give weight to them herself, to concentrate hard on the wish, and to leave the interpretation in due time to me.

"There are many spades," observed Mme Dessain. "And there is an ace of spades, Madame." I was puzzled as to why she insisted on addressing me as "Madame" when I was plainly "Mademoiselle". I was dealing the third cycle. In my conjuring out of the meaning of cards I never go by the tradition. It is true that no one is delighted by the ace of spades but it does not necessarily mean a personal death. It might mean the death of a hope, or the end of a fear. Everything depends on the combination. Anyway, I was dealing the third cycle. I said, "Leave it to me," and finished.

Now I gathered up Mme Dessain's cards.

"Will the rain never stop?" said Mme Dessain, her eyes wandering to the enormous French windows. She was putting this on, this absent air as if she didn't care in the least about her fortune.

"Concentrate on your wish, Madame," I said.

"Oh, I am concentrating. The rain is a tourist attraction if they like the flooded fields, very beautiful." So she laughed off her fortune-telling, but I could see she was eager, even a little agitated. Her husband, too, watched with care. I wanted to remind them it was only a game, but I refrained; I didn't want to bring their nervousness to light.

I dealt the cards under their seven headings, which naturally

I didn't pronounce. Thirteen cards had emerged from the process of selection. I noticed the high proportion of court cards in Mme Dessain's set.

Now, in the first round to her secret self, came up the eight of spades, to her known self the six of spades.

"Spades in my wish!" said Mme Dessain immediately.

"Have patience," I said, setting forth the cards. It was obvious to me now that she was trying to penetrate my method for when I put down the king of hearts she said, "a fair, handsome lover." But I gave no sign, although I felt annoyed at the interruption.

Her cards finally came out as follows:

Secret self: eight of spades and six of clubs
Known self: six of spades and nine of diamonds
Things hoped for: king of hearts and ace of spaces
Self-ignorance: five of hearts and king of clubs
Present destination: queen of hearts and three of hearts
Affairs of the heart: queen of clubs and three of diamonds
The wish: knave of hearts.

Mme Dessain was really perplexed. She saw all seven sets of cards placed out before her, but she had no way of guessing the private headings I had placed them under. Her eyes were bright upon the cards as if she were telling my fortune, not me hers.

"You have got your wish," I said at once, seeing that she had come in for one card only, the knave of hearts, under that heading, and there was no opposition. "However, it is a wish that you should not have made."

"Which cards represent my wish?" she asked, almost in a panic, strange for such a grand lady.

I wouldn't tell her. I smiled at her and said, "This is only a game, after all."

She put on an air that she was pacified, pulled together. But I could see that she was not.

Altogether, from this moment what her cards told me was one thing and what I told her was another. I had reason to be cautious. As I looked at the whole picture that was formed by the seven groups of cards it was at first a coloured mass, changing into a tableau of patterns until one idea protruded larger and more brilliantly than the others. And so, it appeared to me all in a quick moment that Mme Dessain was herself a natural clairvoyant; she was able to read my mind perhaps better than I was able to read her cards. What had been to me a laughing matter, a game, seemed now to veer rather dangerously towards myself, and I knew that her wish had been in some way connected with me. I say connected with me, not directed at me, because there was something indirect about it; at the same time it was distinctly malevolent.

I braved out the performance. I told her a certain amount of nonsense, but as I spoke I could see she discerned that I wasn't as frank as I might have been. More specifically than before I could now see under the heading of the secret self that she was clairvoyant.

Now, for instance, I looked at the known self in a special way. I felt that her very attractive, haggard and aristocratic appeal was by no means as artless as it had seemed when she was working around the outhouses or busy with the vast baronial pans in the great stone kitchen. She looked airily up at the beautiful windows, now, those tall windows with leaded corners. I was aware of her husband's attention upon her and thought he seemed jealous, wondering what had been her wish and looking for her reaction to everything I said.

I continued to say many sweet things with a grain of what seemed probable. "You are hoping," I said, "for a visit from a tall bearded man, I should imagine an Englishman, who has an interest in gardening—" Indeed I received from Mme Dessain's cards a very strong premonition concerning the garden.

"That's Camillo, our odd-job man,' said the anxious husband. "He's been away for five days, and he's overdue. But he's Italian."

"Alain!" rebuked Mme Dessain. "Let Mme Lucy continue."

I continued. It did seem to me very plainly that Mme Dessain had set her heart on a visitor. He would be about her age, probably an American or an Englishman (he could have been a German but for the fact it was extremely unlikely that a woman of Mme Dessain's age and ethos would have a German lover). She was, however, moving towards this love affair full tilt. I was sure he had been a guest at the château, certainly married then, if not now, and decidedly rich. It was a disastrous enough attachment for her house and family.

All this I saw, and Mme Dessain knew that I saw it. What she was unaware of, or was bound by her infatuation to ignore, was the vast amount of bother and anxiety this course was leading her to. Her husband, though not in the least faithful to her, would make nothing but bitterness of the affair.

"You may be unaware that certain benefits will come to the house as a result of your visitor's appearance," I said. And I told her the visitor would be poor, and warned her against unforeseen expenditure. The husband rejoiced to hear these words, and I wound up, "Tomorrow you will receive a very important family letter,"— one of the few honest comments on Mme Dessain's cards that I chose to make. Indeed, I thought it was harmless, for the husband said, "That will be from our son, Charles," and Mme Dessain once more cried out "Alain! You interrupt."

I said, "I've finished."

Mme Dessain was looking beyond me. "Here comes Madame's husband," she said ambiguously; anyway, I looked round and saw Raymond approaching. I guessed he had quarrelled with Sylvia who, leaving the room, looked round smiling with that deplorable angry leer of hers, which quire ruined her appearance.

I left next day. The tense atmosphere between my married friends was not to be borne by me. When I went to pay my bill Mme Dessain sent a maid to take the money and with the message that she was occupied.

But Raymond came running after me as my luggage went into the taxi. His face was fairly frantic. It struck me that he would have been rather handsome without his beard.

"Lucy," he said. "Lucy."

"I'm sorry, Raymond. But I have to go."

He was really inarticulate and I thought it quite civil of him to feel for me and my embarrassment at being on the scene of a messed-up marriage.

"Lucy."

"My apologies to Sylvia," I said. "She'll understand."

That was the last I saw of Raymond, watching my taxi depart, as he did.

Everything but the physical memory of the lovely château went far away to the back of my mind in the general nuisance of changing my holiday plans. The next week I returned to London and took up my life. Mme Dessain and the telling of her cards slept latent for year after year, but with each detail regularly arranged in case it should ever be needed, as is the way with memory.

Some time over the following year I heard that Sylvia and Raymond had finally separated; I was told that Sylvia was married again, to a social worker much younger than herself, and that after the divorce Raymond had given up his good job and gone to live abroad. Abroad is a big place and the rumours were equally too large and amorphous for me to take any account of, so busy with my own life as I was. When occasionally I thought of that holiday I shared with them I thought of the beautiful château, but a cloud came over my thoughts when I remembered how uncomfortable I felt as the third party. I didn't know till much later that they stayed on at the château for another week.

Not long ago I came across M Dessain. I didn't recognize him at first. I was aware only of a little wizened man walking out of the Black Forest at Baden-Baden. I should say that it isn't unusual for anything whatsoever to walk out of the Black Forest, so I took no particular notice. Moreover he was dressed in beige, and I might say that every visitor to Baden-Baden wears beige, both men and women. Their clothes and their shoes are beige and their faces are beige; in which respect they are quite lovable.

But I noticed him again that day seated alone at a lunch table in the dining room of my hotel. Even then, I failed to see anything familiar about him; I only noticed that he looked at me once or twice, briefly, but in a decidedly curious way.

That evening I was sitting in the public room of the hotel playing with my cards. I was alone, waiting for a friend to join me there the next day. I shuffled the cards and dealt them out in my own style which seems so haphazard; I don't ever tell my own fortune, but I can't keep away from the cards. I shuffle and deal and see what comes up, and in the meantime my ideas take form as if the cards were a sort of sacrament, "an outward and visible sign of an inward and spiritual grace," as the traditional definition goes.

Up to me at my table came the wizened guest, him of the Black Forest. He sat down on the edge of a sofa, watching me. I felt he was sad, and I was about to ask him if he would like me to tell his fortune.

"Mlle Lucy," he said.

Then I recognized him, the once chubby little husband of Mme Dessain, and I saw how the years had withered him. In all its formal detail of ten years ago or more, I remembered the features of the room in the château where I told Mme Dessain's fortune while she, intense and distressed, perceived in her clairvoyance all that I was about. I remembered the two chess-players sitting quietly apart, the tall shapes of Sylvia and Raymond moving away impatiently from the scene, the worn floral fabric on the chairs. I wondered if Mme Dessain's lover had materialized, and I recalled vaguely some of my light-hearted predictions which hadn't fooled Mme Dessain one bit. "You are hoping for a visit from a tall, bearded Englishman, interested in the garden." And my own sincere prediction, "You will have a family letter."

I looked at M Dessain and said, "What a long time ago. Are you on holiday?"

"I am here for my health."

"How is Mme Dessain?" I said.

"She does very well. As you predicted, the letter came next day."

"Oh, dear. I hope it was a good letter."

"Yes. It came from her cousin Claude. It announced his engagement. I was delighted, because Claude was my wife's lover."

"Oh," I said. "Well, that must have solved the problem for you, M Dessain."

"It was a good thing for Claude," he said. "And a good thing for you, Mlle Lucy."

"For me?"

"My wife changed your destiny," said the sad and withered man. He repeated, "Your destiny, Mlle Lucy. She saw that you were destined to marry your friend Raymond, and she intervened."

"Marry Raymond? I never thought of such a thing. There was nothing at all between us. He was on bad terms with his wife but that had nothing to do with me."

"Nevertheless, my wife foresaw the outcome. You would have married Raymond, but after your departure, before the week was out she had him for her new lover. He is still at the château. She forestalled your destiny."

"Not my destiny, then," I said, "only my destination." And seeing that he looked so sad and so beige, I asked, "Would you like me to tell your fortune, M Dessain?"

He didn't answer the question. He only said, "Raymond is very good in the garden and in the grounds."

Men Friends

Angela Huth

Conrad Fortescu, on his way to the church, trod on a beetle. In the silence of the Norman porch he heard the tiny crackle as it crushed beneath his foot. Looking down, he saw the smashed shell, each fragment shiny as his own highly polished black shoes, linked by a web of blood. Damn, he thought: how Louisa would have hated this—Louisa who would rescue dying flies from summer window-panes. Conrad felt his throat clench, He coughed. Up until this moment he had been all right, in control. Death of the beetle shattered his calm.

He made his way into the church. He was early. Walking up the path banked with expensive wreaths of flowers at the foot of yews, he had been pleased to think he was probably first. He wanted time to himself to think about Louisa. But he was not the first. Half a dozen others were already seated, curious vulture eyes upon him, people behaving as if the gathering was for a party rather than a funeral. Conrad took a service sheet from an usher, chose a seat by a pillar from which he would not quite be able to see the coffin. *Louisa Chumleigh*, he read: *1st Sept 1956—2nd April 1992*. Not a long life. The organ began to play a Bach prelude. Conrad closed his eyes.

They first met seven years ago, one of those smudged summer afternoons when the tremor of heat makes everything illusory. He stood on a thyme-planted terrace, leaning over the balustrade to admire the descending shelves of impeccably mowed lawns. Friends had brought him to the house for tea, drinks—he couldn't remember which. He had stood transfixed as he watched Louisa, in the shimmer of heat below him, take the arm of an old man with a stick. She supported him as he stepped from the lawn on to the path. Her solicitousness—she had no idea she was being watched, she later told him—was mirage-clear even from so great a distance. She kept hold of the old man's arm—Jacob, it was, her husband. They walked towards Conrad, joined him on the terrace. As Jacob pointed his stick towards the arboretum, spoke lovingly of trees, Conrad regarded his wife. It was a case of instant enchantment. Something unknown to him before.

They had had five years. Five years of adultery, though Louisa would never use such a word. She had made it easy for him—writing, ringing, taking the initiative to get in touch, so that he was spared taking the risk of contacting her. She never involved him in her deceits. She even managed to make him feel, sometimes, that the woman in his arms was *free*. But that was the one thing she was not, nor ever would be until Jacob died. Until that time, her husband came first. If she did not ring Conrad for a week—and the agony of silent days never lessened—he knew it would be because Jacob had made some demand that she would not dream of refusing, although when she did ring she gave no explanation for her silence. And Conrad knew better than to ask.

Once, they had managed three whole days together: Jacob was on business in America. Louise took the opportunity to visit relations in Paris. Conrad followed her on the next flight. Louisa saw little of her relations. On a warm spring afternoon in the Bois, Conrad declared his intention to wait for her: to wait until Jacob, thirty-six years her senior, died. He saw at once his mistake. Louisa, who had been laughing only moments before, retracted from him, though she kept hold of his hand. Conrad, apologising for his clumsiness, felt a lowering of the afternoon "Who knows what will happen—then?" Louisa said, "It's something I can never think about, Jacob's dying."

Soon she was laughing again. Back in England nothing seemed to have changed. Conrad accustomed himself to the imperfections of loving another man's wife, and privately determined to wait, however many years it might be.

Then, two years ago, there had been such a long silence that Conrad had been forced at last to write. What had happened? Louisa rang at once, her weak voice apologetic. Some wretched bug, she explained. She hadn't wanted to worry him. She had been forced to stay in bed for two weeks.

The bug needed treatment—radiotherapy. Conrad visited her occasionally when Jacob was away. He observed her thinning, beautiful skin gleaming with an incandescent menace. Noticeably more frail each visit, she lay back against a bank of linen pillows in the huge marital bedroom whose windows looked on to the garden. Conrad would look down on the lawns, misted with rain, and see the brilliance of that first summer day. A nurse filtered in and out, filling water jugs, straightening covers. Conrad brought pansies, in which Louisa silently buried her face, and elderberry jelly. She spread it thinly on toast, but could only eat a mouthful to please him. They held hands, talked about the past. But mostly sat in silence watching the rain on vast window-panes. Sometimes, Louisa felt like being up for a while. Once they walked down to the lake and back, which exhausted her.

Conrad learned of her death in *The Times*. None of their mutual friends knew of their affair so, not surprisingly, offered no condolences. He had written at once to Jacob, who replied by return, a stiff polite letter in an infirm hand, inviting Conrad to the funeral and lunch afterwards at the house.

Now Louisa was dead, Conrad would never marry. She was the only woman in whom he had found all the qualities he had never known he needed until he found them in her. He doubted he would ever love anyone else.

The church was filling up: men in black ties, women in dark hats. A large man with extraordinary wide shoulders sat in front of Conrad, uncomfortable on the narrow bench of the pew, shifting about. Conrad recognised Johnnie Lutchins, a childhood friend. Louisa had sometimes talked about their times together in Cornwall.

Cornwall, Scotland, the south-west of Ireland—Johnnie and Louisa had spent many holidays together. Johnnie's widowed mother had been the best friend of Louisa's mother. She and her son spent much of their time with Louisa's family. Johnnie remembered his first sight of Louisa, a skinny angel in filthy dungarees. *Feeble*, he remembered thinking, at ten: but within a day he had discovered she was tough and daring as any boy. They climbed trees, sailed in brisk seas—the rougher the better, Louisa used to say. They teased an old donkey, put pretend spiders in the cook's tea—always laughing, always daring the other into greater mischief. At fifteen, Johnnie kissed Louisa in the greenhouse among unripe tomatoes. Then he couldn't stop kissing her. When he went up to Oxford three years later, she would visit him several times a term. He was the envy of all his friends, and showed off the beautiful creature at every opportunity. After he had graduated, and found a decent job in antiquarian books, he finally declared his love and proposed. But he had been beaten to it by Jacob—Jacob, a man older that Louisa's own father. When Johnnie had recovered from the shock, he had tried to dissuade her from such madness. Then he had turned to teasing. "I can only conclude you're marrying the old boy for his money and his house," he laughed, bitterly. Louisa denied this. Neither Johnnie nor anyone could stop her from becoming Jacob's wife.

Still, as Johnnie soon found to his delight, the marital state made little difference to their friendship. Jacob, who had known Johnnie since he was a boy—indeed, he was Johnnie's godfather—issued constant invitations to the house. Johnnie was urged to look after Louisa, keep her amused, when Jacob was away on business. Which meant that with a half-clear conscience they could go out together in London. Opportunity was on their side: Johnnie considered himself the luckiest man in the world. He knew Louisa loved him, even if not in quite the same way as he loved her. It was only a matter of waiting ... sometimes she had frustrated him by her silences, but he knew they meant she was being dutiful to Jacob, and he had no right to be either impatient or greedy. When she had become ill he had spent hours, days, by her bedside, laughing at the many flowers and cards sent to her by "admirers" whom, she claimed, she hardly knew. Johnnie believed her.

He saw her the day before she died—asleep, but holding Jacob's hand. The old man sat with fresh tears replacing dried tears on his cheeks, making no effort to brush them away. But when he rang Johnnie the next morning with the news his voice was firm as usual. He was a dignified old boy. He would have been horrified by Johnnie's uncontrolled weeping.

To deflect his thoughts, Johnnie glanced round the church. Hundreds of pansies were woven into ivy round the pillars, and along ledges where they mixed with the reflections of stained-glass windows, and twined into edifices on the altar. Candles burned as if it were Christmas Eve. The pews were full. People were hunting for seats in the side aisles. Many of them resigned themselves to standing. One of those, Johnnie realised, was Bernard Wylie. Johnnie had met him and Louisa one day in Bond Street, very briefly. He had only just caught the name. Later, he remembered to ask Louisa about him. She said Wylie was a solicitor—something to do with her late father's affairs. They had both laughed about the slickness of his coat, with its too-wide velvet collar. Today, Johnnie recognised the coat before the face.

Bernard Wylie wore his favourite coat accompanied by expensive black leather gloves, and a black satin tie lightened with the tiniest white spots which he had judged would not be offensive. He stood clutching his service sheet to steady his hands, staring straight ahead, feeling the uncertainty of his knees. And he wondered for the millionth time what it was about Louisa that had so bewitched him that his life, since meeting her, had fallen apart.

She had come to his office one November afternoon—some trivial matter to do with her father's estate—wearing a hat of grey fur sparkling with rain. Completely confused by the legal niceties of the matter, she had suddenly said, "Oh, I give up, Mr Wylie," and had laughed her enchanting laugh. "In that case," he had said, "let's go and have tea while I explain it all to you very slowly."

So slowly that their tea at the Ritz drifted into champagne, and then dinner. He had driven her back to her flat, come in for a drink, stayed the night. There had been dozens of nights since—nights and lunches, little notes and presents from her, calls from parts of the world when she was travelling with Jacob. Then, a year or so before she fell ill, there was the final note. "I'm awfully sorry, darling B, but we can't go on. I realise now it was all *infatuation* on my part … and know it was not real love for you either, but great fun, and thank you."

For the rest of his life, Bernard would regret not having made his declaration—Christ, he had loved her from the moment she walked into his office. But he had bided by Byron's principle of never telling your love, merely conveying it. Had his conveying been invisible? Too late he wrote to her, pages of the long-contained passion now set free. But she did not reply. The last time he saw her was at a party, laughing in the distance with some unknown man. She had not seen him. Bernard had left at once.

And now instead of Louisa he had a second-best wife at his side who would never know the loving man he once was … She nudged him, this loyal, unexciting wife, her sense of occasion offended by the sight of a young man standing not far from them in a dark jacket, grey trousers and no tie. In the unknown youth's eye, Bernard thought he saw reflected the same despair that lodged in his own heart: but it may have been his imagination.

The young man, Felix Brown, had cried for many nights. Cold, exhausted, drained, he feared he might faint during the long service, but there were no seats left. He it was who late last night, and at dawn this morning, had transported pansies from the greenhouse to the church, and arranged them on his own. Only three years ago, Lady Endlesham—as he still thought of her, as he would always think of her—had come into that very greenhouse and admired them. Said they were her favourite flowers. They had talked of planting and pruning, and made plans for the south bed. Felix had done his best to conceal the mesmeric effect the shape of her breasts beneath a pink cotton shirt had had upon him. He had told her how happy he was to be working in the garden. He could scarcely believe he had been promoted to being in charge only two years after leaving horticultural college, he said. Lady Endlesham had smiled, and said they must make more plans. Then he gave her a pot of pansies for her desk.

Some weeks later she came into the tool-shed, admired his clean and gleaming tools that hung in order of height on the walls. The warmth of that evening was almost tangible. In the stuffy air that smelt of dry earth Felix was embarrassed by the pungent smell of his own sweat. He could also smell Lady Endlesham's scent, a mixture of fragile flowers. In the shadows it seemed to him she hesitated, planning perhaps to mention some gardening matter. Then she put out her arms, and said, he thought—though he could never be quite sure of the exact words—*Come here, you handsome thing.* Handsome? Gathered to him, Felix could hear the racing heart of his employer's wife. They ran like children through the orchard to a hidden place

Felix knew. Lord Endlesham was away, she assured him, but not in a rejoicing way. She sounded almost lonely. Felix was twenty-one at the time.

Since then they'd made love in every corner of the garden, and, in winter, in the hayloft. Felix would marvel how one moment his mistress (as he liked to think of her) was laughing in his arms covered in grass or hay, and the next he would see her in the distance walking beside her aged husband, immaculate, admiring the flowerbeds whose geography she and Felix had discussed between a thousand kisses.

When she was ill, no longer able to come downstairs, he sent up a new bowl of flowers to her room each day. The last time he saw her she was standing at her bedroom window—looking for him, perhaps. He was raking the terrace. He glanced up, saw her wave. Then she disappeared. She disappeared, and with a crescendo in the organ music Felix knew at last she was gone. Never coming back to their garden. He took about his handkerchief, blew his nose, realising he was the only man in the church to resort to such weakness at this stage. Through tear-blurred eyes he watched the shuffling procession of coffin-bearers hesitate up the aisle, and caught the eye of his employer, Sir Jacob, seventy-two at Christmas. He was a good man to work for. Felix respected the old codger, but wondered if he could bear to continue the job now the inspiration of the garden no longer existed.

Sir Jacob, seeing young Felix, the first face to come clearly into focus, gave the briefest nod to acknowledge that his floral work in the church was appreciated. Louisa would have been amazed. She loved decorating the church. She and Felix, before the illness, had done a grand job always at Christmas and Harvest Festival. She had been wonderful with the boy. In her usual generous way she had inspired him, encouraged him, suggested his promotion—typical of her, always seeing the best in people, bringing out their qualities.

Sir Jacob trod very slowly, in time to the gentle music. In front of him on the coffin lay a single gardenia. He had chosen it with Felix—the best in the greenhouse. Inside, placed in the stiff hands, was the equally stiff card with its private message of love which would not fade until long after the body had perished.

Beside Sir Jacob walked Louisa's mother, a bent old lady with a still-beautiful profile that had been inherited by her daughter. It occurred to Sir Jacob, as he put a finger on the knife-edge of his collar that cut into his neck, that they might look more like man and wife than he and Louisa ever did ... Louisa could have been his granddaughter. Walking down this same aisle, their wedding day—but he hadn't cared then, or ever, what people thought. All that mattered to him was their mutual, perfect love for each other. Which turned out to be proven. While Sir Jacob recoiled at the thought of his own smugness, he couldn't help reflecting that never once in their sixteen years of marriage had Louisa ever let him down, disappointed him, betrayed him. He knew he came first in her life, just as she did in his. He had trusted her absolutely. The only worry they had ever had was about her life after his death. She often said that no one ever could replace him.

The coffin-bearers reached the altar, placed it on its plinth. Sir Jacob and his mother-in-law took their places in the front pew. A shaft of sun, at that moment, pierced the roseate glass of the window above the altar. Sir Jacob remembered Louisa remarking on the strength of its colour—"a small pink pool on the altar steps, darling—did you notice?" In truth he had never noticed, in all the Sundays he had been coming to this church, until Louisa had pointed it out to him. She had drawn so much to his attention that gave pleasure. She had opened his eyes to the extraordinary qualities of the ordinary, and made him the happiest of men.

The vicar clasped his hands. In the moment's silence before the first prayer, Sir Jacob looked round at the congregation—so many people who would always remember his wife. It occurred to him there was a large proportion of men. Men of all ages, he saw, all with that sternness of eye that strong men employ to conceal grief. He knew some of them: others were unfamiliar. Darling Louisa: untouchable to all but me, he used to say. And she, kneeling on the library floor beside him, would laugh her thrilling laugh in agreement. How proud of her he was! There was nothing like having a wife who was desired by all, but faithful only to the man she loved, her husband.

May the vanity of such thoughts be forgiven, Sir Jacob found himself praying. They he joined in the general words of thanks for Louisa's life. He could not close his eyes: in his disbelief they never left the coffin. Like so many of Louisa's men friends in the church for her funeral that day, Sir Jacob could only picture her alive.

Copyright Notices